**Praise for *I'***



'A dark triumph

**Heather Darwen**

**author of *The Things We Do To Our Friends***

'Alert the paparazzi and set up a velvet rope for the future fans of Sutanto, who is poised to become a top-tier thriller writer.' ***Washington Post***

'Not since *Gone Girl's* Amy Dunne has a sociopath been this bewitching. Utterly brilliant, deliciously devious, and absolutely unputdownable with whiplash plotting and a twist that will make you gasp.' **May Cobb, author of *The Hunting Wives***

'It's a twisted tale that will find you switching allegiances and who you believe.' ***Glamour***

'This is toxic female friendship at its most terrifying best.' **Laurie Elizabeth Flynn, author of *The Girls Are All So Nice Here***

'This is a wickedly enjoyable treatise on the dark sides of female friendship.' ***Publishers Weekly***

'Deliciously dark, wittily provocative, with twist after twist that will leave you reeling, Sutanto weaves a dangerously clever tale about friendship, rage, and the mind-games people play.' **Amanda Jayatissa, author of *You're Invited***

'Sutanto expertly manipulates time, moving between difficult childhoods to perplexing adult lives, dexterously revealing puzzle pieces that calculatingly don't fit. Meanwhile, crazy rich Asians, the publishing industry, and fatal misogyny all crack under Sutanto's deadly glare.' ***Booklist***

**Jesse Sutanto** is the author of books for children and adults. She is the author of YA novel *The Obsession*, and *Theo Tan and the Fox Spirit*, the first book in a middle grade series. *Dial A For Aunties* was her debut adult novel and won the 2021 Comedy Women In Print Prize.

Jesse received her masters' from the University of Oxford. She grew up in Indonesia and Singapore and currently lives in Jakarta with her husband and two daughters.

Find out more about Jesse:
Website: jesseqsutantoauthor.com
X: @thewritinghippo
Facebook and Instagram: @JesseQSutanto

*Also by Jesse Sutanto*
I'm Not Done With You Yet

*The Aunties series*
Dial A For Aunties
Four Aunties and a Wedding
The Good, the Bad, and the Aunties

*The Vera Wong series*
Vera Wong's Unsolicited Advice for Murderers

*YA*
Well, That Was Unexpected
Didn't See That Coming

# YOU WILL *NEVER* BE ME

JESSE SUTANTO

HQ

ONE PLACE. MANY STORIES

This novel is entirely a work of fiction. The names, characters and incidents portrayed in it are the work of the author's imagination. Any resemblance to actual persons, living or dead, events or localities is entirely coincidental.

HQ
An imprint of HarperCollins*Publishers* Ltd
1 London Bridge Street
London SE1 9GF

www.harpercollins.co.uk

HarperCollins*Publishers*
Macken House, 39/40 Mayor Street Upper,
Dublin 1, D01 C9W8, Ireland

This edition 2024

1
First published in Great Britain by
HQ, an imprint of HarperCollins*Publishers* Ltd 2024



Jesse Sutanto asserts the moral right to be identified as the author of this work.
A catalogue record for this book is available from the British Library.

ISBN: 9780008683764

MIX
Paper | Supporting responsible forestry
FSC™ C007454

This book contains FSC™ certified paper and other controlled sources to ensure responsible forest management.

For more information visit: www.harpercollins.co.uk/green

This book is set in 9.5/15.5 pt. Brother 1816 by Type-it AS, Norway

Printed and Bound in the UK using 100% Renewable Electricity at
CPI Group (UK) Ltd, Croydon, CR0 4YY

To Anji, my best friend for over half my life. Our friendship is everything Aspen and Meredith pretended theirs was.

# Prologue

There is a game I like to play on my own. It's a game we're all playing, but most people don't know they're playing it. It's called: How Much Is Your Life Worth? If you were to drop dead right this very moment, how big a hole would there be in my life?

People often say things like, "I can't live without you." They rarely ever mean it. But I did. When I said it to you, I meant every word. I'd thought about it, really considered everything—the you-shaped hole that would be left in my life if you were gone. It would devastate me. Obliterate everything like an imploding star turning into a black hole, sucking everything into its gaping maw. Your life was worth so much.

Just not as much as mine.

# Chapter 1

# MEREDITH

I'm stalking my best friend. There's no use denying it. When I first started, I told myself we were so in sync that we were like the same person torn into two halves, and those two halves were linked by an invisible thread that was always pulling us back to each other, so of course we'd constantly be running into each other. Simpatico. That's what we always used to say. *Simpatico!* Followed by a wink, content and smug, because out of almost eight billion humans in the world, the two of us somehow managed to find our soulmates in each other, and what is that if not pure and beautiful magic?

And anyway, it's not really stalking, not like the kind you see in the movies with the stalker prowling in all black (contrary to popular belief, black is *not* for everyone; it certainly does my skin tone no favors), a chloroform-soaked rag in one hand and zip ties in the other. I'm not trying to kidnap Bestie. It's more like . . . Stalking Lite. I just want to know how she's doing. I need to see if our earth-shattering fight mauled her the way it did me. That's reasonable. And I sure as hell won't find out anything through her social media accounts, which are all glossed over with giddily jubilant content. No, if I want to see signs of the wreckage underneath, I need to see her in person—catch a glimpse of the tightness around the right corner of her mouth, or the way she licks her lips like a lizard does (a rapid twitch that does nothing to moisten them).

And that's why I'm sitting in my car around the corner from the twins' school, waiting for her car to appear out of the drop-off line. Damn it, I know it sounds bad; I'm literally parked outside of her kids' school. But this has nothing to do with her girls, even though I miss Noemie and Elea so much (and I'm sure they must miss Aunt Mer), and Luca misses little Sabine.

"Don't you, Luca?" I coo, glancing back at my eight-month-old son. "You miss baby Sabine, don't you, sweetie?"

He's too busy sucking on his toes to give me a reply. But I can tell. I know he misses Sabine. Sabine is two months older than Luca, and he hasn't spent a single day away from Sabine's side up until her mother and I had our catastrophic fight. It's not fair to the kids. Why can't she see that?

I tap the steering wheel impatiently, my eyes scanning each car as it leaves the school. Have I missed her already? I'm not cut out for this spy shit. What if she sees me? What if she recognizes the car? I was careful-ish. I switched cars with Clara this morning, telling her that I had plans to drive up to Griffith Park for a shoot and needed her four-wheel drive. Of course, I've driven my sister's car a few times, so maybe Bestie will still recognize it. Maybe I should drive home. What the hell was I thinking?

But just then, I spot it. Her SUV pulling out of the school driveway. My breath catches in my throat, emotion welling up at the painfully familiar sight of her car. I can practically smell the inside of her car already—her Miss Dior perfume, the girls' raspberry shampoo, and homemade kale chips. Then, as it drives past, I catch sight of her face, her eyes hidden behind her oversized Chanel sunglasses and her hair falling in loose mahogany waves down her shoulders, and tears rush to my eyes (behind my similarly oversized Jimmy Choos). Damn it, but I miss that bitch, Aspen. A bitter snort tumbles out of my mouth at her name. Aspen. I gave that to her. What's in a name? Well. A name is the beginning of your brand, so, what's in a name? Everything. In a way, you could say I made Aspen into who she is today. She owes me everything.

*Eight Years Ago*

I know it's en vogue to hate LA—the dry heat, the fake cocaine- and wheatgrass- and matcha-fueled cheerfulness of everyone, the way that the checkout girl at the supermarket looks like she just stepped off a runway—but honestly? I love it. I can be as manically cheerful as the best of them, and I don't even snort coke (except when I'm trying to lose weight, but ever since I started doing the celery juice fast, I haven't done any lines). Back in Ohio, I was always "too much," but it turns out that in LA, you can never be "too much." Everyone here loves me. Some people—I won't name names—even describe me as their "happy pill."

I'm invited to so many parties that some evenings I literally spend just five minutes at each venue—just enough to make the rounds (*Hi, sweetie! Oh my god, you look FAB! Ah! OMG, it's been too long! We must catch up soon. We MUST! Oh, let's take a selfie, you look AMAZING!*) kiss cheeks, and make sure we're photographed—before I make my exit (*Sorry, gotta run. Chell is celebrating her birthday at the—yes, we MUST catch up soon! Okay, love you, bye! Bye! Kisses!).* Then I zip down the 405, billboards grinning and winking at me like we're all in on some great secret, to another party, glitzier than the one before; then to another party, more exclusive; then another, and another.

(Do you hate me? You mustn't. I'm just a girl trying to make it big. Trying to *thrive.*)

It's at one of these parties that I meet her. Ryleebelle. I only notice her because among the skinny, shimmering LA bodies and glinting fake smiles, she looks so out of place. Picture this: a nonskinny Asian woman in an ill-fitting black dress (black is less cruel to her than it is to me, but still—who wears an LBD to a party in LA, for fuck's sake?), both hands clasped around a martini glass that she's holding against her chest like a shield. Too much eye makeup. A terrified look on her face. I'm about to glide past her when she glances up and I catch the look that crosses her face.

Pure and unadulterated admiration. Imagine a fan being called backstage after a BTS concert. That's the look on her face. More than just a fan. A worshipper. It seizes me (and do not try to tell me that it wouldn't have seized you too).

I give her a kind smile. I'm gracious, generous. I like to help. There's a special place in hell for women who don't help other women, etc. When she sees my smile, the relief that goes through her face is that of a drowning person who's just been thrown a lifeline. I go to her.

Pause for a second. I need you to fully understand what a huge favor I'm doing here. Because the other thing is that I'm Asian, but she looks very clearly like an Asian person from Asia, and not even the right parts of Asia—not the ones that inspire weeaboos or Koreaboos. I was born and raised in Ohio, and I had to learn a long time ago how to fit in—which parts of my Asian-ness to highlight and which ones to hide. One of the things I quickly learned to do was to dissociate from other Asians who weren't conforming. It might sound cruel, but know what else is cruel? High school kids in Ohio. It was a long and brutal road for me to become The Right Kind of Asian. The kind who doesn't bring anything with a face on it for lunch. (One time, Raj Singh's mom packed him a fish head curry in fifth grade. I looked Raj up on Twitter the other day; he is now an alcoholic. I bet I can trace everything that went wrong in his life back to that fish head curry. It smelled dope, though. I'll give his mom that.)

So for me to now approach this plump—okay, she's not plump, but her collarbones aren't jutting out the way that LA likes them to—this nonskinny Asian woman is a huge risk for me to take. She has everything to gain from catching my eye; I have next to nothing to gain from being kind to her.

Anyway, so I go to her with a kind, empathetic smile and say, "First time at one of these things?"

The "one of these things" we happen to be at is a rooftop mixer for models / actors / singers / social media influencer wannabes, with agents and photographers prowling among us like sharks. She's actually quite pretty under the heavy makeup, but like I said, not skinny, so obviously she's not a model. I bet she has a luscious voice and thinks she can win *America's Got Talent* or whatever horror talent show they've got going on nowadays.

She gives me an apologetic smile. "That obvious, huh?"

Only the slightest hint of an accent in her voice. And it's actually a nice accent, not one that would get her made fun of. A point in her favor. One less thing to change. "Only because I've been in exactly your position before."

"Really? You?" She gives me a once-over that's overflowing with admiration. "I don't believe that."

I brush imaginary lint off my sequined dress. "Hey, I'm from Ohio, so when I first moved here, I was probably the epitome of uncool."

"I know," she says. Seeing my look of surprise, she adds, "I know you're from Ohio. I follow you on YouTube and Instagram. Your beauty advice is amazing. I'm such a fan."

Clearly, she hasn't taken my beauty advice to heart, though. Is that a mean thought? Damn it, one of this year's resolutions was to stop being so mean, and it's not even February yet.

As though she's read my mind, she flushes a little and says, "I know, I probably have too much makeup on. I know your mantra: less is so much more! But when I get nervous—god, it's like a tick—some people bite their nails, I dab on a little bit more makeup."

"Let me guess: you were *very* nervous tonight?" Oh my god, why am I being so catty?

Instead of telling me what a bitch I am, she laughs. A full-on laugh-shout from deep in her belly. And I find that I really like her, this woman who doesn't mind laughing at herself.

"Dude, I was so nervous, I almost chickened out of coming out here tonight. I mean . . ." She gestures at everyone else around us, and I see them through her eyes. How ridiculously, painfully beautiful and fashionable everyone here is. How stunningly blonde. "I don't belong here, do I? I can't believe I moved all the way to America thinking I might make it."

"Hey, just because you don't fit in yet doesn't mean you won't ever fit in. I wasn't always this fabulous. You should see my middle school photos. I wore mom jeans. Like, seriously, I was a twelve-year-old who wore mom jeans and thick glasses."

She's laughing again, and there's nothing I like more than making people laugh, so I keep going. "I mean, where the hell did I even get those jeans, right? They don't make them in kid sizes. They're called mom jeans for a reason."

"Well, you've come a really long way."

"It's been a hell of a journey." The unspoken question between us: Am I going to take her on that journey? Make her my mentee? Maybe this can be my good deed for the year.

"I'm Ryleebelle," she says, holding out her hand.

I take it. She has a surprisingly strong grip. I like her. And I promise it's not just because she follows my Facebook and Instagram accounts. In this moment, I make a decision. I'm going to help her. "No, you're not," I say.

She blinks. Laughs hesitantly. "Sorry?"

"What are you trying to be?"

"Huh?"

"Singer? Actor? No offense, but obviously not a model."

"Oh. Right! Um, singer. Well, trying to be."

"So you're on YouTube?"

She nods eagerly. "Yeah, I'm Ryleebellesings on there."

Ryleebellesings. Dear god. "And how many subscribers do you have?"

"About five thousand."

"Change your name and you'll probably get another five thousand." Okay, I mean, I don't know that for a fact, but I'm willing to bet money that her name is holding her back.

Her eyes widen. "But—"

"No one is going to take Ryleebelle seriously." I tilt my head, appraising her. "I'm thinking . . . some sort of plant? Not a flower, ugh. A tree name. Rowan? Hmm, you don't strike me as a Rowan. Oh, I know! Aspen."

The moment I say it, I know we both feel it. The click. The puzzle piece slotting into place. It fits. The uncertainty melts away from her face and she gazes at me with wonderment. She really does look quite pretty. After my makeover—or rather, my makeunder—she's going to look stunning.

"Huh," she breathes out. "I like it. Aspen. It sounds so . . . American."

I know exactly what she means. In many Asian cultures, people like to give their kids Western names. But they don't have a good grasp on Western culture, so then they reach for the "fancier-sounding" ones and make the spelling "unique," and that's when you get atrocities like "Ryleebelle." They don't get that, like makeup, with names, less is more. And because Aspen gets it, I know she's going to get everything I'll do for her. She'll get that I am giving her the most valuable gift. The gift of fitting in.

# Chapter 2

# ASPEN

It is not yet nine in the morning, and I've almost snapped at Elea three separate times.

The first was when I was trying to get a photo of the beautiful stack of sourdough pancakes to post to my Stories, and she stabbed her fork through it before I said they were okay to eat. She totally knew what she was doing too; I could tell from that glint in her eyes. Taking a deep breath, I said, "Sweetheart, wait, please," and she moaned, "But Mommy, I'm hungry. And Noemie's blood sugar is probably getting low." Weaponizing Noemie's diabetes is a recent tactic that Elea's picked up. It drives me insane because let's face it, Elea doesn't give a shit about Noemie's blood sugar. She only does when it suits her.

"I'm okay," Noemie said softly, next to Elea. I gave her a grateful wink, and she smiled at me. My sweet girl. Elea ignored me and ripped out a huge chunk of pancakes. I sucked my breath in a sharp hiss, barely holding myself back from snapping at her, but somehow, through some superhuman effort, managed to bite my tongue.

Ben glanced up from the table, where he was feeding Sabine

mashed peas, but he was wise enough not to say anything. I saw how his mouth pressed into a thin line, though, and it was enough to get my hackles up. I ignored them both, my silently critical husband and my rebellious six-year-old, and focused on taking the perfect shot of the pancakes.

*Never mind the ruined shots,* I thought. *The news I'm about to share is going to make everything okay.*

I served the pancakes and fruits and yogurt, then, as everyone tucked in, I cleared my throat and said, "I have some really exciting news to share."

Ben barely looked up, he was so uninterested in what I had to say. I ignored his rudeness and said, "A producer contacted Mommy this morning. His name is Damien Kim, and he's shooting a Netflix show about influencers and their lifestyles. Each influencer will get a thirty-minute episode to themselves, and he wants to meet with me to see if we'd be a good match." I ended the announcement with an expectant smile, but not even Noemie looked excited at this. Instead, my family stared at me like I'd asked them to clean the toilet with their bare hands.

"What does that mean, Mommy?" Noemie said finally.

"Well, it means we might have a show that's all about our family," I said brightly.

"And have a bunch of cameras recording our every move?" Ben said. "I don't think so."

"Ben, please," I said, and even I hated how pathetic I sounded. Groveling and begging for my family's cooperation, like always. When I read Damien's email, I'd been so exhilarated, so carried away by all of the possibilities, that I hadn't paused to think that my family might not be on board. But why wouldn't they be? If we played this right, our single episode could be so well received that we could end up with our very own show. Then maybe I could finally stop feeling like I'm on a hamster wheel, needing to come up with nonstop content to feed to the perpetually hungry social media machine. But my family, spoiled by my success, had no idea how I was breaking my back to earn as much as I could for their sake. This huge opportunity was nothing more than a blip in their day. I couldn't afford to get into an argument with Ben over this right then, though, so I merely said, "You know what? Let's discuss this later this evening, okay?"

The second time I almost snapped at Elea was when I tried to get a photo of Elea and Noemie in their matching outfits—powder-blue dresses with little strawberry prints all over them, cream-colored knit cardigans, black leggings, and red ribbons in their hair to match the strawberries. They looked so Instagrammable. They always look Instagrammable; that is the whole fucking point. But while Noemie stood there smiling obediently—my sweet, darling Noemie—Elea kept making horrible faces at the camera. And you know what? I rolled with it. I took photos anyway and uploaded them to my Stories with the caption, "Sugar and spice, lol." As I was uploading the photos, Elea shouted, "LET'S GO, MOM, COME ON I'M SICK OF THIS," and once more, I begged, "Please be patient, Elea; you know I need to do this."

Inside my head a voice whispered, *I'm sick of her*, and although I didn't say it out loud, hot shame burned through my entire being.

Number three: As I plopped baby Sabine down on the front yard next to Elea and Noemie, I noticed that her strawberry-red headband was gone. I groaned; I'd put that headband on Sabine to match the twins' ribbons. Without it, the entire photo would be ruined. Then I saw it sticking out of Elea's cardigan pocket. I snatched it out and said in a barely controlled voice, "Sweetheart, why would you take this off? You know how hard it is to put a headband on your sister."

Elea lifted her chin defiantly. "Yeah, because she hates it, and you shouldn't make her wear it if she hates it. No means no, Mom." Never has the word "Mom" been said with so much venom.

I took a deep breath, forcing myself to calm down before I snapped at her. When the girls were born, I made a promise to myself never to raise my voice at them except when they were in danger, but by god, Elea was testing me.

"Well, please don't do that again, okay?" I said through a gritted smile. I stretched the headband and put it on Sabine's bald head. A frown scrunched her chubby baby face. She pulled at the headband, and it went over her eyes, which made her fuss. Great, just great. "Come on, pumpkin," I cooed, adjusting the headband. "Please, just for one minute, okay? Do this for Mommy, please, baby girl." Not that she would understand anything I was saying, but hopefully the soothing tone of my voice would help calm her as I put the headband back in place.

It didn't. She started wailing. I dipped into my Luna's All-Natural Vegan Leather Mommy's Hands-Free Purse. Really it was just a glorified fanny pack, but Luna Rose, the company that paid me over fifty grand to advertise it, had been insistent that I never call it a fanny pack, so I made a habit of calling it my "hands-free purse," even in my head. When you've got over five million followers watching your every move, it pays to be meticulous. And anyway, the Luna Hands-Free Purse really was a genius creation. It was divided into three sections, and into one section I had dumped a handful of sugar-free, freeze-dried yogurt melts. I fished out one of the yogurt melts and offered it to Sabine.

"My teacher said you shouldn't use food as a reward," Elea said.

I ignored her and the twinge of guilt because she was right. But, I reminded myself, at least it's sugar-free. Sabine took my offering and sucked on it happily, letting me adjust her headband. Once it was in place, I ran back a few paces and raised my camera. No time to hesitate; the yogurt melt would only buy me fifteen seconds, tops. I took a dozen photos from various angles and was rewarded with smiles from Sabine and Noemie. None from Elea, of course, but I could Photoshop the corners of her mouth later on to give her a less surly look.

Then it was a mad rush to bundle everyone into the car; a quick snap of them safe and snug with me tagging the company that had paid me to advertise their car seats. I posted them to my Stories, and the Likes poured in before I was even out of the driveway.

Elea refused to give me a hug at the school drop-off, so I—fully conscious of the judgy stares from the other parents around me—made sure to lavish Noemie with a tighter hug and smoochier kiss than usual. She squirmed and said, "It's okay, Mommy. Don't be sad."

"I'm not sad," I said brightly, and she just looked at me knowingly. Noemie has always been an old soul. "Don't forget your morning snack, sweetie."

She gave me a thin-lipped smile, and the crack in my heart widened. *It's not fair,* I thought to myself for the millionth time. *It's not fair that my beautiful, perfect child would be diagnosed with diabetes. She's not even fat!* As soon as the thought came, I chastised myself for fat-shaming. I silently recited my mantra:

*don't think any thoughts that you wouldn't say out loud.* That way, there could be no way that I would slip up and be canceled. Anyway, it's a good thing that Noemie is learning to eat every three hours. It's healthier this way. She'll set a good example for her peers.

I saw the other moms making their approach, and dread lurched up my throat like bile, so I quickly waved to them and called out, "Sorry, ladies, I'm late for a meeting! Lunch soon? Love you all!"

And now, as I drive away from the twins' school and enter the 405, I can't help going over everything that's happened this morning—all of the tiny details that went wrong. Elea's acidic remarks, peeling away layer after layer of my defenses. Ben's unspoken judgment. The way the other school moms approached me, grinning like sharks, their eyes calculating. I can't help feeling like everyone knows. My dark secret. My hands tighten around the steering wheel. I force myself to release my breath. Take a deep inhale. Exhale.

Just as the tension starts to leave my shoulders, Sabine gurgles. I smile at her through the rearview mirror, and she smiles back. My sweet baby. Then her eyes suddenly focus, and her face turns pink. "Oh no," I mutter, just as she lets out a massive, wet fart.

I recognize the sound of a diaper blowout when I hear it. "No!" I cry. "Not today, baby."

But Sabine doesn't give a shit (or rather, she gives a *lot* of shit) about what day it is. She doesn't know we're on our way to meet with Bodacious Babies, a meeting weeks in the making. It would be Sabine's first ever official modeling contract. I held off long enough so I wouldn't be accused of exploiting my newborn, but now she is sturdier, with thigh rolls to die for, and she adores the camera. It would be a crime not to let her shine.

Of course, right now, those luscious thigh rolls are covered in crap. Sabine starts wailing. "I know, baby," I coo, searching for someplace I can stop to clean her up. There is nothing. Of course there's nothing; we're on the freaking 405. I could take the next exit and pray there's a Ralphs or something I could go to, but then we'd be hopelessly late for the meeting. And I pride myself on my professionalism; influencers get enough bad rap as it is, and I've set myself aside from all the others by taking my career seriously. Turning up to a meeting like this one this late is unacceptable. I take a deep breath and immediately regret it as the stench of Sabine's blowout has now filled the car. I look at her crying face in the rearview mirror and say, "I'm sorry, sweetie, but you're just going to have to endure it for now, okay?"

It doesn't help. She screams throughout the entirety of the remaining journey. By the time I take the exit for Wilshire, Sabine's usually cherubic face is covered with snot and tears and sweat, and she's so tired from wailing that her cries are all gaspy—closer to whimpers than full-on wails. I spot a Natural Foods and swerve into the parking lot. I should've stopped off earlier. God, I am the worst mom.

*Stop that. She'll be fine. It's just a little poop, that's all.*

Except when I finally get to her, it isn't just a little poop. It's the mother lode of diaper blowouts. I can't help gagging when I see the mess. "Oh, sweetie, it's okay, it's fine," I say, more to myself than to Sabine. I lift her from her car seat, but now I have no idea what I'm supposed to do. There is just so much. Sabine's whole bottom half is covered in it. Her car seat is covered in it.

For a second, I stand there, arms out, holding my baby, both of us just as stunned as the other. Then, as though being lifted gave her a second wind, she opens her mouth and starts screaming once more. And now, Natural Foods customers are staring at us. As though Natural Foods customers need more reason to be judgy assholes. I snap out of it. *One step at a time,* I remind myself. *This is nothing.* I shoulder her diaper bag and hurry her into the supermarket, being careful to still hold her away from me because the last thing I need is for me to get shit all over my outfit right before a meeting. More judgmental stares. A couple of them seem to recognize me. I ignore them all, locate the bathroom, and rush in.

It is carnage. By the time I've changed Sabine into a clean diaper and clean clothes, I am drenched in sweat. My makeup isn't just running, it's speeding away from my face. I try to salvage it as best as I can, but it's next to impossible with one arm keeping a squirmy Sabine on my hip, and the other shaky after all the stress. *Don't fall apart now,* I scold myself. *It'll all be okay. You always land on your feet.*

"We're so late," I moan to Sabine as I speed walk back to the car. "Goddamn it!" I cry when I see her car seat. Somehow, I'd managed to forget that I still needed to clean it. Again, I try my best, one-handed, Sabine fussing, twisting, arching her back and shouting right in my ear. People looking, always looking. I could've sworn I saw a glimpse of someone's camera phone aimed at me. And I roll with it. I always roll with it. I give them my best *oh god, it's one of those days* smiles and wave. The woman taking a photo smiles back and puts her phone in her purse before coming toward me.

"Do you need a hand?" she says.

"Oh, thank you so much. It has been . . ." I gesture at the mess and give a harried smile. "One of those days."

"I know those days," the woman laughs. "My life is nothing but 'those days.' Want me to carry her while you clean up?"

I almost hand Sabine over to her, but catch myself in time. I can just see the uproar online: *Aspen Palmer gave her baby to a STRANGER!* I force another smile and say, "I think I've got most of it out though, thank you so much." I haven't gotten most of it out. Most of it has been absorbed into the car seat, and no amount of baby wipes, no matter how savagely I scrub, is going to get it out. I shake out a baby blanket and drape it over the car seat before putting Sabine back inside. "Thank you *so* much," I say again over my shoulder to the woman as I wrestle Sabine into the car seat. Not that she has done anything to help, but I am always nice. Always.

I can't speed the rest of the way to the meeting (*Aspen Palmer SPEEDING with a baby in her car!*). By the time we get there, we're twenty-seven minutes late, and both Sabine and I look like shit. We also smell like it—something I realize as the receptionist's nose wrinkles when I get to her desk.

"Hi, I'm Aspen Palmer, and this is Sabine. I'm here to see Michelle Reyes."

Recognition dawns on her face. "Oh my gosh, you're All Day Aspen!" The disgusted nose wrinkle is instantly gone, replaced by an expression I'm more familiar with: admiration.

"That's me," I say cheerfully, resisting the urge to apologize for the way we look and smell. I learned long ago to stop apologizing so much for everything. It doesn't endear you to people. I do, however, apologize for being late, because that's common courtesy.

"Hmm, let's see . . . Miss Reyes is supposed to have a meeting in three minutes' time. Your slot is almost over," the receptionist says apologetically. My stomach drops. But then she adds, "You know what? That meeting is actually flexible, so let me just move it . . . Okay, you have twenty minutes with Miss Reyes now."

"Thank you so much!"

"Of course. I'm such a huge fan," the receptionist says. "My little sister has diabetes, and I really appreciate you raising awareness about juvenile diabetes."

I give a sympathetic "Aww" and nod, and she smiles as she leads me into the main office space. Bodacious Babies is a modeling agency for babies, and the walls are adorned with framed photos of their clients, all of them plump and cherubic with chunky thigh rolls. None of them holds a candle to my beautiful Sabine. Of course, you wouldn't know it from looking at her now. Sweaty, cranky, still whimpering in my arms.

The receptionist knocks at the corner office door. "Come in," Michelle calls out.

"Good luck," the receptionist says.

"Thank you." I take a deep breath and enter with a confident smile. I've got this. How many of these meetings have I taken? She should be glad that I've taken the time to come and see her. She'll grasp my hand warmly and fall in love with Sabine, because how can anyone not?

Instead, the first thing Michelle Reyes does when I walk in is to give a very pointed, very calculated glance at the clock.

"I'm sorry we're late. Poor Sabine had a diaper blowout," I say with an apologetic laugh. I hadn't planned on telling her about the blowout, but it's something I'm betting that, as a mother, Michelle would empathize with.

Except Michelle turns out to be a sociopath, because the mention of a blowout doesn't make her sympathetic, it only disgusts her. God, how have I misjudged this so badly? I try to recover. "But I've cleaned her up now!"

Michelle still wears the look of distaste as she regards Sabine, and I get a sudden urge to take off Sabine's diaper and smack it into Michelle's face. I fight it off and settle into the seat opposite Michelle's desk. "We're both so excited to be here today."

A fake smile appears on Michelle's face. "Yes, so am I."

"Sabine loves the camera. You can tell she grew up with it." Sabine writhes in my arms and shrieks, and I jump back to my feet and bounce her on my hip. "Sorry, like I said, we had a difficult morning. She's usually really easy. The easiest! She hardly ever cries." At this, Sabine screams even louder. Sweat trickles down the back of my neck. *Come on, Sabine. Please don't do this right now.* "Sorry, just—" I rummage through the diaper bag and locate a bottle of formula. "Freshly pumped," I sing to Sabine as I put the rubber nipple in her mouth. I pray that Michelle can't tell the difference between breast milk and formula. With the twins, I managed to breastfeed them until they were a year old. But with Sabine, my breasts gave up three months in, and ever since then, she's been on formula. But try telling any other momfluencer that. I'd be stoned for being a terrible mom. Thankfully, Sabine settles down. "See? Easy." I smile at Michelle.

She gives a terse nod, looking far from convinced. "The thing is, Aspen, as much as we love your brand, we're very concerned about the number of trolls you've attracted."

My gut twists. Anger flickers, searing hot. Goddamn Liv. How many times do I have to tell her to take care of the hateful comments that plague my accounts? I'm going to fire that useless moron. I force a laugh. "Isn't it a mark of success to have trolls? I think every influencer—the ones who are big enough, anyway—have them."

"Yes, but you have more than an acceptable number of them. It's actually quite worrying. Aren't you concerned about your family's safety?"

And now I'm not just angry, I'm furious. How dare this smug, condescending bitch sit there and accuse me of not caring for my family's safety? It's a struggle to keep my voice even. "My family's health and safety is my top priority. Ben and I have made damn sure to do everything to keep our kids safe."

Michelle leans back, clearly unconvinced. "See, the thing is, your trolls seem more . . . personal. My team has combed your accounts, and these comments . . ." She picks up her iPad and scrolls, sucking in a breath. "'Fake bitch,' 'fake,' 'fake,' —we don't like these, because your brand is all about authenticity, but at least they're not alarming. But these ones: 'I know where her kids go to school and trust me when I say they are total brats,' and, 'The twins are so beautiful, especially in those little skirts I saw them wearing on Monday on the way to ballet.' They're not . . . typical, Aspen. I don't think it's a good time for you to be getting more exposure. We don't want to further endanger your family."

The rage is almost blinding. My whole body is so hot that I'm surprised I haven't burned a hole right through the chair. "Every influencer has them," is all I manage to say, and I know I'm just repeating myself. I know there is no changing her mind. "Why did you—why set up this meeting if you were just going to reject us?"

Michelle shrugs. "I wasn't aware of the magnitude of the troll accounts when we set up this meeting. It was brought to my attention only recently."

"You're making a mistake." My voice comes out wobbly, lacking conviction. And god, could I have come up with more of a cliché?

"I'm sure we are, but we take our clients' safety very seriously. Thank you for coming by, and I'm sorry not to have better news."

And just like that, I've been dismissed. I lift Sabine up—she's so heavy, and the diaper bag is so heavy, and I just want to lie down—and stride out of the office. I can't meet anybody's eye. Did they all know in advance that I was going in there to be rejected? A huge lump wedges in my throat, and my breath is coming in and out all shaky with tears. I manage to bite out a hushed "Thank you" to the receptionist as I hurry out of the office. It's only when I'm out of the lobby that I let the tears come.

"Fucking bitch," I whisper under my breath. I can't even wipe them off because my hands are full. There hadn't been time to take the stroller out of the trunk of the car, and boy am I regretting my choice now, as I lug Sabine and the diaper bag across the parking lot under the unforgiving LA sun.

I need Mer. The thought hits me like a brutal sucker punch. It's true. I need my best friend. Days like these, all I want is to drive to her place, plop Sabine in a playpen with Luca, and eat Ben & Jerry's (Phish Food for me, Chunky Monkey for her) right out of the carton while we bitch about what a bitch Michelle Reyes turned out to be. God, why did we have to fight? Of all the things I regret, this is the one I can't get over. Our horrible, soul-ripping fight.

Stop it. No use ruminating. I need to move on.

As I near my car, I spot someone peeping into it. "Hey!" I call out. With tears blurring my vision, it's hard to tell if the figure is male or female, but something tells me it's a woman. She jerks away from my car and runs off before I can say anything else.

I hurry to my car, my blood pounding in my ears. There doesn't seem to be any damage done to it, but still, I can't shake off the sickening, nervous sensation lurking in my gut. Michelle's words echo in my head: *Your trolls seem more . . . personal.*

I look around the parking lot, unable to shake the feeling that someone is watching me. Someone who knows what I've done.

# Chapter 3

# MEREDITH

What am I doing? Just what the hell am I doing? This isn't Stalking Lite anymore. I'm in full-on Joe Goldberg mode. In fact, Joe Goldberg would probably give me that judgy stare of his and say, "That's messed up." Shut up, Joe. At least I'm not a killer.

I should stop. This isn't cute anymore. But when Aspen navigates her way out of the parking lot, I start my car and follow once more, making sure to keep some distance away from her. We take the 110 back towards Pasadena. Aspen's place is a couple blocks away from Caltech, a gorgeous home surrounded by a pristine front yard and a backyard complete with a pool and treehouse and a patio to die for. Meanwhile, I'm stuck in San Gabriel. She shops at Trader Joe's. I shop at the San Gabriel Superstore. She buys organic pre-marinated bulgogi in sterile vacuum packs. I buy frozen nuggets and off-brand hot dogs.

"How is that fair?" I say to Luca. He's taken a break from sucking on his foot and is sucking on his fists instead. "This is why we gotta do this, right, sweetie?"

I lose Aspen right as she exits, but I know her route like the veins on the backs of my hands. I don't panic. I take the turn, not even bothering to try and peer around the car ahead of me to see if she's still there. I drive down Mission Street, and just as I knew I would, I catch sight of her Land Rover driving into Trader Joe's parking lot. I nod to myself and drive away. It's lunchtime, and I'm famished. Luca feeds like a fiend, so I'm just constantly hungry. And tired. And cranky. This whole breastfeeding business is bullshit.

When I got pregnant, I thought to myself: *I'm going to be that mom every other mom loves to hate. I'm going to be skinny because I'm going to take on breastfeeding like it's a fucking Olympic sport. My baby's going to suck all the calories right out of me.* And you know what? I really did do that. For the first month of his life, Luca was basically attached to my boobs 24/7. And it was hell. The tips of my nipples cracked, scabbed over, then the scabs were pulled off as he sucked. It was excruciating, like razor blades on my nipples. While milk poured out of me, tears flowed from my eyes, and snot leaked from my nostrils. I was leaking liquid everywhere. I couldn't even bear to use the breast pump because my nipples were stinging so bad, so when Luca wasn't nursing, I hand-expressed the rest of my milk into Medela bottles. Once, as I was squeezing my breast like a cow's udder, I cried so much that a teardrop plopped into the bottle. My scream jerked Luca awake. I picked up the wailing baby and latched him to my other nipple and called Aspen.

"Is it tainted now?" I bawled. "Do I have to throw it out? There's like, four ounces!"

Aspen laughed. "No. Oh my god. Tears are okay. It was only a drop, right?"

"But I've got my eyelash extensions! The tear is probably contaminated with eyelash glue or something."

"Babe," she said, "you know how much crap is on our nipples? Sweat, natural body oils, moisturizer. Give the expressed milk to Luca. He'll be fine."

Relief washed through me. But right on the heels of that surge of relief was something else. Something that had caught on to the patronizing tone in Aspen's voice. Heard the silent laughter in the way she'd said, "Babe." There was something familiar in it. And it was then that I realized it was how I used to talk to her. *No. I was never that patronizing towards her, never.*

She was still talking. "I was like that with the twins. Sterilizing everything. And now, with Sabine, I'm just like, meh. She'll be fine, you know? Yesterday, she dropped her pacifier on the kitchen floor, and I just gave it a rinse, wiped it off, and put it back in her mouth. It'll be fine!"

She was trying to reassure me. Part of me was grateful, but it was only a small part. The major part of me was furious. How fucking dare she look down on me like that? Treat me like a novice? I was the one who made her. When I spoke again, my voice was pure ice.

"No, I'm dumping the milk. Maybe you're okay with giving Sabby dirty milk, but I don't think I could live with myself if Luca got sick."

There was a pause. Jesus. Why did I have to come at her with claws out? She was just trying to help.

*No, she wasn't. She knew exactly what she was doing. Reminding me that the status quo had flipped, and that now she was the expert—the one showing me the ropes.*

Still, the silence stretched on until I wanted to snap. Then, finally, she laughed. "Okay, Mer. You know best."

"I do."

The memory of that day, that almost-fight, scrapes like a knife against raw skin. There have been so many of those moments, especially once I announced my pregnancy. Dozens of little comments from Aspen made to cut me down—to remind me that I am now walking a path she's already sprinted. She had the twins six and a half years ago; she's a total pro at motherhood. And now here I am, stumbling down this path all alone. I'm not like her. I don't have a devoted husband or an assistant. It's just me and Luca against the world.

By the time we get home, Luca is full-on crying. I gather up everything—my purse, the bulging diaper bag, and Luca—and hurry inside my apartment. Inside, I lift up my shirt and yank down my bra and latch him on.

After the first two months or so of breastfeeding, things got better. My nipples got used to it, the wounds slowly healed, and nursing stopped feeling like I was being mauled by a pack of hungry lion cubs. Still, contrary to popular belief, it hasn't helped me lose the baby weight. Sure, breastfeeding burns some calories, but it's not actually that much.

While Luca feeds, I shove all the junk off my sofa one-handed and settle down with a sigh. I open my Insta and clock the number of followers. 861,292. I frown. Yesterday, I had 861,113. I'm still growing, but it's definitely hitting a plateau.

"What more do you want from me?" I mutter at my Insta. I click on the Insights. My latest posts—mostly Reels—are doing okay. Most of them are averaging around five to seven hundred thousand views, which sounds impressive, but considering the number of followers I have, it's not amazing. Unlike Aspen, who has over five million followers—5,152,349 to be exact, but who's counting? Her Reels are getting over seven million views at the very least. What the fuck is up with that, Instagram? And don't even get me started on TikTok. My TikTok presence is abysmal. On TikTok, I'm what's considered a "micro-influencer," which is only one step above "nano-influencer." I have around seventy thousand followers, whereas Aspen has cracked the TikTok code and is already at six million and still growing massively. She tried getting me to move to TikTok when it first became big.

"It's amazing, Mer," she said, her eyes wide. The twins were about three years old then. I remember because that was right around the time that they found out Noemie was diabetic. "TikTok's algorithm is completely different from everything else. They really want to push your content out to new people, not just your followers. I'm growing faster than I ever did on Insta. You need to be on TikTok; it's the next big thing."

"You said the same thing about Snapchat, and look where that went," I grumbled. At the time, Aspen had already surpassed me on Insta, so when Snapchat blew up, I made sure to invest the bulk of my time in it. Then everyone moved on, and all that time and effort just went down the drain. I might as well have focused on Tumblr for all the good Snapchat did.

"Forget Snapchat, Mer. Trust me, TikTok's where it's at."

But I fought it for the longest time. I told myself that while Aspen was focusing on TikTok, I could take that chance to try and catch up to her on Insta. Not that it was a competition, of course. She's my BFF! My ride or die. I just wanted us to do as well as each other. That's not jealousy. That's camaraderie.

Except Aspen was right about TikTok. Her TikTok platform grew ten times faster than any of her other accounts did, and her TikTok followers followed her on other platforms as well. Her Instagram blew up. I could've sworn she gained a hundred thousand followers every fucking week. I was seeing #alldayaspen everywhere I turned. I muted her. (It's not mean. I was protecting my mental health.) Then I unmuted her. Rinse and repeat.

Aspen's girls were born for social media. She's always dressing them in matchy-matchy outfits, and achingly cute ones at that. They look like little ballerinas, or little princesses, or little fairies. I can just see her target audience—women between the ages of twenty and thirty-seven—lapping up all the whimsical outfits she forces the girls into. I look down at Luca, who's already emptied my left breast, and shift him to the right one.

"Why couldn't you have been a girl?" I mutter. "Then you could've worn all those cute dresses too. Look at the twins and Sabine in this one. Oh my gosh, sunflowers all over, to die for." I narrow my eyes at Luca. Maybe I could put him in shorts with sunflowers around the hem? Plus navy blue suspenders. That would be cute. But where would I even find sunflower-patterned shorts for boys? I sigh. Why did I end up with a boy? You know how boring boys' clothes are? You only have to walk into the kids' section of any department store, and you'll see how stark the differences are. The girls' section is full of different materials—lace, wool, chiffon—in every color possible. Bright primary colors, soft pastels, neutral creams. Everything you could ever wish for, they offer it to girls. And don't even get me started on the hair accessories. If you turn around and head into the boys' section, all you find is tan and navy blue stuff. No frills, no flowers. Only animals allowed in the boys' section, and not sweet whimsical ones like ladybugs or kittens. Predators only. Sharks, dinosaurs, lions. Zero accessories. Boring-ass shoes.

Maybe I could put him in a dress anyway?

I quickly bat away the thought. It would end up being

a statement on gender. I have no idea what kind of statement it would be, but whatever it was, it would only invite trolls. Ah, if only I could be honest and caption it with: "This is not about gender politics. I just think girls' clothes are cuter." The thought makes me snort. Oh, I crack myself up. Ha, ha.

It's only when a drop of tear spatters Luca's cheek that I realize I'm crying. What the fuck? I wipe it away angrily. Ever since I had Luca, my hormones have been going batshit insane. I'm crying everywhere, at any time. It's not postpartum. I know it isn't, because I love my baby to death, I really do, and I don't even feel sad or disconnected. I do feel anxious and stressed out all the time, though, but that's only because my best friend decided she was too good for me ever since she became a huge influencer.

Luca unlatches with a small pop, his head lolling, his eyes half-closed. I heft him over my shoulder and pat his back until he burps, then put him in his bassinet for a nap. I'm so tired. Unbelievably so. How the hell does Aspen do it? She's got not just Sabine, but also the twins to deal with. Then again, she has Ben and Liv, so maybe that evens things out a little. I stretch out on the sofa and close my eyes. I should nap. At almost seven months of age, Luca still wakes up every two hours through the night. Sabine, on the other hand, is the perfect baby, because of course she is.

But when I close my eyes, numbers whiz through my head. Six million. Seven million. Eight million. I wonder if she'll move out of Pasadena once she hits ten million. How much money do influencers with over ten million followers make? Aspen stopped talking about money a few months after she surpassed me. Whenever I asked how much she was making per sponsored post, she'd give me this pitying smile and say, "Oh, you know,

I can't complain!" Bitch, I'm not complaining, I'm just comparing notes. But I know she feels sorry for me, which makes me even angrier. *It used to be the other way around*, I want to rail at the universe. How did things get so backassward?

I give up trying to nap. No, I need to see Aspen again. I need to—I don't know. I need my best friend. Or at least, I need to know what my best friend's up to.

Less than fifteen minutes later, I'm at my sister's door. She doesn't smile when she opens it. "Hi, Auntie Clara!" I say in a baby voice, lifting Luca's carrier close to her face.

Clara sighs. "Seriously? Again?"

"I've got a really important meeting to get to. A potential sponsor."

"Okay, but isn't your 'brand' Single Mom Does It All?" Clara says, putting rabbit ears around the word "brand" and spitting it like it's a cockroach crawling out of her mouth. "So shouldn't Luca come with you to the meeting?"

She has a point, but I recover quickly. "Oh, this one's more Single Mom Looking Fabulous and Having a Healthy Life Outside of Being a Mom."

Clara doesn't look impressed. "I've got a really full day."

"Really? It's not wedding season." Clara's a wedding photographer, and she's usually busiest in the summer, although, LA being LA, weddings do tend to happen all year round.

"Yeah, but I started doing family portraits, too, remember? So I've got pictures to edit, and—"

"Oh yeah, that's right! Hey, that's perfect, you can practice with Luca. Isn't he the most photogenic baby you've ever seen? Come on, you can't say no to that face." I push the carrier even closer to her.

Clara sighs again, but the corners of her mouth are lifting ever so slightly, and I know I've won this battle. "He is pretty damn cute," she says as she takes the carrier from me. "But I swear, Mer, next time, I'm saying no."

"Love you, sis!" I kiss her on the cheek and hand her the diaper bag before jogging down her driveway back to her car.

"And I want my car back by tonight," she calls out. "I don't like the way yours smells."

"Got it, sis!" I almost speed out of there in my eagerness, but since I'm in Clara's car, I take care to drive out slowly, waving at them and throwing kisses as I go.

The drive to Aspen's house takes twenty minutes, since there's very little traffic at this time of day. I park a block away from her house, and for a few moments sit in Clara's car, drumming my fingers on the wheel. What am I doing? I check my Apple watch. It's ten minutes to two. The twins' school lets out at two twenty. So Aspen will leave the house any time now.

I get out of the car and stroll down the next street over to Aspen's, my thoughts repeatedly going *What am I doing?* over and over like a heartbeat, faster and faster as I near her house. I'm two houses away when I hear the clang of her garage door opening, and I slip behind a tree. Her Land Rover backs out of the garage and drives off. The garage door is only halfway closed. I quickly run over—*what am I doing what am I doing*—and before it shuts, I kick out and put my foot under it. For a moment, I think my foot is going to be squashed. But then the safety sensors kick in, and the door stops rumbling down and starts to open again. *Phew.*

Aspen had the safety sensors installed the year the twins started walking. She was terrified that they might get squished under the garage door. I had laughed at her then, calling her a paranoid helicopter parent, but hey, I have to admit, I'm not laughing now. Or rather, I am laughing now, because look who just got inside your garage, Aspen? There are two doors in the garage—one leading straight into the house, which is locked, and the other leading into the backyard, which is unlocked. Since I haven't acquired the skills to pick door locks, I choose to go out into the backyard.

And now what? I feel ridiculous. For a few moments, I stand there in Aspen's magazine-worthy backyard, frozen. Her beautiful pool shimmers before me, so utterly inviting in the LA heat. Before our falling-out, I used to come here every day and plunge into the pool with Luca. His face would light up as he splashed around in the clear blue water with Sabby. The memory cuts at me, and I have to look away from the pool. *Maybe I can go inside through the patio doors.* I try them, but they're locked as well, and I don't want to set off any home alarms. It would be très awkward if Aspen had to rush home because an alarm went off and found me in the middle of her house.

With a sigh, I plop down on one of the lounge chairs. There's a damp towel scrunched up on the lounge chair with a print of Princess Elsa from *Frozen*. Probably Elea's. She's a hardcore Elsa fan. Has an Elsa everything—lunch box, water bottle, even underwear. I smile sadly—god, how I miss the girls—and pick up the towel to hang it up neatly over the back of the chair. It'll get moldy otherwise. But then I freeze. Because there, underneath Elea's towel, is an iPad. Presumably hers. I pick it up and hit the Home button. It asks for a swipe code, and I figure out quickly that the swipe code is an E. I'm in.

As expected, there are all the usual apps. The kid-friendly

educational games, all of them shouting about how they promote STEM. I swipe again, feeling stupid for snooping inside a kid's iPad. What *am* I doing? But then I tap on the calendar and freeze. Holy shit. They have a family calendar. Everything is connected. Everyone's schedule is spelled out clearly, in painstaking detail.

There's Ben's work stuff, the houses he's showing, the chores he needs to do, the twins' extracurriculars, Sabine's pediatrician appointments, but most importantly, there's Aspen's schedule. Aspen's meetings with potential sponsors, with fellow influencers, with photographers. Times and dates and locations. Notes on each one. Hand shaking, I go back to the home screen, and this time, I tap on Instagram. It opens, and I stop breathing. *I'm in Aspen's account.*

I have access to everything. Her drafts. Her scheduled posts. Her DMs. And I know then, clear as lightning, that the universe has decided to give me this one. Because I have taken the back seat long enough. I've been in her shadow long enough. I've endured enough of her subtle patronizing digs.

Things are about to change.

# Chapter 4

# MEREDITH

Hold up. I can sense the judgment seething from you. You're thinking: *What kind of monster steals a CHILD'S iPad?* First of all, I'm not stealing it. I'm borrowing it. Second of all, Elea (and Noemie, and Sabine) is my goddaughter, and if I asked her to lend me her iPad, I'm one hundred percent sure she'd say yes. In fact, she would insist that I take it, because she knows that would annoy her mom. Third of all, I think you need context. You're sitting there thinking I'm this horrible jealous bitch who can't handle her best friend's success, and that's not at all the case. Let me paint a picture.

*Seven and a Half Years Ago*

With my help, Aspen very quickly realized that there was, in fact, no future for her in music. We quickly became close enough to each other to have regular sleepovers at my place. She shared a one-bedroom in Culver City with three other girls, whereas I at least had my own place: a studio in Glendale. It was during one of these sleepovers that we took a deep dive into her YouTube channel. I pointed out that five thousand subscribers in two years wasn't good enough to cut it—wasn't going to get her noticed by a record label. To my surprise, Aspen agreed.

I very quickly learned that Aspen is one of the most agreeable people I've ever known. She's a compulsive agree-er. At first, I found it a bit off-putting, but now, a year into our friendship, I've grown to appreciate it. Unlike most of the people I've gotten to know in LA, Aspen is low drama—happy to go along with most of my suggestions, even when they contradict hers. Truly happy, not an "I'm *fine*" happy. Being friends with her is like paddling in the kiddie pool: safe and predictable. I do not hate it. It's why, when I was invited to a huge influencer event in Las Vegas, I took her along as my plus-one. The event went as expected: lots of photos and videos were taken, and I signed with two more sponsors while Aspen looked on with naked admiration.

We spend a lot of the drive from Vegas trying to figure out her niche. I'm huge on Instagram already, with over three hundred thousand followers ("I can't even *imagine* what it must be like to have a hundred thousand followers!" Aspen squeals. I give her a humble smile in return, my insides glowing, vibrating with glee at her open admiration), but Aspen has foolishly neglected Insta in favor of YouTube and Facebook. Thanks to me, she's started up an Insta account, but nearly a year in and she's gained fewer than ten thousand followers.

"I think I'm just not cut out for fame," Aspen sighs, gazing out at the desert.

"Bullshit. Look at you, you're beautiful. Of course you're cut out for fame. We both are. We just need to find your niche."

Aspen props herself up on her elbow and gazes at me. "I don't know, Mer, I'm not like you. You've got that . . . X factor."

I snort. "Trust me. If you'd known me back in Ohio, you

wouldn't have said that. It's just that I found my niche: beauty and fashion advice with some sass." I wink at her, and she gives me a small smile.

For a while, neither of us speaks, lost in our own thoughts. I'm mulling over my success in Vegas, caressing the memories of me signing with my new sponsors, when Aspen says, "You know what strikes me about this place?"

"Huh?"

Aspen gestures at the lonely desert around us. "This huge stretch of nothingness."

"What about it?"

"I mean, it's literally an endless expanse of nothing between two major cities, isn't that crazy?"

"Uh . . ." I shrug. The topic isn't catching my interest, so I'm only half paying attention. "Sure, I guess."

"There must be so many dead bodies buried out here. Anyone could just walk off the road, into the desert, and never be found," Aspen murmurs.

"What the hell?"

Aspen gives me an apologetic smile. "Sorry, too creepy?"

"Uh, yeah? Why are you thinking of bodies in the desert? Geez."

She laughs. "I guess sometimes my thoughts just go to dark places. Anyway, I love what you've done with your hair."

"Really?" I take one hand off the wheel and primp my curls self-consciously. One of the many gifts I picked up at the event was a high-tech hair curler that promised me the world. "I think they're a bit too tight."

"You can carry it off," she says, as loyal as ever.

I frown at the rearview mirror, then smile. She's right. I can carry these curls off. "Okay, let's go back to finding your niche. What are your interests?"

She shrugs. "Cooking?"

My frown deepens. It's true that Aspen's cooking is amazing. We often stay in because eating out in LA is horrifically expensive, and plus, she stays over at my place so often that she feels guilty about it, so she's always trying to make up for it by cooking me dinner. But to me, cooking isn't something an influencer does. "I don't know, not glamorous enough. Ooh, how about celeb gossip?"

Aspen goggles at me. "Dude, what? I know nothing about celebrities."

"Yeah, but we live in LA—okay, well, we're LA-adjacent—and we're always running into celebrities at the parties I get invited to."

If Aspen notices the specificity with which I say, "the parties I get invited to" and not, "we," she doesn't show it. She continues looking at me with open admiration. "I know," she says, "but I don't like, talk to them. I have no idea what to say to them."

"Babe, they're normal people, just like you or me. Ask them about their day. Tell them you love their clothes."

She giggles. "I'm not like you, Mer. You're so good at mingling."

"You could learn, like you've learned everything else from me. Look at you now. I wouldn't recognize you from a year ago."

It's true. Thanks to my help, present-day Aspen looks like a true-blue Angeleno. She's dressed in high-end athleisure with slim cutouts right below the collarbone to bring the eye to her chest. And speaking of collarbones, Aspen's are popping now, thanks to the low-carb diet I put her on. I've taught her how to get the Kylie lips by overlining them, and her face is so heavily contoured it would make a Greek sculptor fall to his knees. She is gorgeous, and it is honestly infuriating to me why she hasn't yet been discovered by the morons on Instagram. She deserves fame, damn it!

"You know what?" I say. "When we get back, I'm going to do your hair, too, and then we'll take selfies and post to our Instas. And I'll tag you so my followers know to follow you too."

"Oh, Mer," Aspen murmurs. "Why are you so nice to me?"

I grin at her. "Because we're best friends, of course."

She matches my smile. "Forever."

"Forever."

That same night, after we arrive back from Vegas, we go to a party (that I was invited to, of course, not Aspen), this time at a beach house in Malibu. It belongs to the son of some rock star, someone too ancient for me to know of, and the house is filled to the neck with memorabilia. Electric guitars dominate an entire wall, a drum set is in one corner and literally cordoned off with red velvet rope, and framed magazine covers are everywhere. Kind of over the top, if you ask me. But I play the game well. I greet everyone, throw air kisses here and there, and call everyone "Darling," even the people I don't recognize. Aspen is, as usual, at my heels, clutching her purse like a shield. Despite the contouring and the hair and the overlined lips, she still somehow manages to look out of place.

"Loosen up," I mutter to her. "Some of the people here are the very best influencers."

Her plastered-on smile freezes. "That doesn't exactly help me loosen up."

I sigh. "You're my bestie. Everyone is going to love you." Before

I can say anything else, someone grabs my arm and I turn to see Ever Elle. (Can you believe that's supposedly her official name? Like, the actual name on her birth cert? That's what she claims, anyway, the fraud.)

"Bitch!" she cries gleefully.

"Slut!" I shout back. We laugh and pull each other into an aggressive hug. It's our thing.

"Omigod," she yells over the music. "How are you? Girl, you are growing so fast —what are you at now, one hundred thousand followers?"

I smile and bat my eyelashes demurely. "Try three hundred."

"Omigod, bitch!" she squeals, hugging me again. "I'm only at like, two hundred and fifty. You must tell me your secret."

"No secret, I just try to be as authentic as possible." My go-to answer.

"Of course, yes, authentic, totally. I mean, that's what I always say, myself." Ever gives a vigorous nod. Both her hair and eyelashes are neon pink tonight. "I love your post about mental health. The way you were so real, so raw, about the pressure of looking perfect as an Insta-model. Obsessed!"

I want to give her a huge Cheshire cat grin, but that would be kind of tacky, so I tamp down my glee and battle my mouth into an acceptably humble smile. "Aww, thank you. I was just speaking my truth, you know?"

"Yeah, for sure."

"Oh, this is my friend Asp—" It's only when I glance over my shoulder that I realize Aspen is no longer behind me. I cock my head and turn around, scanning the room full of people for her. Nothing but the usual starved bodies pulsating to throbbing music.

"Uh oh, did you lose your date?" Ever says. Even above the deafening music, I catch the sneer in her voice. I want to hit her.

"She must've gotten lost. Excuse me, I better look for her. She's my protégé." I leave without waiting for a reply from Ever, plunging into the knot of people. I swim through the crowd, making sure to keep the brilliant smile on my face. People say hi to me and I say hi back to them, but my eyes don't stop scanning the crowd, trying to locate Aspen's familiar form. I should just leave her be. I should just enjoy myself. But I'm only now realizing that it's been almost a year since I met Aspen, and we've gone to almost every party together, and her absence is disturbingly noticeable. I got used to having her shadow me. To having her watch my every interaction, knowing that she's admiring my conversational skills; knowing that each smooth interaction I have makes her wilt just a tiny bit, because she knows she can't do what I can. (I'm not being horrible, it's just a fact of life that people adore the knowledge of having something that others don't. If there was no pleasure to be taken from exclusivity, then the rich wouldn't be so into their private country clubs. There is joy from knowing you are blessed while others are not; if you deny it, you'll only be lying.)

Only a short while passes, but already I'm incandescent with rage. I invited her to this party. Without me, she wouldn't even have the measly number of followers she has. And she certainly wouldn't be here, in this jaw-dropping Malibu mansion surrounded by stars. And she has the audacity to ditch me? We are going to have fucking *words.*

But she's the one who finds me. I've just stepped outside onto the patio, which overlooks the crashing waves, when she spots me. "Mer!" she cries from the beach. I turn to the sound of her voice, and my rage freezes in my veins. I've never seen Aspen like this before. Her hair is wild, whipping in the sea breeze, and even in the dark, I can see that her face is flushed. She looks like a wood nymph stepping out of the forest.

The spell breaks, and all my anger comes surging back in a fierce wave. "Where have you been?" I hiss, as she stumbles across the sand toward me.

"I'm so sorry!" she laughs. "Oh my gosh, you wouldn't believe what just happened. I got separated from you—the crowd just swallowed you up—god, Mer, I was terrified. I kept trying to look for you, but the crowd was too much. I got overwhelmed, so I went outside to get some fresh air, and I went down to the beach and—"

"Got swept away," a male voice says. A man I haven't noticed has slipped out from the folds of the darkness. He stands close to Aspen. Way too close for someone she's just met. Unlike everyone else at this party, he isn't beautiful, but there's a steadiness to his gaze that makes you look twice.

Aspen giggles, and I want to smack her. "Literally, Mer! Well, my shoe did, anyway." She lifts her right hand, from which dangles a single shoe. "God, those waves. I wasn't expecting them to be that strong."

"It's a surfer's paradise out here," the guy says. His voice is so deep and rich that your brain instinctively tells you to pause and listen, even if he's saying the most clichéd words ever.

"Surfer's paradise?" What are we, in the freaking Eighties? Who even says that anymore?

"I don't even know what I was doing," Aspen continues. "I think I was screaming and like, rushing in to grab it back." I notice that her voice has gone up an octave and is a little bit more nasal, like a kid's. Once more, the urge to hurt her, to pinch her or shake her out of this, nearly overwhelms me. I swallow it down.

"She was screaming," the guy laughs, "and yeah, she was literally about to dive in after the shoe. I caught her just before the waves took her. Are your shoes made of diamonds or something?" He looks down at her, smiling and shaking his head, and I feel nauseated. The way he's gazing down at her and her up at him, there's so much naked attraction in their eyes that I feel as though I am intruding. And not just attraction, but somehow a history, as though they'd known each other for a long time before tonight.

He finally seems to notice me staring and offers me his hand. "I'm sorry, I'm being rude. You must be Meredith. I'm Ben."

I take his hand and taste bile in my throat. His grasp is firm and warm, and when I look into his aquamarine eyes, it's clear that he's not going to be just some guy we ran into at a party one night. The look in his eyes promises that he's going to be a permanent problem, a constant wedge between Aspen and me. *I'm going to have to get rid of you somehow,* I think as I look at Ben and meet his glowing smile.

# Chapter 5

# ASPEN

I hate Ben's smile. That's an awful thing to think, isn't it? What kind of wife hates her own husband's smile? I used to love it, hunger for it even. I don't know when those smiles of his changed—went from adoring to fake, and now, to disgusted ones. I pretend not to notice it tonight as I place dinner on the table. As always, dinner is a feast, both for the eyes and the stomach. Okay, if I were to be honest, it's more a feast for the eyes.

There's a beautifully roasted free-range chicken with crispy brown skin, perfectly caramelized brussels sprouts with turkey bacon bits, salad with veg freshly picked from the garden, and low GI red rice. Everything is organic and both diabetes and social media friendly.

In truth, the chicken is overcooked because to get that delectable brown shade, I needed to roast it just a tad too long. The brussels sprouts, too, are slightly burned to get those charred edges, and I can already tell from the sharp smell that they're going to be bitter and will most likely end up in the compost bin. Nobody likes red rice; it's dry and brittle, and the whole point of rice is the warm vanilla fragrance and chewy texture, neither of which is present when it comes to red rice. The salad is from a garden, but it sure as hell isn't *my* garden, which has languished under the unforgiving LA heat this year. Not that anyone on social media would know; I am nothing if not meticulous. Ben had watched, incredulous, as I took the carrots I'd bought from the farmer's market and buried them in our garden, only to take a video of myself unearthing them.

"Are you serious?" he'd said, with that disgusted snort-laugh. I'd ignored him. I have long learned that the best way to deal with my husband's derision is to pretend it all went over my head. It's not too big a leap for him to make, to think his wife is too fucking dumb to get anything he says.

Anyway, he smiles as I arrange each deceptively appetizing dish just so at the table. The kids are already seated, the twins on one side, baby Sabine on the other, and Ben at the head of the table. I take a video for my Stories and my mouth pinches at how fake Ben's smile is. He's not even trying to look convincing for the camera. Neither is Elea, of course, but she's six, and he's a full-grown man with an understanding of mortgages, and healthcare bills, and why I need to keep doing this.

As I'm taking a close-up of the chicken, Elea reaches out and rips off a drumstick.

"Elea, please don't." I admonish her as gently as I can, but still she jerks back and looks at Ben with wide, sad eyes.

"It's for Noemie," she says in a small voice. "I don't want her blood sugar to drop. Mommy's taking too long."

It's a fight to keep my voice calm. "You didn't really take it for Noemie." Elea has never shown a shred of concern about Noemie's blood sugar level.

Ben looks at me with—there are no other words for

it—contempt. Then he turns to Elea and says, "That's really sweet of you, Elea. I think you get a star for that."

Elea beams up at him, and my stomach is so tight and sour that I think I might throw up. When I was pregnant with the twins, Ben had kissed my belly and said, "Promise me that you and I will always be a team? We won't undermine each other in front of the baby?" I had promised, and I've kept my promise. But nowadays, it feels like it's the entire household versus me, and I don't understand how it got to be like this when I'm the one keeping everything afloat.

I force a smile—when was the last time my smiles came naturally?—and straighten up. "It's fine. I'm done with the video." I'll roll with the ruined footage, because when have I not? I already know the caption: "Somebody couldn't wait to dig in! #HomeCooked #BestRoastChicken."

There are grumbles as everyone starts eating. Well, I say everyone, but the complaints are mostly from Ben and Elea, who hate absolutely everything on the table. Noemie eats quietly, but I can tell from the way she chews and doesn't meet anyone's eye that she, too, isn't enjoying herself. Guilt and resentment fight for dominance inside me. *What are they complaining about? I do my best to put food on the table every fucking day and all they do is complain.* Then the guilt—a quiet, sharp whisper that slides like a knife across a vein: *Yes, but you know the food sucks. It's purely for aesthetics, but it tastes crap. The chicken might as well be cardboard.*

As usual, the guilt overwhelms everything else, and I end up getting up from the table and fetching a bunch of vegan "chicken" nuggets that I'd dumped into the air fryer twenty minutes ago. "Ta da!" I say, placing the nuggets in the center of the table.

Everyone's eyes brighten, even baby Sabine's, and she's still on purees, so I don't know what she's so excited about.

"How many am I allowed, Mommy?" Noemie says as Elea scoops huge spoonfuls of nuggets onto her own plate. I have to bite back a snarky comment about Elea not waiting for her sister before digging in. I force myself to focus on Noemie and do a quick calculation in my head. "Um, I think four's a safe number. Do you agree, honey?" I add, turning to Ben.

I've caught him spacing out, as usual. It's as though he hates my company so much these days that he'd rather escape into his own head. Anywhere but here. He blinks, then says, "Oh, yeah. Sounds good."

Again, I repress the urge to snark at him and ask what exactly he's saying yes to. There is so much bitterness to swallow these days. At least everyone's eating now, even if it is frozen nuggets. Still, they're organic and vegan, so that's not too bad, right?

The peace lasts about five minutes. "Hey, Daddy, after this, can we go on Amazon and buy me a new iPad?" Elea says.

"Hmm?" Ben looks lost for a split second, his mouth full of vegan nugget, then he shrugs. "Sure."

"Uh, I don't think so," I say, and realize there's too much of a bite in my voice. I modulate it to a calmer tone. "I think it's a good lesson for you to learn, sweetie. To take better care of your belongings."

"But it's literally been forever!"

"Mhmm," I say without much sympathy.

"But I need it!" Elea whines.

I level my gaze at her. "Really? You need an iPad? What for?"

"All the educational games on it," she shoots back. This kid definitely has too much sass for a six-year-old. "You were the one who said that I'm smart enough to get into a STEM program. Did you change your mind?"

"Of course not, but you're taking robotics at school, and engineering. I don't think you need an iPad to teach you STEM."

"Daddy!" Elea whines, staring at him with huge, imploring eyes.

Ben opens his mouth, but before he can say anything, I quickly say, "Mommy and Daddy will discuss this later."

He presses his lips together into a thin line and nods. I press mine into a smile. If there's anything I'm good at, it's pretending that everything is fine. "So I'm really looking forward to the shoot this weekend!" I say brightly.

Elea rolls her eyes, but Noemie gives me a small smile. Ben stares at me blankly, then says, "What shoot?"

It is so hard not to sigh at him. "The one with Maya? For next month's posts." Every month, I book a full-day session with Maya Alexander, my favorite photographer. We go through at least ten outfit changes, all of them matchy-matchy, of course, and all of them of us doing a different family activity. Since we're shooting for October posts, I've already lined up a whole bunch of fall activities: I've bought a dozen pumpkins which we'll paint white, I got orange food coloring so we can pretend to be making pumpkin smoothies, pumpkin cakes, pumpkin cookies, Halloween decorations, Halloween costumes (at least three different sets) and so on and so forth. Maya charges three hundred and fifty dollars per hour, so I have to be ruthless when it comes to planning these shoots.

"Oh god," Ben groans. He actually throws his head back and moans like I've asked him to enroll in a marathon.

I resist saying anything snarky. I just look at him.

"I can't do it," he says, finally. "I've got an open house that day."

*Do not get angry. Do not show how furious you are.* I keep my voice even as I say, "I've reminded you twice about this shoot. You know how important they are."

"So is my job," he bites back.

I want to shriek with laughter. His job. Ben is a midlevel realtor who takes home less than forty grand a year, before taxes. Meanwhile, I'm making close to half a million a year after taxes. Guess who's shouldering the burden of the mortgage on our beautiful Spanish-style home in the heart of Pasadena, and the extensive healthcare that covers Noemie's ongoing treatment, and the competitive private school that the twins go to—the one that boasts at least twelve different kinds of STEM activities? Not to mention the pricey gymnastics and ballet classes?

But I don't throw all of these at him. I've been warned, time and again, by well-meaning people like my own mother, that earning more than my husband does will emasculate him. And I don't want to do that to Ben, not in front of the girls. So I swallow yet more bitterness and rage and say, "I'm sorry, but I told you about the shoot months in advance. It's in our shared calendar. Maya is extremely popular; she won't be able to fit us into another slot last minute."

"Then you'll just have to do the shoot without me," Ben says, with a shrug. "Because I'm not canceling the open house."

"Ben, please," I plead. "The house you're showing—it's the one in Alhambra, right? I mean, it's not . . ." I struggle for the right words to say. I don't want the knife to cut too deep. "I mean, look, October is such a lucrative month for me. I'll earn probably double the usual months. October aesthetics are—"

"If I hear that damn word one more time." Though his voice is quiet, it is dripping with venom. "Aesthetics," he spits out.

"Our lives are nothing but aesthetics." He takes a sharp inhale, as though he wants to throw his chair across the room. But then he glances at the twins, who are watching closely, and says (slowly, enunciating each word like I'm hard of hearing), "I am not rescheduling my open house."

I can taste tears at the back of my throat. More than anything, I wish I could talk to Meredith about this.

"Go on," Ben mutters as he stabs at a vegan nugget. "Go bitch about me to Mer like you always do. Oh wait, you guys aren't talking because you're in high school, apparently."

I jerk up from my seat so sharply that my fork and knife clatter on my plate. "Sorry," I say in a hushed voice. "Just gonna—just—bathroom." I hurry out of there before the tears come.

Once I'm in the bathroom, I lean on the counter and focus on my breathing. I can hear cutlery clanging from the dining room, though no one is talking. The twins are old enough to know that Mommy and Daddy just had a fight. I can't believe Ben said that to me. He didn't pull any punches, just went straight for the jugular. He of all people knows how much space Mer takes up in my life—how much it had ripped me apart when we had that fight. He knows how much I've missed her, the numerous sleepless nights I've spent, my thoughts whirling around the giant hole in my heart.

Tears scald my cheeks. *What am I crying over? My utter shambles of a marriage, or my ruined friendship*? I can't ignore the feeling that neither is salvageable. The problem with Mer and Ben is that they both loved me only when I was a naive girl with stars and sweet inexperience in my eyes, and a pure innocent willingness to drink their every word of advice like it was scripture. As soon as I outgrew them, their kindness and generosity sharpened into jealousy. Each time I dared to share any piece of advice I had learned along the way with them, I was quickly smacked down, reminded that my place isn't above or even beside them. I entered their lives as a follower, and a follower I must stay.

I turn on the tap and splash cold water onto my face. I need to get a hold of myself. I take out my phone and open up my socials. As sad as it sounds, scrolling through my profiles is my favorite pastime. They're a reminder of why I'm doing all of this—why I need to keep posting religiously. I put my favorite filters over this evening's photos and post them to my Stories. The Likes come in almost immediately; many of my followers have added me to their notifications list. I already know which ones will usually be the first to hit Like. I lean against the counter and scroll as the comments stream in.

`Grittme commented: Omg looks perfect!`

`AndOp commented: @heartsandcrafts look how good that chicken looks!`

`tDahir commented: Ahh your family is srsly SO LUCKY`

The outpouring of love is a balm to my soul. It sparks real joy, at least momentarily. A high I'm always chasing.

`Gisssssselle commented: Lol I bet that chicken is dry as shit @fandomgurl`

The high ends abruptly.

Fandomgurl replied: @Gisssssselle SRSLY right? The sprouts look burned too. Like plastic @ Bonnie126376

Bonnie126376 replied: @Fandomgurl Oh this fake-ass bitch and her nasty-looking meals again, FFS someone teach her how to cook. Can't believe she's making her fam choke down this garbage day after day

It takes all of my willpower not to throw my phone across the bathroom. I close the post and open another one that I'd posted earlier in the day: a Reel of me making low-carb keto bagels which ends with Noemie biting into one with a huge grin. I'd captioned it, "Guys, I can't believe how amazing these low-carb, low-sugar bagels turned out! Noemie LOVES them, so happy that we're not letting #diabetes get in the way of her living life to the fullest! #LowCarb #LowCarbBagels #DiabetesAwareness."

The top comments make me gasp out loud.

Fandomgurl commented: Low carb CARBS isn't a thing, you dumb bitch @ninamoon look at this stupid bitch

Ninamoon replied: @Fandomgurl WHATTT? "Low carb" bagels, is she high?? LMAO

Teslalove commented: Making your diabetic kid

eat carbs for Likes, this is literally child abuse

I shut down Instagram, but my hands can't stop shaking, and my chest feels like it's being squeezed like a tube of toothpaste. After making myself take several deep breaths, I compose a text to my assistant.

Aspen 7:42pm: Hi Liv, I just checked my Insta and was disappointed to see that there are still a lot of troll comments being made. We've been over this before; part of your responsibilities is making sure to delete troll comments before their presence encourages more trolls to join in. Please delete all troll comments immediately, otherwise we will have to reconsider your position as my assistant.

I read the message twice over. I have to make sure I don't sound like a huge bitch, because there's always the chance that Liv might screenshot it and post it for clout. After some hesitation, I delete it, then type out a new message.

Aspen 7:45pm: Hi Liv, I'm concerned about a few things. Let's schedule a call tomorrow morning at 9am? Thx. xo

There. Firm, but friendly. The reply comes in almost instantaneously.

Liv 7:45pm: Yes, totally! Maybe I can come over to your place?
Aspen 7:47pm: We can do it remotely. I'll call you then.
Liv 7:48pm: OK, talk to you then!

I sigh and try to release some of the tension from my neck and shoulders. I close the chat app. Then open it again. I scroll down until I find Meredith's name, but stop myself from sending her yet another text. I know she's not going to reply. I can't keep sending her texts.

Instead, I scroll through the dozens of new messages that I get every day. They're all from different people—my mom, the dozens of influencers that I've gotten to know over the years, only one or two of whom I would consider as actual friends. Then I come across an unread message that makes me stop scrolling. As much as I want to ignore it, I know I can't afford to.

Clara: Has Mer spoken to you??
Aspen: No:(
Clara: I can't believe her. I mean, I always knew she was brash, but this is just ridiculous
Aspen: Yeah

It's a challenge not to bite my fingernails as I watch the three dots appear, disappear, then appear again. I can't be too angry about Mer, not to her sister. Their relationship is a tumultuous one, but with siblings, blood often runs thicker than water. The bond between sisters is deeper and stronger than many realize, even if it might appear flawed on the surface. That makes me think of Elea and Noemie, and how Elea had claimed to take the drumsticks for Noemie. Despite everything, the thought makes me release my breath. Maybe Elea wasn't lying. Maybe she really was concerned about Noemie's blood sugar. Maybe there's still a sincere, loving relationship inside this cold-hearted home after all.

# Chapter 6

# MEREDITH

It is harder than it seems to get rid of a guy who isn't ready to leave, especially one as charming as Ben. The problem with Ben is that he and I are cut from the same cloth. Aspen is the sun, and we are flowers greedy for her light, wanting to absorb it all and leave the rest of the world in darkness. There isn't room enough for both of us in Aspen's life, and it soon became clear to me who was winning.

Aspen found her niche in Ben. How ironic is that? He wasn't even an influencer in any capacity. Sure, he was on social media, but he was on it the way most people were—using it to share vacation photos and keep tabs on which of their high school friends got married or divorced or went bald. I'll share a few Instagram snapshots to spare you the boring details.

Seven and a half years ago: Aspen and Ben making an apple pie from scratch, him behind her with his arms around her, kneading a ball of pie dough together while grinning at each other. They even went to an orchard to pick the apples. "The warm scent of apples at the orchard is better than any perfume. #AllNatural #HomemadePie #AllDayAspen #AsBen." 117 Likes. 5,086 followers.

Seven and a half years ago: A Starbucks latte that Ben had gotten for Aspen. "You guys! He remembers every little detail. Tall caramel soy latte with extra foam and two lashings of caramel on top. This boy, I swear. #Love #Starbucks #Latte #AllDayAspen #AsBen." 397 Likes. 8,913 followers.

Seven years ago: Ben down on one knee at the Griffith Observatory at sunset, Aspen covering her obviously gasping mouth, her wide eyes bright with tears. "HE PUT A RING ON IT!!! #Love #MarriageProposal #Engaged #AllDayAspen #AsBen." 4,009 Likes. 26,127 followers.

Seven years ago: Aspen and Ben walking down the aisle, caught mid-laugh in a flurry of confetti. I'm in this photo, actually, in a sapphire silk maid of honor dress, a practiced I'm-so-happy-for-my-best-friend smile plastered on my face. "I married my best friend today. #Love #WeddingInspo #AllDayAspen #AsBen." 24,813 Likes. 52,839 followers. (You married your *best friend* Aspen? I thought I was your best friend.)

Six and a half years ago: Aspen's finger with two tiny hands clutching it. (I did the math right; she was already carrying the twins when she walked down the aisle. Some people might say she shouldn't have been wearing white. I am not one of those people. I don't judge.) "The girls decided to come a little bit early. I didn't think it was possible to love anyone this much, but my heart is overflowing. Guess what their names are? Let me know in the comments! Anyone who guesses correctly will get a surprise gift! #MomLove #Twins #AllDayAspen #AsBen." 72,628 Likes. 139,276 followers.

Five and a half years ago: Noemie and Elea gaping at the camera in matching outfits, holding a sign that says: "WE ARE ONE YEAR OLD TODAY!" In the background, a huge, over-the-top birthday party. I'm in this one, too, a practiced I-love-my-goddaughters smile plastered on my face. "Where did the time go?? How can these two be one already!? Giveaway Thursdays! Today, we are celebrating the twins' birthday by giving away TWO diaper bags from Nana's Secret. To enter, follow the guidelines below! #Giveaway #Twins #NoemiElea #AllDayAspen." 269,643 Likes. 427,821 followers. (I suppose I should be grateful that she dropped that dreadful couple's hashtag. I mean, honestly? #AsBen? It sounds like an ass cream. Instagram should've banned her for having terrible hashtag judgment.)

Four years ago: A family portrait taken at a beach in Phuket, all four of them wearing matching, Fifties-style red-and-blue swimsuits. "GIVEAWAY! Guys, forget Hawaii and come to this part of the world. Crystal blue waters + private beaches + affordable, delicious Thai food? Yes please! To celebrate one million followers, we are partnering up with @ThaiAirways and giving away two tickets from the US to Phuket. How amazing is that?! To enter, follow the guidelines below! #Giveaway #Twins #AllDayAspen #ThaiAirways #Vacation." 2,724,149 Likes. 1,108,468 followers. (I had hinted at tagging along so I could do some collaborative posts with her, but Aspen had shut me down so gently that I didn't realize until much later that she'd rejected me. So much for gratitude. How quickly she had forgotten how much I'd done for her.)

Three years ago: Aspen and two other influencers, each one with at least two million followers, doing an outfit change video. The dresses are stunning, and though the three women cycle through outfits of the same colors, they're all different, complementary styles. "How gorgeous are these outfits from @BeauHouse?? Besties @Aram1s and @Honeybelllle both agree that we can't have enough of them! One lucky follower will be able to win a complete wardrobe makeover. Follow all of us, the details will be shared later this week! #Fashion #LookBook #AllDayAspen." 3,819,231 Likes. 2,128,271 followers. (Interesting how she used to call me her bestie, but ever since she hit one million followers, it's bye-bye Mer and hello other big influencers.)

Have you had enough? I certainly have. I've scrolled through Aspen's accounts so many more times than I care to admit. I know her posts as well as my own. Better, even. Countless nights I've spent scrolling and scrolling, reading her captions over and over, zooming in on every picture. Was I trying to look for flaws? Or maybe secrets to how she grew so fast, practically overnight? Not really. I know all of Aspen's flaws; she's my best friend, after all. And logically, I know how she grew so fast. She did the thing I always told her to do—she found her niche, and that niche happens to be sharing her romantic journey, and with the arrival of the twins, sharing her motherhood journey. I know all that in theory. But still, on a deeper level, I fail to grasp it. Because there is still a huge part of me that refuses to see her as anything more than my understudy, my loyal sidekick, the one person I can rely on to squeal with me when my posts get over thirty thousand Likes. (Hah, thirty thousand Likes for Aspen now would be considered a failed post.)

I was happy for her, you must know this. I really was. I'd been so afraid that if her accounts stayed stagnant that she would give up and go back to Bumfuck, Asia. So when #AsBen, as ass-cream-like as it sounded, started gaining traction, I was overjoyed. Aspen came to my studio, and we polished off a bottle of rosé, and at some point opened another one, and we kept watching her follower count grow in real time. It was incredible to watch; the numbers were ticking up before our very eyes. Like watching a magic show. Our endorphins shot up along with the number of followers, and I threw my arms around Aspen, and she pressed her cheek to mine, and we squealed at each other because we were both doing it; we were both in-fucking-fluencers! (And, as big as she was back then, she was still nowhere near my follower count. All was still right with the world.)

But she kept growing and growing. Like the Very Hungry Caterpillar. Over the following months, as her follower count crept up and up and up, I stopped grinning whenever I checked on her accounts. And as it neared my follower count, a lump formed in my chest, like a tumor pressing down on it. When Aspen surpassed me, the lump bore down, a boulder crushing me, not allowing a single sip of air to pass through my lungs. I couldn't meet Aspen's eye for a week. I felt, ridiculous as this may sound, like a complete fraud. Like her success was somehow directly correlated with my failure. Like I had led her wrong all this time, and it took Ben to pull her into the light. I was furious with myself at first. But then I noticed her starting to look at me differently. With pity in her eyes. She started giving me advice on how to grow online. I was humiliated. I've been in this industry far longer than she has been, and let's face it, she only managed to gain a foothold because she got lucky. Because she and Ben make a photogenic couple, and Ben was only too happy to go along with it because Ben had no clue how to do social media. It was a fluke. How unfair is that? My best friend became a huge social media star through a fluke. Meanwhile, I'm left behind in the dust, forgotten.

So you can't possibly blame me for poring over Elea's iPad

like it's alien tech containing knowledge that will save the world. I mean, it's going to save *my* world, at least.

I pick up baby Luca from a grouchy Clara ("Give me advance notice next time you want to drop him off!") and drive home with my heart thrumming excitedly in my chest like a hummingbird. I don't even know what I'm going to do with Elea's iPad, but it feels like a whole world of possibilities has just opened up to me. At the very least, I'm going to dig out Aspen's secrets, figure out that magic recipe she has up her sleeves and sprinkle a bit of that onto my own career. I glance at Luca in the rearview mirror and smile. He ignores me, too busy looking at his own chubby hands. Once we get home, I plop him in his playpen and settle down on my couch with the iPad.

I open up Aspen's TikTok. She has over forty videos in her Drafts folder. I go through each one. They've all been edited and are complete with captions, and they're all so polished I could just die.

Take this one, for example. It's one of Aspen's Day in the Life series: a montage of her waking up (she looks effortlessly gorgeous, of course), making some Insta-worthy drink (today's is cold brew and she pours in the thick, creamy milk in front of the camera so we get an eyeful of the beautiful brown-and-white swirls), waking the twins up (I notice she keeps the camera mostly on Noemie when the twins are involved), before getting baby Sabine out of her cot. She changes Sabine's diaper, plops her in her high chair, and bustles about the kitchen to prep a perfect breakfast for her perfect family. Caption: "Come prepare for the day with me and the girls! Recipe for the cold brew is in the comments. #AllDayAspen #PalmerFamily."

I snort. Nothing groundbreaking here. I used to do morning

routine videos myself until Luca came along. Whenever I try to do one with Luca, the footage I end up with is awful—me looking harried and obviously lacking sleep, Luca screaming, throwing his pureed veggies everywhere, crying for me to nurse him. How the hell does Aspen make hers look so good and so relaxed?

With a sigh, I close TikTok and stare at Luca, who's crawled to the side of the playpen and pulled himself up. He's now calling out to me for attention. I sigh again and heave myself up from the couch. Ever since I had him, I've let my workout routine fall by the wayside, and now, even simple acts like getting up from the couch are reminders of how out of shape I feel. I really should get back to my diet, but like I said, breastfeeding leaves me ravenous, and Luca wakes up so many times throughout the night that I feel like a zombie in the daytime. All my photos are Photoshopped to hell to give me a more defined waistline.

"Hey, you," I say, crouching outside the pen and resting my chin on top of the plastic fence. Luca coos, and drool dribbles down his chin. I pick up a wooden duck and hand it to him. "Play with duckie," I say. He considers the duck for a second, then, without warning, he swings his hand back and wallops me across the face with the duck. "Ow! Fucking—" I fall onto my ass, clutching my nose, and smack the back of my head against the coffee table. "Goddamn it!" There is so much pain that, for a few seconds, I can barely register anything else.

When the initial shock passes, I realize I'm sobbing, and Luca is crying as well. I look at him balefully as I dab at my nose. No blood. Good. "You hurt Mommy," I moan to Luca, still unable to bring myself to pick him up and comfort him. I mean, I need comforting, too, but no one's picking me up and patting my back and telling me everything will be okay. The thought brings a fresh bout of tears. Why does everything have to be so fucking hard? A tiny, ridiculous part of me hisses, seething: *It's all Aspen's fault. She was the one who made it all look so simple. She was the one who tricked me into thinking I could do this—that I, too, could be a momfluencer.*

The screech from Luca hits a point where I can no longer bear it. I pick him up and bounce him, maybe a little bit too vigorously, desperate to quiet him. It takes a while, but eventually he calms down. He gazes at me and smiles, and my breath releases in a huge sigh. "You are a little stinker," I tell him. "Is it time for your nap yet? It's time for your nap." I settle back on the couch and latch him onto my breast, and he sucks while gazing up at me. I wish I could say he's looking at me with adoration, but his gaze seems more calculating. Or maybe I'm just losing my marbles. A six-month-old baby is anything but calculating.

I pick up the iPad once more, but can't bear to look at Aspen's TikTok again just yet. I swipe through the home page, scanning the downloaded apps idly. How many freaking STEM games can one kid play? I open Google Photos. Like me, Aspen is meticulous with syncing all of her photos and videos to the cloud. I scroll through the photos, glumly at first, but slow down when I realize that these photos are unedited. Aspen's skin isn't glowing as radiantly as it does on her socials, and her arms are definitely less toned, and Elea is openly scowling in most of them. So much for playing happy family. I open them one by one, my smile taking over my face as I absorb the reality behind Aspen's social media accounts. So many videos are interrupted by Elea screaming, "Stop it! I don't WANT to do a Reel!" and smacking the phone away. Those make me chuckle. God, I love that little firecracker.

Then I find a familiar video. Footage of her morning routine—the one I'd just seen in her TikTok drafts folder. Except this one is the uncut version. It starts off with Aspen checking how she looks on camera before lying back and closing her eyes. A moment later, she opens her eyes, yawns, and smiles at the camera. I snort. I knew she didn't naturally look that good when she woke up. This is nothing new; I'm pretty sure that everyone who does these "morning routine" videos actually puts on makeup first before recording themselves waking up. But after Aspen gets out of bed, she pads down to the living room, where, to my surprise, I see the twins on their iPads. What the hell? They're awake already?

"Girls, can you get in bed please? Just for a second," Aspen says to them.

Elea gives her a mutinous glare. "I'm busy."

"It'll take a second. I just need you to pretend that you're waking up, okay? You'll get a star for this."

Noemie puts her iPad aside and slides down from the sofa, and Aspen says, "Good girl." Then her voice sharpens. "Elea, come on."

With a frustrated groan, Elea joins her sister. I watch, mouth agape, as they walk down the hallway and go into their bedroom.

"I am NOT putting on my PJs," Elea snaps once she's inside. "It's four in the afternoon. That would be stupid."

"Don't say 'stupid'," Aspen says. "And fine, you don't need to change into your PJs. But pull the duvet up to your chin so we can't see your clothes."

Oh my god. What the fuck am I seeing?

The girls climb into their twin beds, and Aspen turns off the lights. She walks out of their room, then walks in again, the phone camera still in front of her. She turns on the lights and calls out, "Rise and shine, my beautiful babies!"

Noemie opens her eyes and smiles sweetly at the camera. "Morning, Mommy." Elea opens her eyes and rolls them.

"Elea!" Aspen snaps. "You ruined the shot. Now we're going to have to do it again."

I gasp so hard that it startles Luca, who's dozed off while still latched to my nipple. I shush him and continue watching as Aspen turns off the bedroom lights again before going through the same routine. "Rise and shine, my beautiful babies!" she trills.

This time, Elea refrains from rolling her eyes, though she refuses to give the camera a smile. Aspen's prepared for it; the camera merely glances over Elea before settling on Noemie, who is smiling obediently and reciting her line: "Morning, Mommy."

After a beat, Elea says, "Are we done yet?"

Aspen sighs audibly. "Yes. Thank you for humoring me."

The girls jump out of their beds and run back to the living room. Aspen follows them there, where baby Sabine is in her playpen. She picks Sabine up, carries her to the nursery, and places her in the cot. She turns off the lights. Turns them back on. "Rise and shine, my darling!"

I hit pause. Holy shit. What the hell did I just . . .

I—

It's all fake. All of it.

I mean, okay, as an influencer myself, I've long known, of course, that a lot of what we post online isn't necessarily true. We love to crow about being "authentic," but our authenticity comes in a highly edited, extremely polished package. That's okay. Everybody knows we do that, and they go along with it anyway. Kind of a nudge-nudge, wink-wink situation. But this? There isn't even a shred of truth in her morning routine videos. They weren't even shot in the morning! I look down at Luca. I put the iPad aside, unlatch my nipple from his mouth, pick him up gently so as not to wake him, and carry him into his nursery. I tuck him inside his cot and close the door, then hurry to the bathroom, where I slap on some foundation and swipe lipstick on my lips and cheeks. Then I rumple up my hair, put on my cutest pajama top, and get into bed with my phone. I start recording, close my eyes, and then open them with a yawn and a smile. "Morning!" I say to the camera. "Come get ready for the day with me."

# Chapter 7

# MEREDITH

Here is where I start sounding like a paid ad for Apple. That iPad changed my life. There, I said it. But it's not because it's an iPad. I promise you if it had been an Android or a Huawei it would've changed my life as well. Or maybe not? Sorry, but I am a diehard Apple stan.

Over the next few days, I pore over all of Aspen's TikTok and Instagram Reels before locating the uncut versions in her cloud storage. I figure out everything. Literally everything.

Take this one, for example: a Reel of her putting together the most beautiful lunch boxes for the twins. She even shows herself making the bread from scratch—low-carb for Noemie, of course. The final version has relaxing music as its audio, but in the original version, I can hear all of them talking.

**Noemie:** "Mommy, I can't find my PJs. The ones with the unicorn cupcake on it."

**Aspen:** "Oh. I think—uh, hang on, sweetie. It's in the dryer, I think."

**Noemie:** "Can you get it please, Mommy? I really want to wear those ones tonight."

**Aspen:** "Ask Daddy to get them. I'm putting together your lunch for tomorrow."

Here, I have to pause, because Aspen always captions her lunch boxes posts with something along the lines of "Threw these together in the morning while the kiddos were having breakfast!" But I suppose I shouldn't be surprised to learn that these are, of course, prepped well in advance.

**Elea:** "Are you making that low-carb bread? Yuck. I do *not* want any, Mommy."

**Aspen:** "I know, I know. These are for Noemie."

**Noemie:** "Um . . ."

**Aspen:** "What?"

**Noemie:** "Nothing."

**Aspen:** "What??"

**Elea:** "She hates them too."

**Noemie:** "I do not!"

**Elea:** "You throw them away at school."

**Noemie:** "I—Elea! You promised not to tell!"

**Aspen:** "Seriously? You throw them away?"

(No answer.)

**Aspen:** "I can't believe this. Do you see how hard I'm working to make them for you?"

**Noemie:** "I'm sorry, Mommy."

**Aspen:** "Do the other kids know? Do they see you throwing it away?"

**Noemie:** "No."

**Aspen:** "Okay. Fine. Jesus. Look—can I just—can I have some peace, please, girls? Okay? I'm working here."

She resumes shaping the dough into cute knots. When they're done, she places them carefully in the lunch boxes and surrounds them with beautifully sliced fruit and vegetables in an artful pattern. The results are two lunch boxes that look like they came out of a cookbook. Then she takes out the bread knots and replaces them with store-bought crackers before putting on the lids.

In the final version that she posted, the text in the video says: "The girls' favorite low-carb knots. These are TO DIE FOR! It's no wonder the twins are always begging for these. If you hadn't told me that they're low-carb, I wouldn't even have known! Srsly, best bread ever. Recipe in the comments! #AllDayAspen #DiabetesAwareness #NoemiesJourney."

Again, as an influencer myself, I am of course aware of just how much we fake for the 'gram. But whenever I've tried to make food that looks appetizing for social media, it usually turns out tasting really crap. Take buttercream, for example. In order to make it look really good, to make those gorgeous buttercream flowers, you need to mix in enough sugar for the cream to be stiff enough to stay in the fragile shape of petals. If you didn't, they'd melt, and wilt, and generally look shit. But with so much powdered sugar mixed in, the buttercream tastes awful; hard and sickeningly sweet. There is a metaphor hidden somewhere in here about social media, I know it.

But I didn't know the extent to which one could fake it for the camera. Seems obvious now, but I never thought of making beautiful food that I would later simply throw away and replace with less aesthetically pleasing ones to eat. And as I scroll through Aspen's uncut videos, it becomes stunningly clear that this is what she's been doing for years. Her Reels are . . . productions. They are not snippets of her life or glimpses behind the curtains. They are entire productions that she's composed beforehand and then taken time out of her real life to act out and edit. A complete fabrication of what a life governed for aesthetics looks like.

Another example: a video of Elea as a chubby baby, pulling herself up to a standing position.

**Aspen:** "Oh my gosh, she's doing it! She's standing!"

**Ben:** "Oh wow, go, sweetie pie!" He rushes into the video.

**Aspen:** "Ben, what the—you're in my shot. Ben!"

**Ben:** "What?" He swings around, confusion written all over his face.

**Aspen:** "You're in my shot. You're ruining it."

**Ben:** "In your—what? Aspen, I'm trying to watch our baby stand up for the first time in her life."

**Aspen:** "Yes, but this is such a huge moment. I'm trying to record it for my followers."

**Ben:** "Are you insane? Screw your followers. I'm her father."

**Aspen:** "But they—"

(Pause.)

**Aspen:** "All right. Fine. You're right, it's fine. I'm sorry, I just got carried away."

The video ends, but the one after that is of Elea on the nursery room floor. She sucks on her feet for a while, then sits up and spots the bars of her cot next to her. Babbling, she reaches up for the bars, grasps them, and pulls herself up to her feet.

**Aspen:** "Oh my god! You're doing it, sweetie! You're standing! Oh my god, you guys, this is the first time Elea is standing! Oh my gosh, look at my little baby go!"

She is so fully committed to pretending that she's watching Elea stand for the first time that her voice cracks with emotion.

I remember this video, because she'd WhatsApped it to me and said, "LOOK!! She just stood up for the first time!!!" and I'd totally bought it. Did not question it for a second.

And I think this is the moment that births my fury. Because all these years, Aspen has watched me struggle to get my numbers to grow, and all this time she could've told me how to do it. How to go all the way with the fabrication and make my life an Insta-worthy one, and she didn't. She listened to me whine about why I'm failing to capture so many of Luca's milestones despite my phone being as good as surgically attached to my hand. I'd failed to catch the first time he stood on camera because I was cooking. I'd failed to record the first time he crawled and the first time he rolled over because—oh, I don't know—probably because I was staggering around, fogged with exhaustion and despair those first few months. And I had blamed myself for it. Thought I was neither a good mother nor a good influencer, and I'd cried to Aspen about it, and she'd—she had shaken her head and said, "I know, it's so hard, isn't it, Mer?"

And so you must understand why I did it. Why I created a new account on Instagram, found her latest post—one talking about her skincare routine—and typed out: "OK but most of us have to actually look after our kids and don't have the time to do a seven-step skincare regime. Who's looking after the kids while you do this?? @fandomgurl @Gissssselle."

Then, after hitting Post, I sat there, shaking with adrenaline. What good would one negative comment do? Even though I'd tagged two of the most hateful personalities online, I knew it wouldn't do much to move the needle. I needed to do more. Be proactive. And that was why I went into Aspen's Calendar and tapped on one of her appointments. I hesitated only for a moment before I hit Edit.

Like I said, Aspen owes me.

I sit in the beautiful, airy café and stir my green juice idly with my rose gold straw. The juice is aggressively green. Whenever I make a green juice at home, the pulverized veg always oxidizes quickly into a brownish shade of green, but not this one, at this café that has been built purely to cater to looking good for social media. When the waiter brought it over, I expressed concern about the unnatural shade of green. I can't be seen drinking a juice that's full of food coloring—not I, a momfluencer who is breastfeeding. My followers would report me to CPS. He smiled and said, "Oh, don't worry, it's all natural of course! We just put in a few drops of chlorophyll to keep it looking fresh." Then he left with a wink.

At a different table, two women are taking a selfie with their impossibly pink dragon fruit smoothies. I look around, feeling strangely like I'm being watched, but no one's even looking in my direction. I wonder who'd suggested this place, Aspen or Lilibeth? Luca gurgles at me, and I smile down at him. I hope Lilibeth isn't going to be late. I've arranged everything today around this meeting, even going so far as to nudge Luca's schedule so he'll be at maximum agreeability during the meeting.

I needn't have worried. Of course, no one can keep Aspen the super momfluencer waiting. At exactly eleven o'clock on the dot, the front door swings open, and Lilibeth arrives in a swirl of blonde curls and a flouncy Fifties-style dress. She is striking, her makeup expertly caked on, and her face contoured to structural perfection. Makes sense; she is one of the most sought-after makeup artists for a reason. I can sense the two women in the next table, the ones who couldn't have enough photos of their dragon fruit smoothies (which are still untouched), staring at Lilibeth.

Lilibeth scans the room, her contoured nose wrinkling when she doesn't spot Aspen. A waiter leads her to a table adjacent to mine and brings her a menu. After he leaves, she takes a few selfies. Then she scans the menu. Checks her phone. Maybe Aspen has left her messages? (I know, of course, that there won't be any messages from Aspen. Poor Aspen thinks this meeting is happening tomorrow.) Our eyes meet. I'm ready for this, already armed with a calculated smile—not too wide, not too reserved. I let her wait a few minutes longer, then catch her eye again. This time, the smile I give her is brighter, more inviting. She returns it, and I think: *Here we go.*

"My Bumble date stood me up," I say to her.

She snorts. "His loss. I think I just got stood up too."

I widen my eyes. "Don't tell me, a Bumble date too?"

"Nah. This influencer—anyway, it doesn't matter." She stands.

"Join me," I say quickly. "Stay and have a freakishly green juice. You came all this way."

Lilibeth considers this for a moment, then smiles and shrugs. "Yeah, okay."

I grin and gesture to the seat across from me. "I'm Meredith."

"I'm Lilibeth." As she orders a green juice, I give Luca a bottle.

"And who is this sweet little guy?" Lilibeth coos.

"This is Luca. Say hi to the pretty lady, Luca! Aww, he likes you." I look closely at her and pretend to be surprised. "Hang on, you look so familiar. Are you Lilibeth Rose?"

She gives me a bashful smile, obviously pleased at having been recognized. "Yes."

"I'm a fan! I follow you on TikTok. I love all your hair and makeup tips. That video you did on the no-heat hair curling technique changed my life. Actually, that was how I did my hair today!" I run my hand through my hair, making my curls bounce.

"Oh wow, that's so sweet of you. And your hair looks great."

"All thanks to you." Her juice arrives and I raise my glass. "To no-heat curls and being stood up."

Maybe I'm leaning on the being stood up a little heavily, but I want to remind her that Aspen has ditched her. She laughs and clinks glasses with me. "Hear, hear."

We take a sip of our juice, and I don't let the silence stretch too long. I'm so well prepared for this. "You know, what you do, it's so much harder than most people realize."

Lilibeth's eyes widen with appreciation, and she nods. "It really is."

"Trust me, I know. I used to do beauty influencing, too, and it is a tough industry to be in. No joke. And you're one of the few people who do it so well."

"Oh, I love you!" she cries. "People always assume it's so easy to do—"

"If it's so easy, then why don't they all do it?"

"Oh my god, right?" she laughs. "Thank you. So you used to be in beauty as well?"

"Yeah, but honestly, I was nowhere near as good as you."

"Aww, I'm sure you're amazing at it."

"Eh. But it's okay, I've found my niche now." I gaze at Luca with affection and stroke his round face. "This little guy."

Lilibeth's hand flies to her chest and she awws.

"Yeah, I'm posting about mom life—my day-to-day life with Luca here, trying to build my brand, and well, trying to date as a single mom. The dating isn't going so well, as you can see," I say with an eye roll.

"That sounds awesome. Actually, the person I was supposed to be meeting here is a momfluencer too."

"Oh? Which one?"

"Aspen Palmer?"

I keep my face blank. I shake my head. "Hmm, doesn't ring a bell." I pick up my phone, open up Instagram, and show it to her. "Could you type in her handle for me?" The page is on my profile instead of my feed, and I'm crossing my fingers internally that she'll glance at my profile before doing a search for Aspen.

Lilibeth takes my phone, and her eyes widen. "Wow, girl, you didn't mention you're a major player too! So close to a million followers."

"Oh." I shrug. "That's nothing." It pains me to say that, but hey, needs must.

"That is not nothing," Lilibeth says. She scrolls down my profile, looking through my posts. Fortunately, when Aspen and I had our fight, I deleted all of the posts that featured Aspen from my profile. In the last couple of years or so, there hadn't even been that many posts featuring Aspen. Oh no, she'd grown too big to collaborate with me by then. "I love your vibe. It's very similar to Aspen's, actually, but more authentic."

My cheeks grow warm with delight. "Authentic" is probably the highest form of praise you could give an influencer, and to be called authentic in comparison to Aspen is icing on the cake.

"Thank you. Yeah, I try to be as authentic as I can. I want to empower other women, not make them feel like they're somehow failing." Luca finishes his bottle right on time, so I pick him up and settle him over my shoulder. "This little guy is an angel, but he can also be a handful, and I want to show all of that, not just the highlights."

Lilibeth reaches out and squeezes one of Luca's chunky thighs. "Oh, he is precious. I love this video of your morning routine. Oh gosh, imagine waking up to that sweet face every morning."

I nod. "I know, he's so cute in the mornings." Actually, Luca is a nightmare most mornings. He wakes up already hangry, screaming for the breast, and usually he'll projectile vomit his first feed. Then I'll latch him to my other breast, and that one he'll keep down. By the time I've burped him and changed him out of his dirty diaper and PJs and cleaned up his vomit, all I want to do is flop onto the couch and sleep away the morning. But of course, thanks to Aspen's behind-the-scenes videos, I now know how to create a "morning routine" video that is pleasant and relaxing to watch. Ever since imitating Aspen's videos two weeks ago, I've gained almost a hundred thousand followers. Again, the thought makes the anger sear my skin. Aspen could've told me this so much sooner. Could've spared me so much heartache.

Lilibeth cocks her head to one side, studying me and Luca for a moment. "You know," she says, "I am glad that Aspen flaked today. Because I would rather work with you. You're authentic, your profile is a lot less manufactured, and you're up-and-coming. I want to support newer voices, not ones that are already super popular."

I resist the urge to tell her that I've been influencing a lot longer than Aspen has. Boy, that took a lot of self-restraint. Instead, I widen my eyes and say, "Oh wow, really? I mean, I would love to work with you."

"For sure!" she cries. "And look at you, you're beautiful. I would love to do your hair and makeup. I can already think of at least three different looks for you."

I so badly want to leap out of my seat and scream and dance around, but somehow manage to compose myself. "That would be amazing. Yes, let's do a collab! I want to help promote you too. Like I said, I love your account. Oh, maybe we could do a bunch of looks that moms on the go can do?"

Lilibeth's face lights up. "Perfect! Yes, we can do a series of tutorials with me doing your hair and makeup, and then a follow-up with you doing it yourself to show how accessible the looks are."

"Bonus points if it's a look that you can do one-handed, so I can carry this little guy on my hip while doing it," I say, gesturing at Luca, who's dozed off on my shoulder.

"Aww, yes, of course. I love this!" she practically squeals it. "Oh,

Meredith, this is total kismet. I'm so glad we both got stood up. Is that okay to say?"

I grin and lift my glass of neon green juice. "To being stood up."

"And finding something better."

I can't help smirking. "Amen."

# Chapter 8

# ASPEN

Is it just me? Maybe it's my mom brain forgetting everything, making mistakes in my everyday life? Ever since I had the twins, it's like part of my brain shut down and refused to get back into action, and after having Sabine, it's become even worse. This morning, I kept wandering around the house, frantically looking for my phone, before Noemie pointed out that my phone was in my hand the entire time. It's getting kind of scary. Maybe I should get checked out.

But this, this isn't my mistake. I know it isn't, because I've double and triple checked my calendar. I show the receptionist my Google Calendar, where the appointment had been locked in weeks ago.

"See?" I say, baring my teeth at her in what I hope passes as a smile and bouncing Sabine on my left hip. "It says here: 'Appointment with Sunflower Cheeks rep' at nine a.m."

The receptionist meets my smile and raises me with an even brighter, faker one. "Yes, I see that, ma'am, but unfortunately, it's not in our calendar. So there must've been a miscommunication."

Tears clog my throat, and I have to take a moment to swallow the lump back down and make sure my voice comes out even. "Um, could you check again? For my name? It's just—I've been really looking forward to this meeting. I'm such a fan of Sunflower Cheeks, and I think we have a great opportunity to do something amazing together."

Sabine twists in my arm and I nearly drop her. I drop my phone instead so I can catch hold of her with both arms. The phone makes a deafening clatter as it hits the floor. Heads turn.

The receptionist sighs audibly. "What's your full name?"

"Aspen Palmer." I pick up my phone. Great. There's a crack going across the screen. I stuff it into my purse and resume bouncing Sabine, praying that she doesn't start fussing.

"Oh," the receptionist says. It comes out with an undertone that makes me freeze.

"What is it?"

When she looks up at me, what little traces of sympathy are gone. Her expression is a cold mask. "Your appointment to meet with Ms. Chang was two days ago. I remember now. You didn't show up."

"What? No, that's impossible, that—" I struggle to get my phone out of my bag one-handed. "In my calendar, it—"

The receptionist presses her mouth into a thin line and shakes her head, clearly giving zero shits about what was in my calendar. I stop myself and take a deep breath. "Okay, um, clearly there was a miscommunication. Can we reschedule? I really think that I could contribute a lot to this company. I have over five million followers—"

"I understand, but you missed your appointment, and Ms. Chang insists that all of our brand representatives work with a high standard of professionalism. She also mentioned that your accounts have a really high number of trolls. I'm afraid that at this time, she's made it clear that she is no longer interested in pursuing a partnership."

The words land like a slap straight across my face. My cheeks burn so hot that for a ridiculous moment, I wonder if I've developed a fever right then and there. I feel so exposed, like everybody in the room is watching my every move. A quick glance about the office space confirms my fears; there is a handful of other people in the waiting room, and I can tell they're all secretly listening in. I catch a couple of looks being exchanged, and oh my god, I have never felt such humiliation. Part of me wants to stay and explain, once more, that it isn't my fault, that I didn't mean to miss our appointment, that I pride myself on behaving professionally, that—

But I know that they'll all end up sounding like excuses. I know that nothing I say can salvage this. Nothing can get me into a meeting with Sunflower Cheeks. I've probably been blacklisted by them. The fastest-growing producer of locally sourced, organic baby foods, and I've managed to royally mess things up with them. How did this happen? I thought I'd fixed everything. I manage to choke out a small, "Thank you, and please let me know if she changes her mind," before scurrying out of the office building with Sabine in my arms.

My breath comes in and out in wobbly sips as I make my way back to the car. Thankfully, Sabine doesn't fight me as I strap her into her car seat. Maybe she can sense that I'm this close to breaking down and is deciding to give me a break. I get into the driver's seat and release the world's longest, heaviest sigh. Then I open up my email and do a search for Sunflower Cheeks. I find the email setting up the meeting and yep, the receptionist was right; the appointment really was set for two days ago. It's on me.

With a frustrated cry, I toss my phone to the passenger seat and bury my face in my hands. How the hell did I mess things up so badly? Did I miss things somehow? Fear stabs into my chest like an ice pick. I don't understand how this is happening. Did someone . . .

No. It's not possible. It was my mistake. I was careless. I've been distracted, I know. I should've known better. I should've cross-checked it with my emails. I shouldn't have—I should've . . .

So many "shoulds" and "shouldn't haves" cramming through my head, fighting for domination. All of them amounting to the same conclusion: it was all my fault.

No. It's not all my fault. The receptionist had mentioned a second factor in their decision-making process, one that probably played an even bigger part than me missing the appointment. *The troll comments.* The thought lands like an asteroid, cratering my brain, obliterating everything else. Nothing else matters. The fact is, if I had no troll comments, I could miss any meeting and they would still be begging me to partner up with them. I have over five million bloody followers, for god's sake! They should be coming to me; they should be working their schedules around mine. But they're not, and it's because of the damn trolls.

There's a text message notification from my phone.

I feel like you know something you're not telling me. Call me back.

Wincing, I hit Delete and put my phone on silent mode before calling my assistant, Liv.

God, it's a struggle keeping my voice calm.

"Hi, Aspen! What's up?" she chirps.

Oh, if I could scream at her. But no. I'm nice. I'm always nice. It's part of my brand. All Day Aspen never loses her temper. "Hey, Liv. So I just came out of a meeting . . ." Okay, so technically it's a meeting that never happened. "And they mentioned the troll comments on my accounts." I let the silence hang for an uncomfortably long time before saying, "We've been over this. Is there a reason why you're not performing your task? Can I help in any way?" Technically, part of Liv's job is also overseeing my schedule, but after everything that happened, I became too paranoid to ask Liv to go through my calendar. Instead, I've been relying on myself to keep up with my schedule, which I guess is proving to be a mistake.

There's another long silence, then Liv finally cries, "I'm so sorry! I've just been so overwhelmed. There are so many of them, and it's so mentally and emotionally exhausting to have to go through them."

My stomach churns with the idea of just how many trolls there are coming for me. Why do they hate me so much? "I understand, but we really, really need to stay on top of them. Is that doable?"

Liv releases a shaky breath. "I guess. I'm sorry. Are you going to fire me?"

"No." Despite everything, I genuinely like Liv. And more than that, I trust her. It's hard to find someone I can trust. "I get that this stuff can be overwhelming. You don't even need to read them, just scan quickly and if it sounds like it's going to be a mean comment, hit Delete."

"Okay. But . . ."

"Yeah?"

"It's nothing."

"What is it?" I press, grinding my teeth. "Look, whatever it is, you can tell me. You know I'm not the kind to shoot the messenger."

"Well, um. It's just—maybe you should think about why people are coming for you?" Liv says, her voice scratchy with hesitation.

I squeeze the phone so hard I wonder if it'll shatter in my hand. Keep. Voice. Calm. "Why do you think they're coming for me?"

"Well." I can practically see Liv mulling over the words before she spits them out like they're poison. "Um, well, a lot of them are saying you're sort of, you know, a little bit fake?" Then she quickly adds, "I disagree, obviously, but uh. You know. I'm just saying, that's what a lot of the comments are saying. Uh. Yeah."

It's a struggle to not fling my phone at the windshield. Fake? Me? Of course I'm fake. And whose fault is that? When I first started, I thought what it took was to share the real me online. I avoided trends and focused on staying true to myself. None of my posts were curated; all of them were achingly real, no filters. And what did that get me? Five thousand measly followers, most of whom couldn't even be bothered to Like or comment on any of my posts. Most of them were probably just bots.

Nobody wants real. They are hungry for the fantasy. They want to believe that an average person like me can have the dream life—can find the perfect man and be suddenly whisked away from mundanity and find herself in a fairy tale. They don't want real Aspen; real Aspen is boring as shit. You meet real Aspens every day, dressed in saggy sweatpants at the supermarket, gasping for breath in sweat-stained oversized shirts at Zumba class, and sitting with a defeated, dead-eyed stare while her kids run wild at the playground. They want Instagram Aspen who makes it all look easy, who assures you that things will get better, who is proof that you can have it all.

But twenty-six-year-old Liv isn't going to understand any of that. She's too young to see why my brand is so successful. She still thinks that authenticity can be found by scrolling through her For You Page on TikTok. Sometimes, I look at Liv and I hate her because the world hasn't broken her yet.

"Thank you for letting me know," I say after a while. "I appreciate your honesty."

I can almost hear Liv's sigh of relief.

"I'll think about it. What they're saying." I won't. "But in the meantime, please stay on top of the comments, okay?"

"Okay, Aspen." I'm about to hang up when she says, "How come you're calling me now?"

"What do you mean?"

"Aren't you supposed to be at the pediatrician? Sabine's due her MMR shot today, right?"

"What? No, I was supposed to meet with—" Belatedly, I remember that I wasn't supposed to meet with Sunflower Cheeks today. There had been that whole mix-up. "Oh god. Sabine's MMR? You're sure it's today?"

"Yeah, you texted me to help you make the appointment months ago, and I put it in my calendar so I wouldn't forget to book it. I would've sent you a reminder, but you told me not to be involved with your calendar anymore." Am I just imagining it, or is there the slightest tone of reproach in her voice? "Let me see . . . yeah, it's—oh, it's supposed to be twenty minutes ago."

"Thanks, bye!" I don't wait for a reply before hanging up. As I drive out of the parking lot, I ask Siri to dial Dr. Rensburg's office. It rings and rings, but no one picks up the phone. I drive five miles over the speed limit, even though I'm dying to floor the gas pedal. But no, Sabine's in the car, and I'm a responsible mom now. A responsible mom who's just forgotten her baby's vaccine appointment. Oh my god. I am the worst mom. And how the hell did this mix-up happen? I don't understand it. Worry and fear crawl up my spine like spider's legs, and the whole time, a little voice whispers at the back of my neck: *Why does this keep happening? Why? Someone knows something.*

By the time I get to the clinic, my chest feels like it's being crushed by a giant hand, and I've sweated through my bra. Sabine has fallen asleep in her car seat, and I'm in such a hurry to get her out that I don't bother to be gentle. I pluck her out, jerking her awake, and she starts wailing. I rush through the parking lot, into the blessedly cool, air-conditioned clinic.

"Hi, I'm Aspen, this is Sabine Palmer, we're here to see Dr. Rensburg for her vaccine shot," I call out at the receptionist before I'm even at her desk.

She glances up and taps at her computer. "Ah, Sabine Palmer. Sorry, you missed your appointment."

"But—" I give her my best smile, even as Sabine shrieks right into my ear. "Could you slot us in, please? I mean, it shouldn't take any time at all, right? Just a quick jab."

This receptionist is a tad more sympathetic than the one at Sunflower Cheeks, but that doesn't count for jack. She shrugs and says, "Sorry, today's schedule's full. We can book you in for another slot later this month."

"I can't—" My mind scrambles for something, anything, and

pounces on the first story it can think of. "She's in day care and they need to have her up-to-date with all of her shots. Can you do tomorrow?" I say, bouncing Sabine on my hip as she grabs a chunk of my carefully styled waves and yanks.

"Nope. This whole week and the next are all fully booked."

Anxiety claws up from my guts to my chest, a giant spider stabbing my insides. "Please."

The receptionist gives me a *What do you want me to do, lady?* look. She says, "Sorry, I can't help you there. Best thing I can do is make a note, and if we get any cancellations, I can slot you in."

"But—" My voice cracks, and I stop talking. If I say anything more, I'm going to lose it I know I will. I nod my thanks at her and turn away, and when I do, I see that everyone in the waiting room is looking at me, all the moms and dads and their kids. The familiar fear rises up again, painfully acidic. *They know. They all know.*

And worse than that, one of the women has her phone aimed right at me. She doesn't even look sorry when our eyes meet. She just raises her eyebrows a little and continues recording me. Sabine arches her back again, her signature FML move, and screams. Her whole face is red and wet with tears. I glance over at the woman again. Her phone is still trained on us, the camera following us with ruthless, unwavering interest, and something inside me breaks. It's just too much, all of it. Not to mention my home life—my husband resents me and my kids hate me, and I can't take it anymore. Sabine writhes in my arms. I am so close, so close to lunging at this woman. The cruelty of others astounds me. Who reacts to someone who is clearly distressed by recording them? "You are a ghoul," I spit at her, and stride out of the clinic, my blood rushing through my veins in a rhythm of fear. *They know. They know.*

It's only when Sabine and I are safe inside the cocoon of my car and she's sucking on a bottle of formula that it hits me. Oh my god. What have I done? I showed my anger to a complete stranger in *public*. I should've known better than to do that. I never let my mask crack in public, never. I'm always All Day Aspen, all smiles, easy breezy. But losing Mer has been like having half my soul ripped away. I'm off-balance without her. Tears burn my eyes at the thought of Mer. I miss her so much. She's the only one who would know how to fix this.

I take my phone out and open up our WhatsApp text chain. Our last messages sent to each other seem like they were sent a lifetime ago. The sight of it chisels at my heart. How could we have let this happen, when once upon a time, we used to chat with each other throughout the day, every day? And the times we weren't chatting, it was because we were actually with each other. Why did we have to have our fight? I type out "I miss you." But my thumb refuses to hit Send. Instead, I close WhatsApp and open up TikTok.

And there it is. On my notifications tab, I see that the woman at the clinic has wasted no time in posting about my meltdown. She recognized me, of course she did—was probably a fan before she saw All Day Aspen unmasked.

The footage is horrific. I look unhinged, bouncing Sabine aggressively while she shrieks. I could've sworn I was pleading with the receptionist nicely, but in the video, I sound shrill, on the edge of hysteria. A choked gasp escapes my mouth when video-Aspen whirls around and her furious gaze lands on the camera. The words "Uh oh" appear on the screen, followed by

"Guys I think she's seen me." Video-Aspen marches closer to the camera, and it adjusts its angle to take in my face. Now I'm towering over the phone camera. "What the hell are you recording?" video-Aspen says, and I put a hand over my mouth to keep from screaming because video-Aspen's voice is a witch's snarl, as rough and sharp as a serrated knife. The caption says: "The REAL #AllDayAspen!"

"No," I whisper to myself. The Likes are only trickling in for now, but I'm sure it'll turn into a torrent in no time. "No, no, no."

This is hell. I know it. I've somehow landed myself in hell, and I don't know how to get out of this.

# Chapter 9

# MEREDITH

I did it. That magical M that every influencer dreams of, hungers for, would probably kill for. Oh, that beautiful, glorious, wonderful M! "1.2M followers," it says, underneath my Instagram handle. I can't stop gazing at it, that M. It's exactly where it belongs, right under @MerryMeredith. In the last few weeks, since Elea's iPad fell into my lap, I've gained over half a million followers. I've shaken off the K and graduated to M.

I hope you don't think it's all because of Aspen, do you? I don't want you to think that all I had to do was copy everything Aspen has been doing and steal her meetings. Simply catching a glimpse of the behind-the-scenes of Aspen's life wasn't enough; but they inspired me. They led me to shattering my boundaries—to embracing creativity when it comes to making my Reels. I was always so bound by what I thought was common sense. Of course "morning routine" videos would be recorded first thing in the morning! I never thought to break down those shackles of reality. A whole paradigm shift. And, okay, the meetings were set up by Aspen, but if I didn't go to them prepared with a whole lot of research and armed to the gills with charm and wit and flattery, they wouldn't have done anything for me. But here I am, with three new sponsorship deals and four collaborative relationships with huge influencers, and I am finally doing it. I am turning into my own success story. And it all happened thanks to my ingenuity. Okay, and Elea's iPad.

I crouch down outside of Luca's playpen and smile at him. He grins back, drool trickling out of his mouth. "You are a little stinker, aren't you? But I'm so glad we're in this together." Having him was definitely the right decision to make.

Before, when I was still struggling to make it as a momfluencer (oh, how easily I shed that past struggle! In the Before Times, when I was still struggling . . . ha! As though it has been years and not mere weeks since I managed to turn things around. But that's success for you; it's frighteningly easy to get used to), I'd sometimes look at Luca and wonder if I'd made the right decision to have him. Is that awful for a mom to think? No, I refuse to believe that I was the only mother to ever pause and think, during the lowest moments of motherhood: *What the hell have I done?* (Yes, maybe those thoughts occurred a lot more with me than what's socially acceptable, but who's counting?)

Can I tell you a secret? One so deep and so dark that I have never told a single person this, not even Aspen, and we were inseparable right up until our friendship ended. I'm hoping that you understand, by now, why I did it. That you might not judge me so harshly. You have heard of the painful years I spent toiling away at growing my brand, at passing on all of my hard-earned knowledge to Aspen.

*Mer,* you might say, *stop delaying, I already know you stole a child's iPad and used it to sabotage her mother, who is supposedly your best friend. What could be worse than that?*

All right, here it is. After years of striving in the beauty and fashion genre of social media, I realized that I simply didn't have what it took to stand out in that department. Plus, at twenty-nine, I was getting too old. Most of the people who are interested in beauty and fashion are on TikTok, not Instagram. The ones left on Insta are all new moms who don't have the time to keep up with the latest beauty trends. They wear their hair in messy mom buns and spend what precious little time they have on social media trawling Instagram for the latest infant products. I knew this because I watched Aspen's accounts exploding with new followers as she hawked her babies and her recipes online.

I can sense your impatience. *You're stalling*, your eyes are saying. *Out with it.*

I just needed to give you the context, okay? I knew that if I didn't do something—something big, something drastic—that my career as an influencer would soon be over. And so I made the decision to shift from beauty/fashion to something more . . . age appropriate. Like being a mom influencer. Except I didn't have a baby, so. Yeah.

*No*, I did not decide to have Luca solely for social media purposes. That would be insane. (Or would it? People have had babies for far stupider reasons, haven't they?) I was also lonely. Aspen was my best friend, but I could sense her slipping away from me, sucked into the ever-growing vortex of her family. And when she announced she was pregnant again, I just—I knew that she would soon be gone. With three children, a husband, and her millions of needy fans, she wouldn't have time for me. Not unless I was on the same journey she was.

You must give me some credit. I didn't just hook up with randos at some LA club. I went to a fertility clinic and chose a donor (Caucasian, 6'2", UCLA Law graduate, blue eyes, brown hair. Mixed race babies are so adorable, don't you think?), and two months later, I told Aspen that her baby would have a playmate for life. Never mind about the baby's daddy, I assured her. I was determined to do this on my own. With my bestie right beside me, of course. Then I set about shifting all of my content from Beauty to Pregnancy.

Why am I telling you all of this? I guess I just wanted someone to understand why gaining that M was the best moment of my life. I needed someone to know just how much I sacrificed for that moment. But I digress.

Life is very different for someone with a K behind their follower count versus someone with an M. I know, I thought it was an exaggeration—that the change, if there even was one, would be so subtle and so gradual that I wouldn't even notice it happening. But it was more like a light switch being flipped. Darkness at first, feeling your way through uncertainty, groping blindly, then suddenly a voice whispers, "Let there be light," and the stage lights thrum on, the music blares, and the entire production springs to life.

DMs galore! Okay, I always had DMs galore in the Before Times, but now, those DMs are from people with blue checks next to their names. People belonging in the M club. People who are Someones.

In the last few years, my invites mostly dried up. Especially after I moved on from beauty/fashion to the world of moms. No longer was I spending my evenings party-hopping the hottest locations in LA. But I wasn't getting invited to any mom gatherings either. Stuck in purgatory.

But not anymore. It's only Wednesday and already, this week

alone, I've received five invitations to various events. There is a maternity brand launch party, a baby shower for some mom-fluencer, a party at a mega-influencer's Hollywood Hills mansion, and two others I can't even remember.

I stand and give myself a once-over in my full-length mirror. Tonight is the house party, and I've rented a gold-colored, long-sleeved midi Fendi dress. Underneath it, I'm wearing shapewear so unforgiving that if I dared take a deep breath, my ribs would crack. I look phenomenal. With not a small amount of difficulty, I bend down slowly, wincing at the way the corset bites into my belly, and pick Luca up from his playpen.

"Ready to go to Aunt Clara's?"

He tries to go in for a kiss, but I shy away from him. "Sorry, little guy, your kisses are really drooly, and Mommy spent an hour on her face. Tomorrow, there will be all the kisses in the world, okay?"

I sing along to "Baby Shark" the entire drive down to Clara's. Luca, sensing my good mood, is all grins and lovely coos. Everything is falling into place for me, just the way it should've done so many years ago.

Clara accepts Luca with a smile, but when she turns to face me, the smile fades a little. "You look nice," she says in a way that somehow turns it into not-a-compliment. "Big date?"

"No," I laugh, waving her off. "No time for dates. I got an invite to this big mixer in the Hills."

Disapproval lines Clara's features. "You know, I thought that when this little guy came along, you'd give up on this whole thing and settle down."

I'm dressed in Fendi and my makeup and hair are immaculate, but somehow, Clara knows just what to say to make me feel like a piece of crap. An acidic retort makes its way up my throat, but I swallow it back down. If I piss her off, she might refuse to watch Luca. So I just nod and say, "Yeah, well. It's work. Thanks, Clara." I don't wait for a response before heading back to my car.

"What time will you pick him up in the morning? I've got my tennis lesson at nine."

"I'll be back way before that!" I call out, already sliding into my car. I throw kisses their way and back out of her driveway. As I drive away, I see their silhouettes in the dim glow of the sunset—Clara lifting Luca's little fist and making him wave *bye* at me. There is a small twinge at the sight of my son, so tiny in my sister's arms. But then I make the turn to the main street, and the twinge is replaced by a spark of excitement. I'm headed to Tanya Dylan's mansion, and I want to scream at the thought of it.

With over thirty million followers on TikTok, Tanya Dylan is one of the biggest momfluencers there is. She used to be a runway model, which was how she first became an influencer. When she got pregnant, she quit the runway and focused her content on anything and everything that had to do with raising kids. She's still drop-dead gorgeous and LA-skinny, of course, and her fashion sense remains as sharp as her cheekbones.

But that's not the only reason why I've got pinpricks of excitement zinging through my body. As if the thought of meeting Tanya Dylan in person isn't nerve-racking enough, guess who else was invited to Tanya's party? Yep. Aspen. You must've seen this coming, right? Despite my meddling, Aspen still has over six million TikTok followers. She's been part of the M club for quite a while now, and Tanya is one of Aspen's many momfluencer buddies. Not that she would ever deign to introduce me to Tanya. Oh no, Aspen keeps her contacts very close to her chest–yet more proof that Aspen was a shitty friend. I was tempted to fudge the date of Tanya's party on Aspen's calendar, but in the end, I left it alone. Tanya's party is a huge deal that people keep posting about. Aspen might get a reminder about it and find out that her calendar's borked. I am trying to minimize the number of appointments that I mess up on Aspen's calendar. I'm not a total monster. Also, I don't want her to get suspicious.

Tanya's mansion is a stunning glass structure overlooking the Hollywood Hills. She hired a valet service for the event, but I end up parking one block away because I don't want anyone to see my beat-up Honda. One day, my career will be so smashingly successful that I'll turn up at events in some flashy sports car. (It's important to dream big, you know.)

God, when was the last time I came to a house this beautiful? It seems like forever ago that I was invited to places like these. But this is different from all of the gorgeous homes I used to go to. Those had been bachelor and bachelorette pads, all sharp angles and minimalist decor. This house is a family home—a Pinterest-worthy place of light grays and whites with touches of bright colors here and there. Instead of avant-garde art, the walls are hung with pastel-colored photographs of Tanya's children caught mid-laugh, all of them framed in sleek gold. The kids aren't around, though; this is an adults-only party. The music is loud enough to drown out any awkwardness, but not so loud that you have to shout to be heard, and there are enough people to fill the space, but not so many that you end up feeling squished. Servers slip through the crowd, carrying trays of drinks and canapés.

There is a horrible, cold moment where my anxiety goes almost into overdrive, and every cell in my body screams at me to leave, because surely they will all see that I do not belong in this gorgeous crowd. They'll kick me back down, I know it.

But then my social skills, honed through years of gliding through party after party, kick in, and a dazzling smile finds its way onto my face, and I plunge into the crowd. I embrace its energy without a second thought, mirroring the other partygoers. Are they air-kissing? One or two-armed hugs? Are they calling each other "Hon" or "Babe" or "Bro" or—? And within minutes, I remember just how good I used to be at this stuff. I am in my natural element once again. It feels like I've been yanked out of a deep slumber and back into the light. I have come back to life.

I'm chatting with a DJ who has just under two million followers (hey, I did my homework before coming to this party) when I spot Tanya Dylan. She looks amazing, her platinum blonde hair swept back in a tight ponytail, sporting the "clean girl" look with minimal makeup that, nevertheless, looks like it took three hours to get just right. She's wearing a silver jumpsuit that hugs every curve of her body, and it's only in person that I get to fully appreciate just how unfairly gorgeous she is—how genetically blessed. I must talk to her. But that's easier said than done, because, of course, everybody in this room has the same thought I do. Everybody is gravitating towards her, calling out her name and touching her arm and flocking to her.

But I'm not like everyone else. I've done my homework. Yesterday, I spent over four hours scrolling down Tanya's accounts, going all the way to the very first posts she made on Instagram and TikTok. Her latest posts are mostly TikTok dances with her ridiculously talented kids, but the ones from six, seven years ago had her talking about how hard it is to raise a kid with ADHD. She has three children—a boy and two girls—and it seems that the boy has ADHD. She doesn't talk about it as much now, maybe because those videos didn't get that many views compared to the dancing ones.

I wait until the knot of people around Tanya untangles, leaving a bit of breathing room available, then I quickly slide in. No time for hesitation. I catch Tanya's eye, smile, and say, "You look like you could use a drink." Pause. Apologetic laugh. "Oh my gosh, that sounded like such a bad pick-up line."

Please laugh, plea—

She laughs. I release my breath. "I've heard worse," she says.

I pluck two flutes of champagne from a passing server and hand one to her. "Yeah, sorry about that, I swear it sounded way better in my head, but I recently got diagnosed with ADHD, so my mind's like—ack, you know?" I mime a mess in my head.

Her eyes widen. "Oh, wow. Really? That's so interesting, because I actually got diagnosed with ADHD myself a few years ago."

"Seriously?" I cry. "No one else I know got diagnosed with it as an adult. What are the chances?"

Tanya nods. "Yeah, I—well, my son has it. He was diagnosed when he was four. So, of course, I had to educate myself on the condition, and the more I read up on it, the more I was like, hang on . . ."

"Oh my gosh, right?" While we talk, I'm smoothly navigating us towards the patio, away from the hungry crowd. I'm an expert at this. I do it so gradually and so subtly, keeping up our easy-going chatter the whole time, that I doubt Tanya even realizes it. Then we're out of the house, away from the din, and on her beautiful patio. There is a handful of people out here as well, but it's far less crowded and the noise level is more manageable. Tanya leads me to a sofa and we sit down, drinks in our hands, and I work my magic on her.

There is a very fine balance to go for in conversations where you want to be appreciative, but not fawning. People love to be flattered, but nobody likes a sycophant. I am a master at this. I'm not bragging; it's just how it is. I've never been good at sports, but getting people to like me, that's my superpower.

Within half an hour, Tanya is saying stuff like, "Oh my god, where have you been all my life?" and calling me "Mer" instead of "Meredith." I am glowing. I am fully in my element, my humor charmingly self-deprecating and oh so relatable, and I do not want this night to end. I do not want to return to my messy apartment and sleep in my twin bed and wake up to pick up my cranky baby and then spend the whole day tending to said baby. I want to capture the magic and glitz and glamor of tonight and bottle it. I want to—

A flash of dark brown curls appears for a moment in the crowd inside the house, and I lose my train of thought. I don't have to catch more than a glimpse to know that she's here. Of course, I know who it is immediately. I know Aspen probably as well as my own reflection. Probably better, because we've spent almost every day together for years and years. My brain has memorized the way she moves, the way she stands. And seeing her again after all these weeks of not talking to her is electrifying. Quite literally, it feels like an electric shock to my system. So many emotions jolting through me. A yearning for our old friendship, and resentment, and jealousy, and of course, thrumming through everything else, there is guilt.

"Whoa, you okay? You look like you've just seen a ghost," Tanya says.

I tear my eyes away from the small figure swimming through the crowd and force a smile. "Oh, yeah. I'm fine." Then it hits me—people bond over negative things so much easier than positive ones. Just look at how Tanya immediately warmed to me when I told her I'd been diagnosed with ADHD. Still, I know I need to step carefully. I don't think she and Aspen are close—heck, I don't think she's close to most people at this party—but there is a chance that they are a lot friendlier with each other than I know. Aspen is a chronic brownnoser; she wouldn't be able to resist sucking up to someone like Tanya. "I think I saw my ex-best friend in there."

Tanya's eyes widen with curiosity, and she straightens up. "Oh, who?"

"Oh, it's—" I flap a hand casually. "It's Aspen Palmer, not sure if you guys are friends?"

"All Day Aspen? Of course, yes, I know her." Tanya narrows her eyes at me and leans in. "Ex-best friend?"

I raise both my hands. "Zero drama. I still love her to death."

Tanya nods vigorously. "Yes, zero drama, totally. Love her."

"Yeah, it's just . . ." I let my voice trail off before sighing and letting my shoulders droop. "It's just one of those things, you know? We used to be like this—" I curl my index and middle fingers together. "Inseparable. Her husband hated me because we were basically joined at the hip," I give a sad laugh before pressing my mouth into a thin, sad line. "But then um, well, I guess she got too big for me." Another bright smile, so brave of me. "It's okay, though. I'm fine. I'm so happy for her; she deserves every bit of her success."

"Wait, what?" Tanya says. "So you guys used to be besties, then she got big and dumped you?"

I cringe. "It sounds awful when you put it that way. I'm sure she has her reasons."

"Bullshit!" Tanya snaps. "Ugh, I hate people like that. I'm like, if I'm going up the ladder, I'm taking as many of my friends up with me."

"Same!" I say. "But not everyone feels the same way, obviously. And it's not like I'm even hoping for a handout or anything. I just . . ." I modulate my voice so it's nostalgic, but not pathetic. "I just miss my best friend."

"Well, you don't have to, because I have decided that we are going to be besties."

I giggle as Tanya wraps one skinny arm around my shoulders. "I love this girl!" she hoots at nobody in particular. "She is literally my new best friend." She lowers her voice. "And this Aspen bitch? She is dead to me. I always thought she was super fake. She is done in this industry."

A cold shiver crawls down my spine, guilt nearly choking me. Part of me wants to tell her no, it was all a mistake, Aspen's fine. But the other part of me spits out memory after memory of Aspen's little snubs over the past couple of years, ever since she became so much bigger than me: Aspen turning me down when I ask if we can hang out, Aspen posting Stories of her hanging out with her mega-influencer buddies, Aspen giving me social media tips and advice like I'm an amateur (when I was the one who taught her how to do social media properly in the first fucking place). Each terrible memory seethes with poison, its toxicity swirling around the curves of my brain, clouding my senses.

I meet Tanya's eyes and I nod. And later, much later, when

the story has spread all over the party like a noxious fume and someone says to me, "Should we do something crazy?" I seriously consider it. Because let's face it, Aspen deserves every bit of what's coming to her.

# Chapter 10

# ASPEN

Deep breaths. Everything's fine. Act normal. Don't think about how my life seems to be falling apart at the seams, threads somehow unraveling while I scramble to retie knots here and there. I'm okay, my marriage is lovely and my children are delightful and I must be happy-happy.

But the whole way to the party, I can't quite shake off the feeling that I'm being followed. And even after I get here, the feeling doesn't fade. In fact, it intensifies. Am I imagining it, or are people slightly cold towards me? From the corner of my eye, I keep catching lingering looks that are less than friendly. Cold stares that are broken as soon as I glance over. Snippets of whispers, bringing me right back to high school—a place crawling with bored, hormonal teens on the prowl for someone to hurt.

No, stop that. I force a smile, make myself lift my chin. I'm just imagining it. These are my people. Fellow influencers who have chatted with me, who have proclaimed me as their "bestie" or their "sis."

I'm clutching my champagne flute in front of me like a shield and have to remind myself to lower it. My phone buzzes with a text message.

> `Something is very wrong. Why aren't you more worried???`

I stuff the phone back into my purse, squashing the feeling of dread as deep down as I can. Scanning the room, I catch sight of a familiar face.

"Remy!" I cry with delight. Remy is one of the OG momfluencers, a glamorous blonde who also happens to be a successful party planner. Our friendship began about a year ago, and we DM each other a few times a month. Hers was one of the many friendships that Mer had accused me of upgrading to when my social media accounts became huge. The thought of Mer and our fight threatens to tug the corners of my mouth down. With a little shake of my head, I banish all thoughts of her. "It's been so long."

Remy looks somewhat taken aback to see me. "Aspen!" It takes only a split second for her to conjure up a dazzling smile, but it feels like eons. We kiss the air near each other's cheeks. "How are you?"

I give a dramatic sigh. "You of all people know how it is, what with the kids and the photo shoots and all. And Elea is still going through her rebellious phase." It's part of our thing; Remy and I bonded by commiserating with each other about our crazy schedules and how surprisingly hard and lonely it is at the top.

But instead of laughing and agreeing with me, Remy only gives me a close-lipped smile. "Yeah, I hear you." Her gaze scans the room.

Again, I shake off the uneasy feeling that's been plaguing

me the whole evening and fight to keep the smile on my face. "Enough about me, what about you, lady? Congratulations on the new partnership with The Orangery, oh my god, you superstar."

"Thanks, Aspen." Remy catches sight of someone over my shoulder and waves, her face brightening. "Sorry, girl, I just saw someone I need to say hi to. I'll catch you later." She squeezes my arm and is gone before I can say another word.

What the hell? That wasn't normal, was it? I turn around to see who Remy ditched me for. It's Tomas, an up-and-coming comedian. What the hell is a momfluencer like Remy talking to a comedian for? That's someone you talk to if there's no one else in the room, not someone you ditch a fellow momfluencer for! Then—my skin prickles, my whole body freezes—the two of them, still speaking to each other, look at me.

And it is not a friendly look.

They both catch me watching them, and Tomas says something in Remy's ear, and she giggles behind her hand before shaking her head. Embarrassment sears my skin. My scalp crawls like it's about to writhe right off my head. They are talking about me.

I tear my eyes from them and the next thing I see is another party guest staring at me while whispering something to the person next to him. I cast my gaze desperately, searching for a friendly face, but find none, and the stares and whispers skitter across my skin like insect legs, creeping and cutting their way right into my chest, burying themselves in the cavity of my flesh.

I can't quite get out of the living room fast enough. There is no networking to be found here. For whatever reason, this crowd has turned its back on me, and its toxin is burning into my skin. Have they seen the footage of me at the doctor's today? I've been monitoring it, and it hasn't quite gone as viral as I'd feared. But it's only a matter of time before it completely blows up, right? What am I even doing here? I escape outside and walk to where my car is parked, hoping that the cold night air will refresh me. In the distance, I catch sight of a familiar figure walking rapidly away from the direction where my car is parked.

Meredith?

The dark, waist-length hair is unmistakably hers, but when I try to call out, her name catches in my throat like a sharp fish bone, choking me. The sight of her tears what is left of me into ragged pieces. I wish I could run to her and grab her and beg her for forgiveness. Explain to her that I didn't mean to alienate her, that the only friendship I hold dear, that means anything to me, is hers. That without her, everything is turning to shit. That I need her. That I miss her so fucking much.

She's walking too fast for me to catch up, and before I know it, she's turned down a corner and disappeared. I stand there for what seems like ages, my thoughts churning in a confused mess. It can't be Meredith. My breath releases in a defeated sigh. There is nothing left for me here. I should go home, be with my family. My steps are slow, heavy with exhaustion.

I'm a few feet away from my car when I notice something weird about it. It seems—I can't put my finger on it. I quicken my pace, and when I get to my car, a gasp escapes my mouth. It's sitting lower, closer to the ground. Because all of the tires have been slashed. Vicious lacerations that leave no room for interpretation, no possible way this was an accident. Fear smothers me, its stench drowning all of my senses. The slashed rubber tires look gruesome, like an open carcass. Who could've done this? *The party, everyone staring, whispering*. Who hates me this much? *The woman who looks so much like Meredith from a distance, hurrying away.* No. There's an explanation for everything, there must—

"Aspen!"

A scream lurches out of me before I can stop myself. I jerk upright and raise my arms defensively.

"Whoa, you okay?"

My heartbeat is thunder, my eyes wild. It takes a moment for my brain to catch up to my flight-or-fight instincts and register who's in front of me.

"Liv!" I squawk. "You scared me."

My assistant gives a nervous laugh. "Yeah, obviously I did. Sorry, I didn't mean to. I was just so surprised to see you here."

"What are you doing here?" The question, meant to be casual, comes out accusatory.

"One of my friends invited me as her plus-one. But it got a bit too much for me—there are so many huge stars in there! I came out to get some air. I was looking for you the whole evening, actually."

Now that my heart is no longer trying to squeeze its way up my throat, I feel a little bit better. Well, less like I'm about to have an anxiety-induced heart attack, at least. Having Liv here helps; she's so bubbly in a wear-her-heart-on-her-sleeve way, and after the pointed looks and snubs at the party, it's a welcome change.

"Are you off home now?" Liv says.

"Well, I was, but . . ." I gesture at my tires. Liv's gaze follows my hand, and her eyes widen.

"Wow, what the fuck?" she gasps.

Somehow, seeing the shock and horror on her face eases the

weight that was crushing my chest a little. It feels comforting to share this horrific incident with someone.

"Yeah, I know," I mutter.

"Who would do this? That's messed up!" Liv cries.

For a moment, I consider telling her about Meredith, but I quickly dismiss the idea. The last thing I want is for someone else to know about my fight with Mer. As ridiculous as it sounds, it feels like a betrayal to Mer. I could never bad-mouth her, not now, not ever. No matter how bad our fight was, Mer will forever be my best friend, my other half.

"I don't know," I say finally.

Liv shakes her head and looks around the neighborhood. "I bet it was some teens playing Truth or Dare. They probably thought they were such badasses. God, that sucks. I'm sorry, Aspen. Come on, I'll give you a ride home. It's late. You can deal with this tomorrow. Or better yet, ask Ben to do it for you."

I manage a weak smile. Hah. Yeah, ask Ben to take care of this for me. Unlikely. He was so grumpy about me coming to this party in the first place, loading the dishwasher so angrily that I wondered if he would break the crockery. Made snide little remarks about having to stay in and look after our kids on a Friday night. Made other little remarks about how the others would probably bring their spouses to the party. He's not wrong; many of the attendees did bring their spouses. But I didn't want to bring Ben, not this Ben, not unhappily married Ben. Old Ben—Breadwinner Ben, Head of the Household Ben—was very fun at parties. Current Ben is full of bitterness, his jokes coming out sour with resentment, his eyes full of contempt for anything social media related. I can't bring Current Ben to a party of influencers, for god's sake.

Liv keeps up easygoing chatter as we make our way to her car. It's a comfortable SUV with a car seat in it. Although she's worked as my assistant for quite a while now, I'm ashamed to say that I hardly know anything about Liv, aside from the fact that she's got about a hundred and fifty thousand followers on TikTok and has a baby. A boy? A girl? Their age? I have no idea. I know, it's awful of me, but Liv mostly works remotely, and I've kept our conversations pretty strictly about work only.

Now, as she slips into the driver's seat, I take in little details about Liv that I haven't noticed before. We've only met two or three times, and each time I was so focused on giving her tasks that I hadn't stopped and considered her as a person. Liv isn't naturally pretty, but her makeup and hair are so on point that she does end up looking very attractive. The way she talks is easy and welcoming, and before I know it, I'm relaxed in my seat, watching the LA lights as Liv guides the car down the Hollywood Hills.

Liv glances at me. "You okay? Still thinking about your car?"

"Yeah," I sigh. "I know, it's probably a stupid prank, but it really scared me back there."

Liv gives me a sympathetic grimace. "I bet. I would've been freaked out too." She pauses, then says, "You know what? We're going to make a pit stop."

I'm too tired and defeated to argue. It's almost eleven p.m. now. Usually, I would be in bed reviewing my social media accounts, replying to a few comments, before I turn off the lights and go to sleep. I sit up when Liv drives to an In-N-Out. "Really?" I haven't had fast food in years.

"Come on, the food at that party was like 'organic sea foam on a bed of air.' I'm starving," Liv says. She considers the drive-thru menu and orders two double-doubles with fries and chocolate milkshakes.

My willpower crumbles as soon as the bags are in the car and the scent of the burgers hits my nostrils. I mean, seriously, can anyone resist double cheeseburgers?

"I thought we'd have it in the car so no one sees us and posts about how we're terrible mothers for eating fast food," Liv says.

I laugh through a mouthful of meat and cheese. "God, this is so good. Orgasmic."

"Right? Fuck the organic shit, give me processed meat and cheese anytime," Liv says. "Not that I would ever tell my kid that."

I roll my eyes. "Tell me about it." I hesitate, wondering if I should pretend to know more about her child, but something about Liv makes me not want to lie. "How old is—uh, your . . ." Son? Daughter? God, I really know nothing about her. I suck. "Sorry, I should know this already."

"Don't worry about it, why would you know? You're busy with your family and your business." Liv wipes her mouth with a napkin and says, "My daughter is eleven months old. Her name is Rain." She takes out her phone and shows me a picture of a grinning baby.

"Aww, she is adorable," I say, smiling. "That's really close in age to Sabine. We should have a playdate sometime."

"I would love that."

"Tell me more about you." I don't know if it's guilt talking, or if it's the endorphins from this delicious meal or what, but I find myself being genuinely interested in Liv's life.

Liv takes a sip of her milkshake. "Okay, hmm, let's see. I have an eleven-month-old daughter, I've been married for three years . . . I have a degree in computer science from Berkeley—"

"What?" I practically shout, making her jump. "Seriously?"

Liv looks at me. "Uh. Yeah? Why, what's wrong?"

"Nothing, just that you're a bona fide genius!"

She laughs. "Oh god, hardly. I mean, am I using my degree? Nope, not at all."

I cock my head. "Why not?"

"Well, after I graduated, I interned at a tech startup in NorCal for a while, and it was brutal, man. All that crap you hear about tech bros? It's true, every single one of them. Like, completely insufferable."

I snort. "Really? More insufferable than influencers?"

We're both cackling now. "About the same," Liv says when our laughter fades. "But in a different way. And maybe I would've been okay with it if I didn't realize something." Her face turns serious.

"What?"

"That . . . I hate programming."

I stare at her. "Seriously?"

She nods. And again, we both burst out laughing. "You'd think I would've realized that sooner, right? Before I devoted four years of life to computer science?" Liv cries. "But I didn't! I guess like, I loved learning about it, but actually having to do it, and stare at the code for hours, sifting through it looking for bugs? Fuck, that was boring as shit. And I just thought—this is it. This is what my life will be for the next forty years. And I kind of uh—went through a depressive episode."

"A quarter-life crisis," I say.

"Yeah, exactly. And I was vlogging about it, you know, just putting my thoughts out into the ether, and I started gaining followers. When I got to thirty thousand followers, I decided it was now or never. I was going to make the jump and become an influencer, see how it goes."

"Wow." I'm genuinely blown away. Who would've thought? "That's amazing."

Liv smiles at me. "You know, you were a huge part of that decision."

"What?" I goggle at her.

"Yeah, when I got pregnant, the algorithm started suggesting all this mommy content to me, and some of it was yours." Liv's eyes are bright as she gestures enthusiastically. "That was when I started following you, and your content was just so amazing! I loved everything; your videos were such a highlight to my days. Your yummy recipes, your super cute kids—you made it all look so fun and easy. I was like, 'This is the kind of mom I wanna be.'"

"Aww, that is so sweet." A small part of me feels ever so slightly guilty because that's exactly the problem—I make it *look* fun and easy. The truth is a different matter entirely. But hey, Liv's an adult. She should know it's all smoke and mirrors.

There's a moment's silence, then Liv says, "I'm so glad I ran into you."

I realize then that I am, too. It's been so long since I've been able to have a heart-to-heart like this with anyone, even with Mer. In the months leading up to our fight, there had been a barrier I didn't understand, our friendship rotting slowly from inside. Chats with Mer had gone from an easy flow to an awkward friction where I found myself bracing for her to take offense at some innocuous remark, or for her to take a sudden blow at me. My throat closes up at the memory. Why did things get so bad between us? How did it happen? I miss her, but maybe it's time I let go of the ghost of her. I look at Liv and say, with all sincerity,

"I'm really glad too. And . . . maybe you could work from my house some days? I could give you a few pointers on how to come up with relatable content."

Liv brightens up. "I would love that! Really? I don't want to get in the way—"

"You won't." There is such a huge hole in my life since Mer disappeared from it. It's time for me to fill it. "And bring Rain; she and Sabine can entertain each other while us moms work."

"It's a date."

My good mood disappears the moment I get home and see Ben's sulky expression. He's nursing a beer.

I keep my voice even as I take off my coat. "Hi," I say, "how were the girls at bedtime?"

He barely glances up at me, eyes still glued to the TV. "Fine."

Okay then. I guess that's that. I go to the kitchen, where there are two empty bottles of beer sitting on the counter. Typical. He can't even be bothered to throw them away. Sighing, I rinse them off and put them in the recycling bin. I'm about to go upstairs when Ben says in a very pointed tone, "How was your night out with the 'influencers'?"

He doesn't actually do the air quotes, but the way he says it, you could practically see his fingers doing them. So much venom in that one word alone.

"It was okay."

"Huh." He takes another sip of beer. "Yeah? 'Cause it looked like you had a great time. When you came in you were smiling real wide. And I noticed someone dropped you off?"

"Oh!" Somehow, after that great chat with Liv and the In-N-Out and coming home to my poisonous husband, I'd managed to forget about my slashed tires. "Oh my god, I forgot to mention—someone slashed my tires. That's why Liv had to drop me off."

Now, finally, Ben looks at me, the sulk temporarily replaced with confusion. "Liv? Your PA?"

"Yeah. She happened to be there as well, which was really fortunate, because—my tires! My god, how crazy is that?"

Ben frowns. "How do you know someone slashed them? Maybe you ran over something."

I bite back my frustration. Of course, his immediate guess is that I did something wrong. "No," I say slowly, "they were slashed, Ben. Someone literally took a knife to them."

"All of them?"

"All of them." I don't know what I was expecting from Ben, exactly, but it would've been along the lines of shock, horror, concern. Any of the normal reactions that should come from a husband whose wife told him her tires were slashed.

Instead, Ben merely snorts before taking another swig of beer. Then he says, "Wow. I guess you pissed someone off."

I stare at him, my husband of seven years. What happened to us? I know in my heart we weren't like this before. One of the reasons I fell in love with him was because he was so generous, so gentle, so supportive. I remember how, when we were dating, I got a mean comment (ha! How naive I was back then, how soft, to let one negative comment ruin my day). Ben had been so sad to see me so heartsick over it. He'd whisked me away for a day at Venice Beach to take my mind off it. He plied me with churros and shaved ice, and kissed the top of my head and told me I was perfect, and that people were being ugly only because they knew how imperfect they were in comparison. If Old Ben had heard about someone sabotaging my car, he would've jumped out of his seat and fussed over me, making sure I was okay before telling me he'd take care of everything. The thought makes me want to sob.

I'm too tired to get into anything with him right now, though, so as usual, I swallow my anger. I tell myself it's fine, he's probably tired, too, after a night of looking after the kids all by himself. And maybe the whole tire thing is too bizarre for him to grasp in the moment, especially after three beers. *He still loves you,* I assure myself as I trudge up the stairs alone. He just needs some time to . . . go through whatever it is he's going through. A midlife crisis? Seven-year itch?

As soon as the thought hits, it spreads like cancer. Is Ben having another affair? Maybe that's why he can barely stand to look at me. Maybe every time he sees me, he's wishing I were somebody else. I thought we were beyond this by now. I thought he'd learned his lesson.

My hands are shaking by the time I get inside our bedroom. I sit on the bed alone, gripping the edge of the mattress tight. Mer would know what to say. She always said the right thing. She'd assure me that I'm too hot to be cheated on, or something equally ridiculous that would make me smile. I take out my phone and click on her name. I send just three words.

"I miss you."

There is no reply. She's not going to read it. Nobody holds a grudge quite like Mer does.

# Chapter 11

# MEREDITH

There is a stereotype about Angelenos—well, there are many stereotypes about Angelenos—but the most pervasive one is how fake people are here. I feel compelled to clarify that we are not fake, not in the way Southerners are, where they say, "Bless your heart," when they really mean, "You fucking idiot." Angelenos would totally tell you you're a fucking idiot, but we'd also hand you a kale smoothie while we did it, and tell you it's okay that you're dumb; at least you're skinny. See, Angelenos just get hopped up on oat milk matcha lattes and the endorphins that come with chatting with the Trader Joe's cashier and end up calling everybody their best friends. We make way too many plans with said best friends—plans that we never have any intention of fulfilling—but in that moment, it would be impossible to say no to anything, because that's just the magic of LA.

I know all of this, and yet. And yet, days after that magical night at Tanya's party, when Tanya texts me to say she's sooo bummed but she can't join me for infrared yoga after all, I can't help but feel utterly dejected. The only person I'm mad at is myself, because I should've known better than to believe, even for a moment, that someone as huge as Tanya would want me as her BFF.

Oh god, I just used the term unironically, like a freaking twelve-year-old. To be fair, she used it first. That night at the party, after bonding over our mutual hatred for Aspen, Tanya had introduced me to at least three people as her BFF. Okay, so she was on maybe her fifth glass of rosé, but still. You mustn't judge me too harshly for feeling disappointed.

If I had six million followers like Aspen does, Tanya would never cancel on me. That's the thing about LA. To make meaningful friendships, it is imperative to be somebody. LA is full of wannabes. It is weary of wannabes. Its skin has been hardened by cynicism (and Botox) and it has no time for wannabes.

"What does that mean for Mommy?" I muse out loud to Luca as he bounces happily in his bouncer. He doesn't even glance at me. "It means, my sweet baby, that we need to grow *faster.*"

It is truly incredible how fast the joy that came with hitting 1M followers faded away. The first few days after it happened, I carried that shiny fact like a piece of jewelry in my pocket, taking it out now and again, caressing it lovingly and feeling the warm, secret smile spreading throughout my whole body. I thought (foolishly, naively) this feeling would last me years. Or at least months. But no, within a week, it quickly faded into a mere background fact that I got used to, like the sky being blue. It's pleasant, but it doesn't give me that jolt of happiness anymore. Like an addict, I need a bigger hit.

And for that, I turn to Elea's iPad. (Sorry, kid. I hope you have a replacement by now. If not, blame your mother; she can easily afford one, and the only reason she has for withholding buying it would be spite). Thank god I have this device, because, truth be told, since I rage-blocked Aspen's number, I've been really missing her. Even though she obviously doesn't deserve it.

Aspen's calendar gave me appointments with sponsors I wouldn't otherwise have any access to. Her cloud storage showed me how to divorce myself completely from reality in order to produce the most aesthetically pleasing footage. Both of those things have been super valuable, of course, but I need more. I need ideas for content. Things that would set me apart from the chaff. Not just the same old recipes, the same old workout videos, the same old talking-head videos spouting the same old observations. Aspen was always taking down little fun thoughts and ideas on her phone. Where would they be stored?

I swipe left until I get to the final screen, then swipe right, scanning each app. Then I see it. Notes. I tap on it, and bingo! Lists upon lists of Aspen's ideas. I'm not sure how to describe the sensation of reading through these lists. It feels like I'm peeking into Aspen's head, and I'm torn between love and admiration for my ex-best friend, and also soul-crushing envy because she is so fucking good at this. So naturally good at coming up with ideas with such amazingly relatable hooks.

- Cooking/baking with Sabine (make sure she's wearing cute chef's hat and have everything be within her reach so she can grab hold of anything she wants to for comedic effect. Remember to bake a separate batch that looks good for final shot!)
- Outfit change: Line up the girls and have one tap the other's shoulder, and with each tap, the girl's outfit changes
- Time lapse: Me rushing the twins to ballet when they

were toddlers, them stumbling around in ballet class, and now, them dancing beautifully

Such sweet and cute ideas. And the recipes! Oh my gosh.

- Homemade burrata? Maybe can be used on home-made pizza? (Make sure pizza sauce is made using "homegrown tomatoes")
- Sourdough bread with butterflies on top made out of flower petals
- Beef bourguignon but cooked inside a giant pumpkin

Then there are the sponsor baits.

- Tea company sponsorship: A series where I suffer from various maladies like migraines, digestive problems, etc., then a tea recipe for each one. The recipes will be shot top down, like a baking recipe, with the flowers and leaves laid out on the table in a beautiful pattern
- Any company: Elea and Noemie arguing over the last bag of X, and meanwhile Sabine in the corner with an extra-large bag of X, smiling to herself
- Children's clothes company: The outfit change idea where the girls tap each other, etc.

I scan the list while shaking my head. It feels as though the notes go on and on. There is no limit to Aspen's creative ideas when it comes to content that is refreshing and fun. Ironic, because when she first got started, generating content ideas was the one thing that kept holding her back. "I just can't think of anything!" she'd whine. "How do you do it? How do you come up with so many different makeup looks?"

Hah. How the tables have turned. I used to think it was something she just wasn't very good at, but turns out all she needed was to find her niche, and now it seems she has way too many ideas and not enough time to turn them all into actual content. Well, let me help you with that, Aspen.

I go down the list, this time discarding the ideas that I can't do because, unlike Aspen, I only have the one baby to work with. It still leaves me with more ideas than I can shoot in a single week. And knowing Aspen, she'll add to the list every day. I look over at Luca and smile.

"Come on, mister, let's get you in an apron and chef's hat and we're going to bake cookies."

The video of me baking with Luca and him making a huge mess with everything gets over nine million views. Nine million! The comments are all incredibly positive, everybody gushing over what an adorable little sous chef he makes and how good the cookies ended up looking, despite the mess. I would never have thought of doing a comedic video like that. If you'd asked me to make a cooking video with Luca, I would've set him a safe distance away from the kitchen counter and given him a pile of chocolate chips to nibble on while I did most of the work. But having him strangle the flour bag with both hands and shovel a stick of butter into his mouth while I scramble to stop him is genius; you can't help but stay and watch the carnage. And to have it end successfully after all that leaves the viewer with a pleasant feeling. I really have to hand it to Aspen to think of setting aside a good batch to ensure a positive outcome; in reality, Luca destroyed everything, and I would have had nothing to bake if not for Aspen's note.

I also did the outfit change video with Luca, where we turn and look at each other, then I tap him on his nose and his outfit changes. He taps me on mine (it took about thirty takes with me saying, "Where's Mommy's nose? Where is it? Mommy's nose!" the whole time before he booped me on the nose) and my outfit changes. And so on and so forth, five outfits for each of us. Six million views. Not as many as the cooking one, but considering I have below two million followers, it's still an amazing view rate.

I do her other ideas as well, each time tweaking it enough so that it's ever so slightly different from Aspen's notes. A Moroccan lamb stew instead of beef bourguignon cooked inside a pumpkin. A focaccia instead of a sourdough loaf with butterfly flowers. I tell myself that this way, Aspen won't realize that I'm taking her ideas. When we had our fight, I blocked her on everything, including all of my socials. I tell myself that she won't even be able to see any of my content. But of course, with them going viral and people downloading and reposting them, chances are she'll come across them at some point. And I know she's not stupid; she would totally know that I stole her ideas. I keep waiting for her to realize that I took Elea's iPad. Each time I turn it on, I keep expecting a sign to blare, "THIS IPAD HAS BEEN LOCKED BY ITS RIGHTFUL OWNER." But nothing happens. Her Notes app is updated multiple times daily with new ideas, many of which I help myself to.

And I continue on my meteoric rise.

You'd think that this would make me happy. It's all I wanted—a proper career as an influencer. But instead, the more followers I get, the more hollow I feel. The more anxious, because what happens when Aspen finds out she's being hacked into and changes all her passwords? What happens when I no longer have fresh ideas to rely on? Sure, I could go back to mimicking other people's content, which a ton of influencers do, but there's something about being the pioneer, the one who everyone else copies. And above all, doing this doesn't stop me from missing Aspen. And I do. I miss her so much. I wish I could rip her out of my heart neatly, leaving no traces behind, but instead, I move the other way. I become even more obsessed with her, with trying to find out how she's doing without me.

At night, after putting Luca down, I lie in bed exhausted, both mind and body depleted. What I find hardest about having a baby isn't the never-ending chores. I don't mind changing dirty diapers over and over again. I don't mind breastfeeding. I don't mind washing all of the components that make up a baby bottle. In fact, I enjoy it, because it means I can safely turn off my brain and just wash the damn bottles.

It's the playtime that I find shockingly draining. The pressure of having to come up with ways to encourage learning. Yes, he's not even a year old, and already I need to find a dozen creative ways each day to make sure his brain will develop to the max. Peek-a-boo. Dancing and singing. Sensory toys. It is endless, and each game, requiring me to trill at him in a desperately happy tone, is more mind-numbing than the last. Playing with little children is a special kind of torture where you feel your mind slowly sagging, turning you into some kind of cretin, but at the same time you must be one hundred percent aware and present, because babies and little kids are always coming up with new ways of getting themselves hurt.

The only thing that can ease this excruciatingly boring and yet taxing activity is to have a playdate with another equally tortured mother. Something I used to do with Aspen, but obviously not anymore. I could arrange for playdates with other moms, and I have, but finding the right moms to have playdates with is trickier than it sounds. For one thing, your babies need to actually get along. For another, it's a tough balance to find someone who is just as vocal as you are about how shit motherhood can be. I haven't been able to find that yet, and the more I take from Elea's iPad, the more I find myself being sucked back into Aspen's world, and yet not actually being a part of it.

At night, I lie alone in bed, drained, but instead of sleeping, I pick up the iPad and pore over it, refreshing the Calendar, Albums, and Notes in case there are new updates, which there often are. Sometimes, exhilaratingly, the update happens while I'm watching the iPad. In real time. Those moments always send a shiver down my spine. *At this very moment*—I would tell myself—*Aspen is tapping away on her iPad.* And it's as though I'm right there, peeping over her shoulder. Then the sudden yearning hits me, a sharp thrust straight through my chest, the message clear as day: I am alone. I have no real friends. I had one real friend, and I picked a fight with her and chased her away.

And the tears slide down my cheeks, wetting my pillowcase, and still I sit there while the iPad screen grows too blurry for me to read.

This morning, as I mash some steamed peas for Luca's breakfast, I glance over at the iPad and see that there's an appointment for Ben today. "Open house at 63 Belmont Ave. All day."

Something inside me clicks. I've been toying with the idea of tailing Aspen again, just to see her even if from afar, but maybe it's time for a change. Maybe I'll learn more by seeing Ben. Unlike Aspen, he's always been hopeless at hiding his thoughts and emotions. Maybe he might let it slip just how much Aspen has been missing me.

After a hectic breakfast where most of the peas end up smushed into Luca's wispy hair, I wipe him down and place him in his playpen. He immediately shrieks; he hates the fenced corner, but I ignore his enraged screams and dart off for a quick shower. I blow-dry my hair into loose waves and apply makeup. Part of me sneers at myself. *Are you putting makeup on for Ben? Pathetic Nice Guy Ben?* I ignore her the same way I ignore Luca's screeching, and soon enough I'm on my way to Clara's.

"For fuck's sake, Mer," she says by way of greeting when she opens her front door.

"Clara, language!" I cover Luca's ears and give her a look of mock outrage.

The corners of her mouth twitch like she's trying not to smile. She sighs. "What did I say about giving me advance warning before dropping him off?"

"Something came up suddenly. You know how these things are." I hold Luca up and say in a high voice, "Please don't be mad, Auntie Clara. We'll have such a great time bitching about Mommy."

"Argh," Clara grumbles, taking him from me. "You are such a brat."

"That's not a nice thing to say to your only nephew."

"I'm talking about you."

I grin at her and hand Luca's diaper bag over. "Love you, sis. See you later!" I skip down her front steps while still blowing kisses at Luca. I am definitely thankful for a sister who works from home.

When I get to the open house, I park across the street and stay there for a while, not quite sure just what the hell I'm doing. I think of driving off. Instead, I take a deep breath, check my reflection one last time in the rearview mirror, and get out of the car.

Soft classical music spills out of the open front door, and there is a delectable scent of freshly baked chocolate chip cookies. I've known Ben long enough, been dragged to enough his open houses by Aspen, to know that he takes a tray of frozen cookie dough to each open house and slides it into the oven right before he starts. Tacky, but it works. My mouth is watering.

Ben is in the kitchen, speaking to a young couple. "Hi, welc—oh," he says when he registers who just came into the house. "Meredith, hi. Ah, one minute."

"No worries," I say in an easy-breezy voice, though my mind is screaming, *WHAT AM I DOING HERE?* I wave him off. "I'm just going to look around a bit. Take your time. Hi." I give the couple a friendly, nonthreatening smile, and go deeper into the living room.

The house is a recently renovated three-bedroom that's slightly nicer than what Ben usually gets. I guess he's moving up in the realtor business. Though it's still in Alhambra, so he's not moving up that much. Nonetheless, it's a lot nicer than my current apartment. I stand inside the master bedroom for a long while, imagining living someplace like this. Spacious and modern. Big enough to have a space that's separate from all the baby clutter.

Ben's voice startles me. "Looking to buy a place?"

I turn and see him leaning against the doorframe, his arms crossed in front of him. It's been a while since I saw Ben. I always thought he was good-looking in the way that a math teacher might be—safe and predictable. But now I'm seeing him in a different light. Which just goes to show how much motherhood messes with your head. "Yeah," I lie without much effort. It's not like I can say no; I'm here because I'm missing his wife.

"Cool," Ben says. "I'll give you an overview of the place."

I follow Ben quietly as he shows me around the house, pointing out things like "a newly installed bathtub" and "low-key ambient lighting," and so on and so forth, and it's very strange to see Ben so in his element. So in charge. At the end of it, we stop at the living room, and he says, "So what do you think?"

It takes me a moment to realize he's asking about the house. Of course he's asking about the house. Come on, Mer. I give a noncommittal nod. "Seems nice."

"It is, isn't it? It's good for a small, young family." He starts talking about mortgages, which makes my head swim.

Before I know what I'm about to say, I blurt out, "How's Aspen?"

Ben stops mid-sentence. He closes his mouth, then narrows his eyes. "Did you just—did you come here to check in on Aspen?"

"No," I say, and we both see the lie, plain as day. I wonder if he's going to throw me out of the open house. Ben never really had much of a sense of humor. Or maybe he just didn't find me or Aspen funny. Same thing.

Instead, he snorts. Then the snort turns into a laugh. He shakes his head. "Mer," he mutters, not unkindly.

My cheeks grow warm. I don't know whether I should try to convince him otherwise or give up the ruse.

"Why don't you two just talk to each other? You know, be mature adults."

"Okay, I'm going to overlook the patronizing tone this time.

I—" I fumble for the right words. "I miss her, but . . ." What can I say? Everything I've been ruminating about for months, all of the infractions that have sliced into me, now seem so petty. Like her being buddy-buddy with other big influencers and making content with them and calling them her besties. Every single post she made with them had pummeled into my heart like a battering ram, each Reel a betrayal to our best-friendship. But I can't say that to Ben. What do I even say? That Aspen is supposed to be my best friend and mine only? That would make me look about as mature as a six-year-old. Oh god, it was a mistake coming here. I don't even know what I was thinking.

But before I can make up an excuse to leave, Ben says, "Yeah," and his voice is raw with so much emotion that it makes me do a double take. "I know." There is so much weight in those two words, so much empathy, that I look again at Ben. Really look at him this time, finally seeing him. The tiny frown lines etched into his face, the bitter sadness in his eyes. And I realize that all those times Aspen had gushed about how sweet Ben is, and how thoughtful, and what a doting husband he is, and what a perfect marriage they have . . . were, like the rest of her social media content, nothing more than fucking lies.

# Chapter 12

# ASPEN

If anyone were to tell me that, one day, I would be grateful to have had my tires slashed, I would've laughed and asked just how much weed they'd smoked. But that is actually how I feel. Ridiculously grateful. Because without the slashed tires, Liv wouldn't be coming over to my place for the third time this week, and Liv's presence is a godsend.

Her daughter Rain gets along beautifully with Sabine. Well, about as beautifully as two babies can get along, which is to say they alternate between ignoring each other and sucking on each other's toes. But the most important thing is that the two girls keep each other occupied in the playpen, leaving me and Liv gobs of time to devote to our work.

Liv is a meticulous worker. Her organizational skills are to die for, and she has a natural eye for spotting early trends. I suppose I should've known all of this before she came to work in person, but somehow, when she was working for me remotely, it was too easy for me to miss just how brilliant she is. How capable. How likable. In just a short time, I went from seeing her purely as my assistant to both an employee and a friend.

"You're probably sick of me saying this," she says, "but I still can't get over how Pinterest-worthy your entire house is."

I roll my eyes with a laugh, but inside I'm glowing with pleasure. Because I've poured so much effort into making sure our home is, indeed, Pinterest-worthy. Every choice I made in home decoration was through the eye of a phone camera. What might look good in person doesn't necessarily translate well to the nine-by-sixteen Reels format. And Ben is forever snorting and telling me we need more colors in the house that aren't some shade of nude or gray or white, but the thing with bright colors is that it's too easy for them to end up looking garish on the phone screen.

My phone buzzes then. Another text message.

`Why are you ignoring me?? WE NEED TO TALK.`

I turn it to Silent and work on keeping the smile on my face.

"And Ben is sooo sweet," Liv says, stroking the petals of the fresh vase of peonies in the middle of the kitchen counter. "I can't believe he still gets you flowers for no reason."

My smile wavers as the sadness weighs down on it, threatening to break it. Because of course the flowers aren't from Ben. I have a subscription at a local florist to have new bouquets delivered to my doorstep once a week. But when Liv first walked into the house, she'd assumed they were from Ben, and I didn't have the heart to correct her. And now it's become A Thing. Argh, why didn't I just correct her from the very beginning? There is no shame in getting myself flowers. Surely, it's the feminist thing to do. But it's too late to set the record straight now.

"What's the secret to having the perfect marriage?" Liv says, and she looks so earnest that I almost break down in tears then and there.

I'm this close to telling her that I don't have the perfect marriage. I have whatever's the exact opposite of a perfect marriage. The answer is in my mouth, aching to spill out, but then I hear Sabine's delighted squeal, and I glance over at her in the playpen, and she's so beautiful that it's hard to believe she's real. Ben and I made that, along with our robust twins. Despite the flaws in our marriage, we created something so unbelievably good.

I meet Liv's eye and say, "I don't think any of us has the perfect marriage. But if you want my advice, I think the most important thing in any relationship is to not keep score. I feel like a lot of couples have this pent-up resentment towards each other. They're like, 'Oh, I gave in about X, so you should give in about this thing now.'"

Liv says, "Oohhh," her eyes wide, her eyebrows raised as she slowly nods. "I love that. You're so right. I'm going to bring that up in our counseling session, because Adam and I definitely keep score, and it makes us like . . . almost hate each other." She covers her mouth like she's just let out a burp. "Oh my god, I can't believe I just said that. Please don't judge me."

If I were to judge anyone, it would be myself. At least Liv has the courage to be real with me. "How long have you been in marriage counseling?"

"About two months now. It's really helpful."

I'm about to ask her more about it when one of the girls starts crying, so the chat is cut short, which is probably just as well. But the rest of the day, I can't quite shake the thought of seeking marriage counseling with Ben. By the time he gets home from his open house, I'm ready. Liv is gone and the kids are perched in the living room, watching the Disney Channel. I bring him a glass of chardonnay as he takes his seat at the dining table.

"Oh, thanks," he says, looking surprised by the wine, which kind of pierces at me. Have I really been such a horrible wife that my husband is taken aback when I offer him something as small as a drink?

"Sure. How was the open house?"

Ben shifts in his seat, breaking eye contact. My internal alarm goes off. I'm not the only person in this room who's hiding something.

"It was fine," he mutters, taking off the cling film that I'd put over his plate of food.

Definitely guilty of something. "Any promising offers?"

Ben gives a long-suffering sigh before glancing up at me. "I've had a long day. I'd rather not do this right now."

Do what? The question's on the tip of my tongue, but somehow, I manage to swallow it down like a bitter pill. I nod to nobody in particular. Ben isn't even looking at me anymore to see me nodding; he's hyper-focused on stabbing into his roast chicken. *Well,* I chirp brightly (and silently) to myself, *this is at least a good way to segue into what I wanted to discuss.*

"Um, so I was chatting with Liv today—"

A tiny, mirthless snort from Ben. "Your new best friend," he mutters.

I'm not sure why that feels like such a dig, but I choose to ignore it for now. "And she mentioned that she and Adam—her husband—are in marriage counseling, and that it's really helpful."

Ben stops chewing. His eyes settle on me, and I almost shrink away at the burning malignity in them. How could anyone look at their spouse this way? He chases down the mouthful with a large gulp of wine. "Chicken's dry," he says finally. "Again." His gaze is still searing a hole in my skin. "Looks amazing though. I bet your followers love it."

*Your followers* is said with as much disgust as one might say the words "sex offender."

Again, I swallow the retort clawing its way up my throat. "I was thinking maybe we could see a marriage counselor as well."

"Why? Don't we have 'the perfect marriage?'" It comes out absolutely dripping with sarcasm.

My voice cracks. I can barely hold the tears back when I say, "Ben, please. I'm trying to make this work."

He softens then, at the sight of my raw desperation. Another sigh, though this time, it's one of defeat. As though by pleading with him to see a counselor, I've attacked him. "Fine." He says it to the chicken breast and not to me, but I have to be grateful for what little scraps he gives me.

"Thank you," I whisper. Then, because I find myself ridiculously overwhelmed with gratitude for his acquiescence, I reach out and squeeze his hand.

I pretend not to feel his hand twitch and stiffen, as though mine were a scorpion crawling onto his skin.

Ben surprises me by speaking up when the counselor, Laura, asks who'd like to begin.

"I'll go first I guess," he says. And he gets right into it. "I'm tired of living in an Instagram account."

"Oh? Can you clarify that, Ben?" Laura says. Her voice is very calming. I should learn how to modulate my voice so my questions don't come out too aggressively.

"Well, Aspen here's an influencer." That tone again, like

"influencer" is a dirty word. Ben gives Laura a look and laughs a little, as though he expected her to laugh along with him. She doesn't. I decide that I like her. "When we first met, I thought it was cute, you know? I was so supportive. I did everything I could to help her grow online, and now it's grown way out of control. It's ridiculous. I'm sick of feeling like everything we do is purely for 'aesthetics.' When we bought our house, I didn't have a say at all in how I'd like it to be decorated. Oh no, Ben knows nothing about aesthetics. I wanted some color in the house. I always thought that when I had kids one day, they'd have this vibrant nursery full of every color of the rainbow, but no. The whole house is gray or white or eggshell or whatever the fuck. Even our kids' toys all have to be color-coordinated. God forbid I ever get them a brightly colored plastic toy! No, it all has to be boring Nordic wooden toys that they don't even like to play with. What even is Nordic wood? Is it Norwegian?" He gives a short, shrill laugh before raking his fingers through his hair. "It's—it's exhausting."

Every word in his well-prepared speech slices into me, opening the wound even wider, exposing me to Laura. By the time Ben's done, I feel like I can barely look Laura in the eye. She must think I'm the worst wife and mother in the world. His testament is so scathing and so full of wrath, it's a wonder Laura doesn't just go, "Okay you guys, there is no hope for the two of you. Off you go now in separate directions."

But when I raise my gaze to Laura's, I find nothing but empathy in her eyes. "Thank you, Ben. That was enlightening." She nods encouragingly to me. "Would you like to tell me what you think about what Ben said, Aspen?"

Tears prick my eyes, and I don't bother trying to fight them.

What's the point? "Um—" My voice cracks and I take in a shuddery breath. "He's right. All of it." I turn to him and clasp his hands in mine. "You're right." Ben looks confused. I sniffle and turn back to Laura. "Ben's right. I'm tired of it, too—of having to pretend to have the perfect life. But the thing is, I don't know if I can afford to stop. I'm responsible for most of our finances. The mortgage, the healthcare . . . One of our daughters, Noemie, she's diabetic. The insulin alone is costing us eight hundred dollars a month, and that's with insurance. Then there are the pediatrician costs and other drugs, not to mention the exorbitant school fees, and—" This time, when my voice breaks, I let it. I sit there and cry and don't even bother trying to hide my tears. Laura hands me a box of tissues and I thank her in a small voice. "I'm sorry. I just feel so helpless. What would we do without my income?"

Ben pulls his hand away and shifts uncomfortably in his seat. He looks everywhere but at me.

"I mean, maybe we could downsize to a smaller house," I continue between sobs, "but I've been trying and trying, and I can't figure out a way to afford Noemie's healthcare without my career. And Ben—I'm sorry, babe, but your income . . ."

"Isn't anywhere near big enough," Ben mutters. "I know."

"Ben's a realtor," I say for Laura's sake. "His job doesn't have health insurance. Mine doesn't provide it either, to be fair. I'm paying for our family health insurance ."

She says, "Ah, I see. Right. Well, I think you both have very legitimate concerns."

"It really hurts my feelings," I add, "when Ben treats my career as an influencer as something silly."

"Do you feel that he does that often?" Laura says.

I chew on my lip and nod. "I get the feeling that Ben thinks it's shallow and fake. I think maybe it's easy to see it that way because I have to appear bubbly in my videos, even when I don't feel cheerful. I'm a momfluencer, and one of the many reasons I love what I do is because it connects me to other moms. We help each other feel less alone. Being a mom can be so isolating. I put a lot of thought into my content, and I wish he would recognize that. Especially since I'm the one supporting the family financially."

When Laura looks at Ben, there is, for just a split second, a flash of contempt in her expression. And I wonder how many wives have sat here on this leather couch and told her how dismissive their husbands are of their careers. Ben squirms, his gaze locked onto his lap.

"Ben, do you have anything to say to that?"

He shrugs, his whole demeanor that of a guilty schoolboy.

"Well." Laura leans back and takes a deep breath. "Thank you both for being so honest with me and with each other. I think there is a lot to work with here. There are some issues, yes, but I also sense a ton of love between you two."

Is there? I want to shout at Ben. Is there still a ton of love between the two of us? Or are there only its remains, festering away?

I wish Ben would look up and meet my eyes. Convey to me somehow that he's in this, too—that I'm not the only one fighting to keep our marriage intact. But when he does lift his head, his gaze is trained on Laura's. He's deliberately not looking at me, and his jaw is set in a way I find familiar. A stubborn expression that I used to find attractive and so masculine, but which I now know is nothing more than childish petulance. Despite everything I brought up, or maybe because of all the things I brought up, Ben is even more set in his thinking. He'll continue casting me as the villain, refusing to face the reality of our situation, and resenting me for doing what needs to be done to support the family.

And I know, then, that no matter what Laura says, no matter how obediently we do whatever homework she assigns us, our marriage is over. The only question that remains is which of us will have the courage to say it out loud.

# Chapter 13

# MEREDITH

*What am I doing?* The question hounds me the entire morning, and I still can't come up with a good answer. *What am I doing?* I ask myself as I carefully curl my hair. *What am I doing?* I ask as I swipe on mascara. *What am I doing?* I ask as I slip on a top that shows off my cleavage. Each time, I tell myself I'm just getting ready as per usual. Each time, I know I'm lying to myself. *What am I doing?* I ask myself as I drop Luca off at Clara's. (At least she's less pissy this time because I asked her in advance, and also gave her a luxury gift basket as a thank you for her trouble. The hamper was actually a gift from one of my new sponsors, but I thought it unnecessary to tell her such petty details.)

*What*

*Am*

*I*

*Doing?*

I ask as I drive to Alhambra and park outside of another of Ben's open houses. I'm meeting a friend. You can't judge me. There is nothing wrong about me and Ben being friends. *Except you had years to become friends. The entire time, Aspen was pushing you two to become friends, but you kept rejecting it—kept coming up with reasons to hate him. And this whole time, the real reason was because you were jealous of him. Because you saw Ben as the person who had come in between you and your best friend. And now that said best friend is out of the way, you see Ben as—what? Fair game?*

I shake off the thought, rumpling my soft waves as I walk up the front steps of the house. Kindly shut the fuck up, please, mind. I'm only here to view a house. Because now that my social media accounts are booming, it's wise to be looking for a home to invest in. I can't live in a one-bedroom apartment with my baby forever.

Ben looks surprised to see me, but a delighted surprise, not an "Oh god, what is she doing here?" surprise. At least, I hope it's not that kind of surprise. He excuses himself from the handful of viewers he's chatting with and strolls toward me with his hands inside his pockets. It's a disarmingly adorable move, and I find myself shifting from one foot to the other, trying to present to him my most attractive angle. *Stop that. He's your best friend's husband.*

Well, ex-best friend.

"What brings you to this side of town?" he asks with a smile that says: *I'm glad you're here.*

My insides heat up. *Careful, Mer. You are playing a dangerous game here.* Shut up, shut up. "Well, I heard that there's an open house being held by one of LA's up-and-coming real estate agents, so . . ."

"Up-and-coming, huh?"

I give a playful shrug. "So I heard from the grapevine."

Ben laughs. "It's great to see you again, Mer. You looking for something for you and Luca?" He gestures at the house, which is bigger than the last one I saw. "This one is a bit too big for just the two of you, I think."

Something in the way he says it both stings and excites me. "Who says it's just for the two of us?"

Ben's eyebrows rise. "Oh? Is there a new guy in your life?"

Forget my cheeks, my entire face feels hot. I turn away from him and pick up a brochure from the kitchen counter. "I mean, I'm not saying no. But I'm not saying yes either." I busy myself with flipping through the brochure. Luckily, Ben is distracted by the other viewers who have just finished their tour of the bedrooms. While he chats with them, I take the chance to nip into the bathroom and check my reflection.

I definitely have more makeup on than usual. My lips are fully plumped up and are practically begging to be kissed. The sight of them, so much more pillowy than usual, makes my stomach curdle with shame. Again, the million-dollar question: *What am I doing?*

"Mer, you still here?" Ben calls out from down the hallway.

"Yeah," I say quickly. I swipe my hair away from my face and come out of the bathroom.

The absence of the other viewers is painfully palpable. The entire house is so quiet that I can hear every sound we're making. Ben leans against the counter. "Cookie? They're fresh out of the oven."

"No, thanks." I stand there awkwardly, unsure of what to say next. There's a stiff pause as we both look at each other and grope about for something to say.

"Do you want . . . a tour of the place?" Ben says at the same time as I blurt out, "She got too big for me."

We both freeze. I wonder if that was the wrong thing to say, if he even heard it at all over the sound of his own voice, if I should take it back, if—

Then Ben nods. "Yeah." He takes a deep inhale, holds it for a few seconds, then sighs, long and hard. "She got too big for me too." He pulls out one of the chairs at the kitchen island and gestures for me to take a seat.

I do so, and Ben plucks a glass of wine from a row of glasses he's prepared. He takes one for himself, and we clink glasses. I sip slowly, wondering which of us is going to go first.

"I have to say, I never saw it coming with you two, though," Ben says after a beat. He regards me over his wineglass, his gaze appraising me with obvious approval.

The wine goes down cold but warms up my belly. Or maybe it's the way Ben is looking at me that's getting me all heated up. "Yeah, me neither. I really thought she was my ride or die."

"You wanna know something ridiculous?" Ben says.

"What?" I lean closer.

"I was always jealous of your friendship."

I nearly snort my wine out my nose. "No way. I was jealous of your relationship!" I want to swallow the words back as soon as they're out. I shouldn't have said that. That sounds so pathetic and childish.

But Ben's expression softens, as though I didn't just say something unbelievably petty. He lowers his eyes and strokes the rim of his glass with his index finger. "Yeah," he mutters. "I always got the feeling that I was in the way of your friendship."

I shrug. "You sort of were, in the beginning. But then I saw how good you are for her."

He smiles bitterly. "I don't know about that. I doubt Aspen

sees me that way. Lately, I just feel like I'm a hindrance to her as she blazes down a path to conquer the world."

"Ha! I am very familiar with that feeling." I raise my glass and he meets it with a satisfying clink once again.

"When I first met her, she was so different." His eyes get this faraway look and I know what they're seeing: Aspen seven and a half years ago, girlish and—not so much naive, but fully aware of her naivety, happy to look up to everyone else and play submissive follower. Her eyes and smiles were always open and trusting. *Whatever you think is best, Mer!* She'd say. "I felt like—" He grimaces. "This is going to sound really stupid, I know, feel free to give me a hard time over it, but . . . I felt like a man. Like I was there to protect her." He takes another gulp of wine. "How's that for some alpha male bullshit, huh?"

I laugh. "Wow, Ben. That is indeed some alpha male bullshit. Never took you for that kind of guy, honestly."

"I'm not. I swear, I'm not some chest-thumping, gun-toting meathead. But I just—in some small way, I liked feeling like I could shield Aspen from whatever bad stuff's out there."

*You could protect me. Luca and I are all alone in the world.* The words pop into my head out of nowhere. Fortunately, they don't make it through the filter between my brain and my mouth, but I feel guilty anyway, as though he can read my shameful thoughts. "It's not as ridiculous as you think it is," I mutter, then quickly swallow more wine before I say anything else.

"Well I sure as hell don't feel like that anymore. Not nowadays. I'm just one of the millions of chores that Aspen has to tick off every evening." Ben leans closer to me, close enough for me to smell the spicy scent of his aftershave. "What happened between the two of you?"

"She didn't tell you?"

"Aspen? She's a closed book. And even if I did manage to pry the book open, it would be written in Russian or something."

I can't tell if the fact that Aspen hasn't told Ben means our fight shattered her the same way it did me, or if it meant nothing to her. Maybe she's forgotten about me entirely. "Like I said, she got too big for me. We used to talk every day. Like, from the moment we got up, we'd—"

"Oh, trust me, I know," Ben laughs. "I was so sick of you, Mer."

I grin ruefully. "Sorry, not sorry. But yeah, we were tight. But then she got big, and she found other big influencer friends, I guess. Our chats became more sparse. I would message her, and it would be hours before she responded. I'd ask if we could hang out—I mean, you know better than anyone else, we used to hang out every day! But she started giving these bullshit excuses. 'Sorry Mer, I have a meeting to get to.' 'Oh no, Mer, I'm going to be so swamped today!' And on and on. A million reasons boiling down to the same damn thing: that she no longer had time for me. I wasn't important enough for her." I can't bear to look at Ben as I spill the truth, so I train my gaze at my glass of wine. "I tried to be okay with it for the longest time, I really did. But then one day I just . . . snapped. I exploded on her. I told her she was the fakest friend I've ever had."

Ben sucks in his breath through his teeth, and I grimace. "Yeah, it was bad. I was screaming at her, and she looked so—" My breath catches in my throat, and I have to pause to keep my voice even. "She looked anguished. But also like she pitied me. I couldn't stand having her look at me that way. Who the hell does she think she is? I told her never to call me again and I stormed off." I'm burning with shame now, so I try to lighten the mood by adding, "It was super dramatic." I laugh to hide how much telling the truth has wounded me, but Ben doesn't join in.

"That's messed up," he says.

"I know; I've always had a bad temper, I—"

"No, Mer," he says quietly. "I mean the way Aspen treated you. That's messed up."

I finally look up at him and immediately get lost in his warm aquamarine eyes. There is a connection here, a surprisingly deep one, forged through both of our bitter experiences with Aspen. Here is the one person in the world who understands completely, without reservation, how I feel.

But—god—haven't I done enough to Aspen already? The worst thing she ever did to me was to outgrow our friendship. What am I doing? Stealing her husband? Am I really going to stoop that low? Be The Other Woman?

But maybe it's the wine or the unbearable loneliness gnawing at my heart ever since I lost Aspen, or maybe it's the falling-off-a-cliff feeling that I get when I think of a life with nobody but Luca. One day he'll turn eighteen and leave me, too, and I'll be all alone. Maybe it's all of these things and none of them. Maybe, maybe.

Whatever it is driving that need, the same force lifts my hand and places it on top of Ben's. He shifts, and for a horrifying second, I think he's going to pull his hand away. Instead, he flips it over so it is palm up, my hand now in his, and his fingers wrap around mine and squeeze. I can feel the thump of his heart in the warm palm of his hand, and it is as though we're holding the entire universe together. The space between us thrums with electricity. I'm seeing Ben in a whole new light:

not as my best friend's husband, or her irritating boyfriend, but as his own separate entity. A man.

I notice, now, how his left eyebrow slopes ever so gently downward, just a little. The asymmetry gives his face more depth. I take in the aquamarine of his eyes and the way his brown lashes catch the light, turning them golden. My gaze settles on the curve of his lips, the little notch in his bottom lip that highlights their plumpness. Ben isn't just pleasant-looking; Ben is handsome. He's very handsome.

And his eyes are drinking me in, too, as though, like me, he's seeing the person for the first time. Inch by inch, we close the space between us. All of my senses are heightened. I feel superhuman—so sensitive that I can practically feel every air molecule grazing my skin. Then our lips meet, feather-light, and a soft whimper escapes me because it's been so long since I was touched like this. Then harder; a longer, deeper kiss. I'm kissing Ben. I'm—

*What are you doing?*

I jerk back a split second before the front door opens. In my sheer panic, there is a dreadful moment where I think the person standing at the doorway is Aspen. Then my senses return, and I see that it isn't. In fact, her height and build and the way she wears her hair are probably more similar to mine.

"Liv!" Ben cries, jumping to his feet. He looks about as horrified to see her as can be possible. I mean, the way he's reacting, she might as well be Aspen. "What are you doing here?"

I wince. His voice is too shrill, guilt coursing through it in palpable waves. Come on, Ben. You need to be better at this.

Liv's gaze ping-pongs back and forth between Ben and I, an awkward smile plastered on her face. She looks beautiful in a way that I'm familiar with. There's a very specific type of beauty that TikTokers have—uber plumped-up lips and eyelashes that graze the eyebrows. So, a TikToker. I stand and offer her my hand. "Hi, I'm Meredith Lee. And you are?" I hope I'm coming off a lot more confident than I feel.

"I'm Liv. Aspen's PA." Her grip is strong, her expression knowing.

Behind me, Ben is shifting his weight from one foot to the other. The familiar irritation that I used to feel when it came to anything involving Ben rises up. I feel an inexplicable urge to smack him and snap, *Stop fidgeting.*

I force myself to keep my attention on Liv. "Oh, right! Of course. It's so nice to meet you."

"Hm." Liv nods with a close-lipped smile. Then she turns to face Ben. "Aspen thinks you took her iPad by mistake. I'm here to pick it up."

"Huh?" Ben gapes at her, and I can't believe that only two minutes ago, I had thought he was handsome. What the hell came over me?

"Aspen's iPad," Liv says patiently, as though explaining something to a toddler. "Can you maybe check your bag?"

Ben frowns. "I doubt it would be in there. Aspen hardly ever goes into my briefcase . . ." Then he lights up. "Ah, maybe my car. Yeah, she used it to go to the store last night. I'll go check." He hurries out of the house, obviously eager to get away from Liv and me.

The silence he leaves behind is excruciating. Time to make my exit. I busy myself with gathering my phone and my purse, studiously avoiding all eye contact.

"What brings you here?" Liv says. Her tone is conversational, but her eyes are shrewd. Too shrewd. "Are you looking to buy?"

I force a smile. "Yeah. My kid's getting a bit big for the apartment, so." I shoulder my purse.

Liv considers me coolly. "Weren't you and Aspen close before?"

What the hell is she trying to get at? I feel myself bristling. It's a fight to keep the smile on my face. "Yep. We were."

"And now you're not, so you're seducing her husband for revenge?" Liv says it so casually, in the tone one might use to order a kale and strawberry salad, that it takes a second for my mind to grasp the actual words.

"Found it!" Ben calls out, waving the iPad above his head triumphantly. He strides in with all the confidence of a mediocre man and hands Liv the iPad with a huge grin. "Anything else?" he says.

Liv tucks the iPad in her bag. "No, thank you, Ben. So helpful as always. See you! And Meredith, so nice to finally meet you in person. I've heard so much about you." She gives me a nod and a knowing smile and walks out of the house.

Once she's gone, Ben releases his breath in a loud sigh and mimes wiping his forehead. He widens his eyes at me. "Phew, that was a close call, huh?"

I stand there, frozen. His hand crawls toward mine, and I jump when his fingers wrap around mine. I can't yank my hand away fast enough.

"Whoa, hey, you okay?" Ben says.

I jerk my head up and down and realize only when I follow Ben's gaze that I'm wiping my hand on my jeans, as though his touch sullied it. "I think Liv saw us."

Ben pales, but then he shakes his head and smiles. "Nah, she didn't. I can tell."

"No, Ben, she—"

"Trust me. Liv's so . . ." He mimes fireworks around his head. "She's so bubbly and—you know, kind of ditzy. If she saw us, we would know."

Anger burns an acidic path up my chest. "So just because she's 'bubbly' you think she's too fucking stupid to pretend she didn't see?"

Ben's mouth drops open. "That's not what I said at all. Don't put words in my mouth."

"That's literally what you said," I snap.

"I didn't!"

"You fucking did!"

Ben raises his hands, shaking his head. "You know what? It doesn't matter. I think you need to leave now. You and Aspen are exactly the same crazy bitches."

"The only reason crazy bitches exist is because there's always some asshole gaslighting us into losing our shit," I hiss.

Ben utters a short, mirthless laugh. "Okay, Mer. Whatever. Aspen's right, there is no reasoning with you."

More than anything, this is the one that cuts real deep. The knowledge that Aspen bitched to Ben about me. But of course she would; he's her husband. Her husband whom I just kissed. Whom her personal assistant saw me kissing. God, how did this day get so utterly fucked?

"Fuck you, Ben," I growl, and stomp out of there before he can get a last word in.

# Chapter 14

# ASPEN

Call it intuition. Call it insecurity. Call it whatever you will, but whatever it is, it tells me that Ben is hiding something from me. I know this feeling—am unfortunately familiar with it. A sickening darkness like an octopus writhing in my gut, unfurling its tentacles, stretching them as far as they can go, infecting every inch until my entire body is filled with its poison. It's a knowledge that only a wife would have. An alarm telling me that there is a separate reason why Ben is pulling away. It's not because of us, or rather, not just because of us. There is an external factor involved here. Years ago, when my earnings first surpassed his, Ben had some sort of crisis and started dabbling in stocks. He quickly spent most of his savings, and it was only my timely intervention that stopped him from going into debt in his fervor to outearn me.

I shudder at the memory. Above everything else, financial security is the most vital thing to us as a family—to the girls' future and well-being. If Ben is doing something that might endanger it . . .

I try to shake the thought from my mind. But the whole

morning, it plagues me. I'm distracted, unable to focus even on the simplest tasks. When I try making a pumpkin focaccia for social media, I end up spilling half the dough in my haze. I utter a frustrated cry so loud that it jerks Sabine awake. She rubs at her face and starts wailing. I take in the mess in my kitchen, and I want to cry at the thought of having to clean it up. I can't. I just can't. I can't stay here, trying to make TikToks while Ben is out there doing god-knows-what. I scoop Sabine up and bounce her on my hip while I rush through the house, grabbing things and stuffing them in her diaper bag.

"We're going to go on a trip, sweetie," I coo at her.

Thankfully, by the time I get her into her car seat and deposit a strawberry cookie in her hand, she's stopped bawling. I slide into the driver's seat and consult the family calendar. Right. Ben is supposed to have an open house today. I glance at the rearview mirror at Sabine, who is sucking on the cookie.

"Ready to see Daddy?" I don't bother waiting for an answer before backing out of the driveway.

The whole way there, my thoughts are a scrambled mess. This is crazy. I'm being ridiculous. I'm being one of those jealous, insecure wives who can't stop themselves from snooping through their husbands' phones.

I'm not being insecure. I'm trusting my instincts, and my instincts are telling me that there's someone else. You don't go from loving husband to distracted and secretive unless something is happening. Not that Ben was a loving husband before this. But this is different. He was aloof before, but now the rift is getting wider, and it's because something, or someone, is prizing it open.

A small voice says: *You've been distracted.* Maybe that's it.

*Your mind has been on everything else but your marriage, and he can feel your distraction.*

A loud *honk* shatters my mental argument with myself. Jesus, I just ran a stop sign. My throat closes up and I have to focus on breathing. I just ran a stop sign with my baby in my car. I strangle the steering wheel, willing myself to calm down. Focus on driving, goddamn it.

Somehow, I manage to drive us to the open house in one piece. After turning the engine off, I sit there for a long time, until my heart rate goes back down to something approaching normal. Sabine gurgles and I glance at the rearview mirror. The sight of her makes a sob lurch out of me. "I'm sorry, baby girl. Mommy's so sorry." I can't believe I drove so irresponsibly with her in the back seat. I will do better. I will get my shit together.

For once, Sabine doesn't fuss when I take her out of the car. As I walk down the street towards the open house, I sift through my options. I could tell Ben I happened to be in the neighborhood—though what I could possibly be doing in Alhambra, I have no idea. Maybe I could lean into the loving wife angle? Tell him I missed him so much I had to drop by to see him. Nah, our marriage has deteriorated enough that he'd be suspicious at this sudden show of affection. Or maybe I could use that. Say that I'm making an extra effort to revive our marriage. Maybe even sneak in a quickie? Maybe the open house has a nursery we can plop Sabine in for a bit.

The idea of having sex in a stranger's home sends a tingle down my spine. That's the kind of crazy thing we used to do when we were dating. We used to have sex everywhere—his backyard, a deserted park, the back seat of his car. Now, sex has to be penciled in a week in advance to coincide with the kids' crazy schedules.

There is a spring in my step as I walk. Maybe we'll have super passionate sex on the kitchen counter. Now that would definitely spice things up. Maybe this can be our thing: every time Ben has a house to put on the market, we can christen it. Hope is a beautiful thing. Just a tiny grain of it is enough to change one's whole outlook on everything.

Hope is a cruel thing. Just a tiny grain of it, when dashed, can shatter everything.

I realize that when a glance through one of the windows shows Ben leaning into a woman. His expression is one of such tenderness that I instinctively look away, wanting to give them privacy. Then my brain catches up with me and goes: *What the fuck? Give your husband privacy? To do what? Kiss another woman?* I drag my eyes up and force myself to look—to stare through the glass at the nightmare unfolding before me. For a moment, I stand there, completely frozen. A pillar of salt cursed by a vision I shouldn't have seen. Every muscle is petrified, my mind stuttering in place.

Then Sabine writhes, and I'm yanked back to reality. Panic surges through me like an electric shock, and I dart away from the window. I can't let Ben see me. Not like this. Why? I don't know. All I know is I can't stand to face him and—and that woman. Ben's mistress. Ben is having an affair.

The thought strikes me like a physical blow, and sobs wrench their way out of my mouth as I stagger back to my car. I bundle Sabine into her car seat, slide into the driver's seat, and let my head drop onto the steering wheel as the anger swallows me whole.

Why? I've worked so hard to provide for our family. I starve myself so I can still fit into the same pair of skinny jeans I wore eight years ago. My belly is still as flat as before I had kids, albeit with a little loose skin. I adhere to a seven-step beauty regime with vitamin C and snail slime and essence of whatever-the-fuck, and my skin is as youthful and supple as it has ever been. Whenever I make the school runs, I see the other kids' moms side-eyeing me with open envy while their husbands leer at me. I'm supportive of Ben's every need. I've never stopped him from doing whatever it is he wants to, whether it be golfing or a Vegas trip with his buddies. I look after the kids, cook impressive meals, and keep a pristine house. How dare he?

What do women have to do to make sure their husbands don't fuck other women? And why do we have to do whatever that thing is? Why can't we sit back and be confident, smug, in the knowledge that our husbands won't stray? Why is loyalty from men never a given?

My swirling thoughts are interrupted by a sudden trill from my phone. I grope for it blindly, my vision blurred by my tears, and answer before registering the name on the screen.

"I'm right outside your house," the woman says, her voice as sharp as a knife's edge. "And I'm not leaving until you come out and see me."

Fear claws at my throat like skeletal fingers. "I'm not at home right now," I sputter.

"Then come back now." She hangs up.

Just like that, all thoughts of Ben evaporate from my mind.

# Chapter 15

# MEREDITH

Having Liv catch me with Ben is like having a bucket of ice water dumped onto my head. The reality of what I did shrieks into excruciating clarity all at once. Stunning, unforgiving clarity. The question that I wrapped myself around, twisting myself into an intricate knot so I didn't have to face it, is suddenly answered.

What am I doing?

I'm fucking up.

What am I fucking up?

Everything. But more specifically, everything that has to do with Aspen.

Why?

The answer is cruel in its simplicity. Because I got jealous.

I could tell myself over and over that it's because Aspen went from being my best friend to ditching me, but I can't ignore the truth any longer. It's because she was behind me for the longest time. My little follower. Then she caught up to me somehow, then she surpassed me. And that, I could not accept. Especially not when she flaunted all of the perks that came with being in her position: the famous new friends. The exclusive parties. The glitz and glamor of it all.

Yes, maybe Aspen could've been kinder. Maybe she could've been a little bit more inclusive, but I knew it wasn't all on her. She was trying her best; I see that now. But for the past few months, I've let my insecurities blind me. Because I was jealous. Simple as that. What an ugly sight I am. I've always prided myself as a great friend—someone who reached down into the dust and found Aspen and dragged her up into the light. But now I'm seeing myself in the light, and I hate it. I see everything I've done in the past few months.

I stole my goddaughter's iPad. I wrecked Aspen's calendar. I stole her meetings. I turned people against her. I kissed her husband. And, even before all that stuff with the iPad, I had created troll accounts to incite hateful responses to her posts. What kind of friend would do that? My envy has turned me monstrous. And now, guilt flattens it, pounding at the jealousy and anger until it crumbles into ash; then the guilt overwhelms everything else, choking all of my senses with it. Tears stream down my eyes as I drive.

When my phone rings, it startles me so badly that I actually yelp and swerve to the side of the road. I hit the brakes and rummage through my bag for it. An unknown number. I'm about to hit Reject when something overcomes me, and I pick it up.

"Mer? Please don't hang up."

My breath catches in my throat at the painfully familiar voice. "Aspen?" I gasp. A sob shudders out of me at the weight of her name on my lips. I hadn't realized just how much I'd missed her. How much it had cost me to block my best friend from my life. And all that over what? TikTok followers? God, how I've missed her. "A-Aspen." I force myself to take in another deep breath so she won't know I'm crying.

"Are you okay? Are you crying?" The maternal concern in her voice brings about a fresh wave of tears that I have to fight back.

"I'm okay," I say, then laugh a little because it's obvious that I'm not okay, not even close. "I miss you," I blurt out.

"Oh, Mer," she sighs. "I miss you too. I've been calling and texting, but—"

"I blocked your number."

She laughs. "I know. Hence me using a different number."

There's a short, awfully pregnant silence. A silence filled with a million unspoken thoughts.

"Can we—" Aspen clears her throat. "Can we meet up and talk?"

"Yes!" I say, and I don't even care about how eager I sound. "Tonight? Maybe you could come over to my place, and we'll talk. I'll get dinner, and—and prosecco?" What I wouldn't give to go back to the time when Aspen would spend the entire weekend at my place, and we'd get drunk on prosecco and shriek-giggle over the stupidest shit.

There is a pause, then she says, her voice thick with emotion, "I would really like that. Um, do you think I can stay the night? I could really use a break from the kids and Ben. It'll be like old times."

This time, the tears that come are tears of joy. This is precisely why we're best friends. Because our minds operate on the exact same wavelength. Just look at how she's echoed my very thoughts. "Yes!" I cry. "Of course. I'll have Luca stay at Clara's for the night. And don't worry about bringing food or anything, I'll get everything. Just bring yourself."

Aspen laughs. "Okay. And maybe don't tell anyone about this? I've been going through so much stuff with Ben and you're the only one I trust."

My cheeks warm with pleasure. Despite everything that's happened, I'm still Aspen's rock. The only person she can trust. "Yes, of course."

"Hey, Mer?"

"Yeah?"

"Thank you. I really needed this."

"Me too." I'm grinning so hard when I hang up. Pure joy spreads from my chest to every part of me. Tonight, Aspen is coming over, and I'll tell her the truth about everything, and then we'll make up and everything will go back to the way it was. To the way it should have been. Tonight, everything will be put right.

# Chapter 16

# ASPEN

Clara's silhouette is so similar to Meredith's that it gives me a shock as I near the house. The way she stands, the way she rests her weight on her left foot—it's so eerily Meredith-like. My mouth goes dry at the sight of her, and I have to remind myself to inhale and exhale as I turn into the driveway. She turns to face my car, raising a hand to shield her face from my headlights. There's a bundle in her other arm. Luca, I realize with an ugly feeling in my stomach.

It's a struggle to keep the smile on my face as I climb out of the car. "Hey, Clara," I say, not pausing before I walk to the back door and slide inside to get Sabine out of her car seat. My thoughts are racing, my heart drumming a rapid rhythm: stay-calm, stay-calm, stay-calm. I take my time unclasping Sabine's belts, gathering my thoughts and composing myself. When I straighten up out of the car, with Sabine in my arms, I turn to find Clara right in my face. I almost scream.

Clara's stare pins me in place. She's always had an unnerving way of studying people, like she can see through their skin and bone and read the thoughts zipping through their minds. I hold

Sabine in front of me like a shield, and she smiles and babbles when she catches sight of Luca.

"Do you want to come i—"

"I haven't heard from my sister in over a month," Clara says, and though her voice is cold, I see fear lurking underneath her hard features. "And that's not at all like her."

"I'm sorry, Clara," I say softly.

"You're her best friend!" she cries, gesturing at me. "Why're you so—how can you be so—okay?"

"We haven't—" Emotion catches up with me and I have to pause to gather myself. "You know that we had a falling-out and I haven't talked to her for months. And you said she told you she's going into a rehab or something, right? A tech-free retreat?"

Clara shakes her head and snorts. "Right, and left her only child with me and hasn't bothered to check in on him for over a month." She gives an incredulous laugh. "How crazy is that? No, that's not at all like her."

I sigh. "I'm sorry, Clara. I don't know what to tell you. I wish I could help, but . . ."

"You know something," Clara hisses, her eyes filling with tears. "You two were joined at the hip for years. There isn't a single thing about Mer that you didn't know. I don't buy for a second that she never mentioned anything to you."

"I told you," I say, in the voice I use when Elea is being particularly difficult, "Mer and I haven't talked for months. She's moved on to other friends. Maybe you can talk to them instead."

Clara takes a step toward me, and there's something in her body language that is so purposeful, so focused, like a hunter, that I take an involuntary step backward. Her gaze burns into mine. "I've known you for years, Aspen. I can tell when you're lying. And you know where my sister is."

The thing is, Clara's right. I do know where Mer is.

She is in the lake, deep underwater, her body slowly decomposing, becoming bloated before falling apart gently. Exactly where I left her a month ago.

# Chapter 17

# MEREDITH

*One Month Ago*

By the time Aspen is due to arrive at my place, I'm out of breath, my cheeks red with excitement. I can't think of the last time I felt so much anticipation over meeting anyone, not even a hot date or a meeting with a potential sponsor. No, this trumps them all. I'm waiting for my best friend! The apartment has been tidied up, albeit in a rush, but it's fine, as I'm not expecting Aspen to open up drawers and closets. I dropped an overnight bag for Luca at Clara's and told her I have a big date tonight. I couldn't bear to tell Clara that the "big date" is in fact a reconciliatory meeting with Aspen because, Clara being Clara, she'd just raise one eyebrow and say something along the lines of, "Finally you two are going to get over your little high school spat." On the way home, I stopped by Trader Joe's and grabbed all of Aspen's favorite snacks, a rotisserie chicken, a salad, plus a bottle of prosecco and a bottle of rose. We'll be set for a proper girls' night in. Right after she forgives me for everything, of course.

I jump when the bell rings. I dart from the living room to the front door, where I fling it open. "Aspen!" I shout, and fling myself at her. She's wearing her hair differently (a short maroon bob), but despite that, looks the same as ever, still the same old Aspen, and smells of her favorite shampoo and perfume. And tears fill my eyes because oh my gosh, why did we ever have a falling-out? She seems taken aback by my greeting at first, but then her arms encircle me, and she hugs me back just as tightly. When we let go, we're both laughing and crying. "Come in," I say through my happy tears.

Once she's inside, Aspen lifts a bottle of champagne. "I know you said not to bring anything, but I feel like we're about to have a celebration."

I laugh and take the bottle from her. "Come on in. Have a seat while I open this. You look amazing, I love what you've done with your hair!" My heart is hammering away so hard against my ribcage. Aspen is here. After so long away from each other's lives, she's finally here again, in my apartment. My thoughts clash with one another as I go into the kitchen to open the champagne.

I'm so tempted to not tell her anything. Not about the iPad, the meetings I stole, the trolls I incited, and definitely not about kissing Ben. How easy it would be to simply sweep all of that stuff under the rug. Pretend I know nothing about them. I can see it unfolding in my mind's eye. Me pretending to be horrified when she tells me about the meetings she's missed and the industry people who have inexplicably snubbed her. Me nodding with empathy when she tells me about her marriage problems. Tempting. So tempting.

But then I think of that look on Liv's face. The sheer contempt. Like she knows for a fact that I am beneath her. And can I blame her? I am beneath her. I've betrayed my best friend in countless unforgivable ways. And maybe the first step in absolving myself is to finally tell Aspen the truth. I'm going to do it. Though maybe it can wait until after we've had a couple rounds of drinks. I'm definitely in need of liquid courage.

"I love what you've done with the place," Aspen says as I walk into the living room carrying two flutes of champagne.

I snort. "I literally have not done anything to it that you haven't already seen."

She laughs. "Okay, I guess I was just making nervous conversation."

I lift my glass. "To friendship."

She grins. "To friendship." We both drink.

Before Aspen can say anything, I blurt out, "I'm sorry."

She lowers her glass, staring at me hesitantly. "I lost my shit at you and it wasn't even your fault. None of it was your fault."

Her face softens. "Oh, Mer, it's fine—"

"No, it's not fine. I was a huge bitch and you deserved better. So I'm sorry."

Aspen puts her hand on mine and squeezes it. "Thank you."

I sigh with relief. There. I've apologized, and we can both move on.

"So—" we both say at the same time, then laugh. "You first," I say.

"Okay." Aspen tucks her shiny hair behind one ear. "What's been going on with you? Mer, you've grown so huge! Online, I mean. Not like, in person. In person you're as skinny as ever," she says with a wink.

"Um, yeah, I guess I have been growing online."

"Dude, fuck 'growing,' you blew the hell up!" Aspen cries. "I mean, you have what, three million followers on TikTok now? That is amazing growth. Seriously, I'm so proud of you!" She puts an arm around my shoulders and squeezes. "I always knew you were going to be a huge star."

There is no condescension in her voice. Not a single patronizing note. I look at Aspen and wonder how the hell I could've read her so wrong all those months ago? All I see now is sincere happiness shining through her eyes as she goes on and on about how well deserved my success is. And the purity of her joy is like a knife stabbing right into my chest. Because of course, I don't deserve any of it. The only reason I became so successful in the past couple of months is because of Elea's iPad. I should tell Aspen the truth. But the thought of it crushes me, pressing down on all sides until I'm compressed into one single hard lump.

"Oh, you know," I say, waving vaguely. "I got lucky. Got a couple of good collabs and . . . yeah."

"About freaking time," Aspen says. "You deserve it."

I drain my glass and refill it, then, when the guilt overwhelms me, I excuse myself to run to the kitchen to fetch us more snacks. When I come back, Aspen is pouring champagne into her own glass.

"So what about you? What have you been up to? How are the girls?"

Aspen's smile wanes. I lift the bottle to refill her glass and realize with a start that it's finished.

"Wow, we went through that fast," Aspen says.

I narrow my eyes at her. "I know it's early, but do you wanna—"

"Prosecco?" she says.

We shriek with laughter. Oh my god, it feels so good to have my best friend back. I jump up and go to the kitchen, and Aspen trails behind me, filling me in on the details of her life.

"Noemie's the same old sweetheart," she says, and I smile

at the thought of my quiet, sweet goddaughter. "Yesterday, she saw that I was having a really tough day, and she wrote me this card." She takes out her phone and shows me a picture of a card written in childish cursive. It says, "*Mommy plees don't be sad you are the best mommy in the werld.*"

"Aww!" I say. "Noemieee, god, what a sweetie." I take out the prosecco from the fridge and pour some into two clean glasses. We make our way back to the living room. "What about my little firecracker Elea?"

Aspen rolls her eyes and takes a large gulp of prosecco. "You know what she's like. Six going on sixteen. Oh my god, I can't even imagine what she'll be like as a rebellious teen." She makes a face.

I laugh. "Come on, of the two of them, Elea's the one who takes after you, you know."

She gives a rueful smile. "I know. And Sabbie misses Luca."

"Aww, Luca misses Sabbie too."

Aspen releases a defeated sigh. "And Ben . . ."

Despite the pleasant fuzz from all the alcohol, the mention of Ben makes my stomach clench. Did he mention me to Aspen? The thought sends a cold trail of fear crawling up my neck. No, don't be so freaking stupid, of course he didn't. If he did, she wouldn't be here, sharing a bottle of prosecco with me. I force myself to release my breath.

"Ben's been so distant," Aspen says. "And my accounts aren't growing fast enough. I've been missing meetings and stuff . . . it's all been pretty shit, actually. Oh, and remember those troll comments I started getting a few months back? They've grown even worse now."

My guts are writhing and twisting. I want to throw up.

Somehow, I manage to bite my tongue and keep myself from saying anything.

Aspen laughs, and it's a horrible, wobbly sound. "I don't understand what's been going on. Why I've been so scattered, how I managed to miss all those meetings—it's been horrible." Her gaze locks on mine and my heart stops because I can tell, in this awful moment, that she's going to tell me she knows what I've done.

Instead, Aspen says, "Honestly, Mer? I've been a mess without you," and of all the things she could've said, this is the one that breaks me. Because the only reason why she's been a mess is me.

*Tell her!* Everything inside me screams. And still, I don't. I say, "Me too." And I smile at her.

"I swear," Aspen continues, "I'm on the brink of losing everything. Ben can barely stand to look at me, and when he does, all I see is revulsion." Her eyes shine with tears. "That's crazy, right? But I can't divorce him. The girls would be devastated. And how would it look to my followers? If they leave me, I'll be nothing."

"You'll never be nothing," I cry. "You're All Day Aspen! You'll be fine."

Aspen smiles sadly at me. "Thank you for saying that. Even though you're lying through your teeth."

"No, seriously." I reach out to pat her shoulder, but somehow, all I touch is air, and before I know it, I've lost my balance. I land on my knees on the carpet. "Wow," I laugh. "How much have I drunk?"

Aspen just sits there, staring at me. "Not much. That would be the mix of drugs I slipped into the champagne."

"Whaaaa?" My voice comes out from far, far away.

"Mer," Aspen sighs. "I gave you every chance to tell me the truth."

I try to get up, but the world sways, and one moment, everything is upright. The next moment, I seem to be seeing everything sideways. I blink, and blink again, and try to form words, but they come in a jumble that makes no sense. Something pushes me from my side to my back so I'm now staring up at the ceiling. A face swims into view. I'm confused when I see it. Aspen? But we're not talking to each other. I smile at her. I'm glad she's here even though we've been fighting for so long.

"That day you stole into my house, the security system alerted me that there was movement in our property. I logged on, and lo and behold, what do I see on my screen but my own best friend snooping around in the backyard like a fucking cat." Aspen snorts. "I had no idea what the hell you were doing. Actually, I was so dumb, for a moment, I thought you'd come to apologize. I thought you were going to leave a bouquet of roses or a letter or something for me. Imagine how shocked I was when you stole Elea's iPad. What the fuck, Mer? You know how messed up that is? I had to punish Elea for losing her iPad because I didn't want Ben to know what you did. Look what you made me do. Punish my own kid for something she didn't do. Although maybe that'll teach her not to leave her shit out in the backyard."

Aspen crouches down and picks up the wineglass from next to me. Dimly, I want to tell her not to bother cleaning up, that she's a guest here. A small voice is screaming at me to focus. Something bad is happening, but I don't understand what. Maybe the bad thing is the prosecco spilling on the carpet. I need to get baking soda and vinegar on that before the stain sets in.

"For the next few weeks, I watched my accounts like a hawk," Aspen continues. "Did you never stop to wonder why I didn't change our passwords when Elea's iPad went missing? Did you really think I was that dumb?"

*Of course not,* I want to say. Naive, maybe, but not dumb. My eyes close. Sharp pain whacks into my cheeks, and my eyes fly open.

"Wake up, Mer," Aspen snaps. "You can't go to sleep yet. Not before I explain to you exactly why I'm doing this."

I'm pretty sure my eyes are blinking at different rates. I think I manage to nod.

"I watched as my appointments were switched around. I turned up at the correct time and watched from afar as you swooped in and took all those meetings for yourself. I followed your accounts and saw all the videos you copied."

I open my mouth to explain that yes, I might have copied a few of her videos, but imitation is the best form of flattery.

She's shaking her head and laughing a little. "I didn't even care that I was missing these meetings, some of which took months to set up. All I could think about was what you were doing. And I made sure to turn up at the wrong time, too, in case you were still watching me. And you know what? I don't even really care about the whole Ben thing. Oh yeah, I know you and Ben were sneaking around behind my back. Because I've been following you, Mer, ever since you took Elea's iPad. Seeing what you've been up to. My husband, as it turns out. But who cares? Ben's a fucking loser. If you wanted him, I would've given him to you. You know why, Mer? Because you're my best friend." Her voice shakes then, turning rough, and tears shine in her eyes, which makes me sad. I want to tell her I'm sorry, that I don't want Ben, I just want her, because she's my best friend too.

"But the thing is, Mer, you fucked with my business. My brand is the only thing keeping me and my kids going. What would happen to Noemie's healthcare if I were to lose my brand? Did you ever stop to think of that, Mer?"

Shame burns every part of me. She's right. I didn't. I never once stopped to think about how my actions would hurt my beloved goddaughters.

"You, of all people, know exactly what it took for us to get this far. I waited to see how far you'd go. But I also waited long enough to come up with a plan." She leans down so her face is mere inches away from mine, and now I can feel the cold rage radiating from her. Now I finally feel scared. I try to push her off, but my hands aren't listening to me. Nothing seems to be working. "You're supposed to be my ride or die, Mer," Aspen whispers. "If you're not going to be my ride, then you might as well die."

*I am your ride or die*, I want to say, but Aspen leans to one side and picks up something. A cushion with a gray-and-yellow chevron print. *Wait* I say, but she lowers it onto my face, and I find that I can't say anything much at all.

# Chapter 18

# ASPEN

I have always wanted a sister. A sister would be into the same things I am. Beauty and fashion and the giddy excitement that comes with meeting a hot guy. A sister would commiserate with me about the hardships of breastfeeding or losing the baby weight. A sister would give a shit. Unfortunately, I only have a brother who lives several states away and never sends so much as a card on my birthday. When I met Meredith, I thought to myself, *it's okay that I didn't grow up with a sister, because here is someone better than a sister.* She is a soul twin: someone whose personality is on the exact same wavelength as mine. Someone who fits me like we're two puzzle pieces, curving in and out to accommodate each other precisely. But we all know how that turned out. Life can't help but be disappointing.

Maybe Meredith found it easy to betray me because she had a sister. A sister who she was always taking for granted. A sister who is now on my front porch, nipping at my ankles like a bad-tempered terrier. As I stand here, listening to Clara rant about how I must know where Meredith is, a sense of exhaustion and defeat surges through me, and I just want to crumple up into a ball then and there, and wail at everyone to leave me the hell alone. I am so tired. I've just seen Ben kissing Liv at his open house, and the last thing I need is Clara making a scene.

I let the tears come, and Clara's rant falters. "I'm sorry," I sniffle. "I miss her so much, too, you must know that, right? She's my best friend, and I—look at me, my life's a mess without her. I've been texting her and calling her and she hasn't replied to me. I think she's blocked my number. So I don't know what to tell you, Clara, okay? I'm sorry." I shift my hold on Sabine to a position I know she finds uncomfortable, and just as I hoped, Sabine starts fussing. "Look, I have to go."

Clara looks torn between sympathy and mistrust. "I'm going to report her missing."

Dread uncoils deep inside me, but I've prepared myself for this eventuality. There was no way that Clara wasn't going to report Meredith missing. I always knew that, at some point, Clara would report it. All I can do is wait and trust that I've cleaned up my tracks as well as anyone could. I meet her eyes and nod. "I think that's probably for the best at this point."

This gives Clara pause. She's been expecting me to fight it. "You really haven't spoken to her at all?" Her voice wobbles.

I shake my head, thanking the universe for the millionth time for the fact that Meredith hadn't told Clara that I was going to be at her place that day. "I'm worried too. I think you're right about reporting her missing."

Clara nods. As she leaves, I call out, "Keep me updated?"

She waves and leaves. I take Sabine inside the house and the moment the door closes behind me, I utter a huge sigh of relief. I've thrown Clara off my scent by telling her to call the cops. Hopefully, this means she'll set her suspicions elsewhere.

As I change Sabine's diaper, I mentally go over all of the details that I've been so careful to take care of.

Yes, I killed my best friend. But I think it would be apt to say that she killed me first. Killed my trust, completely spat in the face of our friendship. She destroyed my heart, my soul twin who betrayed me. That day, when I finally did it, I gave her so many chances to come clean. If she had, I wouldn't have gone through with it. I would at least know that she felt remorse for trying to fuck me over.

We met as fledgling influencers. She watched me struggle to grow my following. She was there the times I had sobbed and said I would never make it—that there was no place in the industry for me. She was the one who nudged me to keep going—the one who propped me up. And now, to turn around and try to destroy that?

When I realized what Mer was doing with Elea's iPad, I went from anger, to disbelief, to a whole different realm entirely. It was like I walked into a stark, white room filled with nothing but a tiny, high-pitched sound. A room of cold, quiet, murderous rage. It was this rage that had driven me to begin my planning. To prepare Mer's grave; to line up everything that would lead to her disappearance. When I poured various powdered drugs into the champagne bottle, I was calm—so calm. And when the drugs entered her system and brought her down, I gazed down at my best friend, lying there on the floor, her eyes blinking at different rates and one hand twitching, and I knew that there was no going back. Then I'd picked up one of her cushions and brought it down onto her face, and that was when the grief struck. I'd planned every step so well, thought long and hard about how I was going to do it, but when the time came to actually do the deed, I found it a million times harder than expected. Still, I went through with it, because I'm not a quitter.

I cleaned up well. It was simple, actually. As a momfluencer, I'm very good at deep cleaning. There's an art to it. I knew all the right kinds of chemicals to use that wouldn't leave a harsh ascetic smell in the air. I knew to go down on my hands and knees and scour every corner, even under the cabinets. Wipe down everything I might've touched but not every surface; there still needs to be Mer's prints here and there. Then I washed up all the glasses that we'd used, dried them, and put them back in the cupboards before taking the empty bottles of alcohol out.

The trickiest part was getting Mer's body into her car. I took care to wrap her up in a blanket before lifting her up. It wasn't easy. Like every momfluencer worth her salt, Mer was skinny, but so was I, and I staggered about as I tried to heave her up over my shoulder. I nearly fell a couple of times, but finally managed to find my balance, swearing under my breath the whole time. By then, it was already dark. Outside, I kept to the shadows, my ears pricked for any neighbors who might be watching. But if they were, they'd see a redhead with glasses on. When I got to the car, I dumped Mer inside the back seat. I was panting hard by then. I retrieved my duffel bag from inside Mer's apartment. It contained a spade, water bottles, and a change of clothes. I took out Mer's phone and sent a message to Clara.

I need a fucking break. I'm going to check myself into a retreat for a few weeks. I know you won't truly understand, but I need to do this to replenish my soul. Love you, sis, and `tell Luca Mommy loves him and will be back with so many presents and all the kisses!`

Then I turned it off before Clara could send a reply, took out the SIM card, and snapped it in half. I had turned my own phone off to avoid any GPS tracking earlier on, before coming to Mer's. Then I was off to the desert. The desert I'd told Mer, so many years ago, was surely filled with dead bodies. I still remember, even now, the haunted look on Mer's face when I'd let my mask slip. When I showed her a glimpse of the darkness lurking underneath. She really should've known better than to cross me.

I can't describe, even now, the feeling of driving deep into the emptiness of the desert with the dead body of my best friend in the back seat of the car. Like I said, thinking about it is one thing. Actually doing it, and knowing that it is done, and that there is no going back, is a whole other thing. A couple of times, the oppressive emptiness almost got to me, and I considered driving away and never coming back myself. I wailed as I drove, keening my sorrow into the starry sky. My best friend was dead, and I had to bury her. I pounded at the steering wheel and sobbed and sobbed. My tears burned endless trails down my cheeks.

I'd prepared so hard for this. I'd driven out here a couple of times in the past few weeks to dig. I had to go deep. I wouldn't make the rookie mistake of digging too shallow a grave. But when I veered off the freeway towards the hole I'd dug, I saw tire tracks in the dirt. My chest squeezed, my instincts rearing up, and I turned around and drove away. My insides churned. The hole I'd dug, the grave I'd so carefully prepared for Mer, had been found. Maybe I could dig another hole at a different spot? The desert was vast. I dismissed the idea quickly. When I'd dug the original hole, I'd been taken aback by how difficult a task it was. How back-breaking. It had taken me hours to go about four feet down. I'd had to come back a second time to go deeper. I didn't have the luxury of time now, not with Mer's body in the back seat. I would only manage a shallow grave.

*Think, Aspen. Do not panic.*

I took a map out of my duffel bag. It wasn't like I could do a Google search. Less than twenty miles away from where I was, there was a lake. I could get rid of both the body and the car there. Right. I could do that. I got back on the road and navigated my way to the lake. By the time I got there, it was eight-thirty p.m. It was pitch-dark out here. I checked to make sure no one was about, then I dragged Mer's body out of the back seat and shoved it into the driver's seat. The sight of her face brought a new wave of tears, hot and furious. I tried my best to stifle my sobs as I aimed the steering wheel at the large body of water and set the car to D. I had no idea what to expect; it wasn't like I'd done this before, but once I let go of the brake pedal with the shovel, the car rolled forward so fast that the shovel was almost wrenched out of my hands. I only had enough time to jerk it out of the window.

"Wait—" I said, knowing that it was futile. *I hadn't even said goodbye*, I thought stupidly, as the car trundled down the bank and into the water. There was hardly a splash. It kept going and going at a steady speed. What if it stopped now, halfway into the water? But before the thought could take root, the car was completely submerged. Bubbles popped on the surface. I stood there for some time—I wasn't entirely sure how long—then I shook myself. I had a long trek home. I hadn't planned on leaving Mer's car out here. I was going to bury her out here, drive back to the city, and leave her car with the keys inside. In a city like LA, her car would be snatched off the streets, repainted, and sold within twenty-four hours. But now, I had no such luxury. It wasn't like I could call an Uber to pick me up all the way out here. No, I had to walk back to the city. I checked my watch. It was only nine p.m. I could do this.

I went at what I thought was a sensible pace—brisk but steady. Still, by the time I made it to the nearest city, every joint in my body was screaming; it felt like my bones were scraping against each other. I stopped at a gas station to use the bathroom. I washed my face and refilled my water bottle, then styled my hair the way Meredith used to do hers before pulling a cap over it. Outside, I found a trash can and threw the spade in there, after wiping it down. I took a burner cell from my bag and ordered a cab to take me to the next city. I didn't speak to the driver and kept my head low the entire ride. I tipped him generously, but not so much that he'd remember me. Then I ordered another cab to take me yet closer home. Two more cabs, and I was finally back at Mer's place. I stumbled back to my car and drove home, numb with exhaustion. I crept into the nursery and curled up next to Sabine's crib.

In the morning, her soft waking-up snuffles woke me, and I hurried into the bathroom, where I stripped off my clothes and took a scalding-hot shower. When Ben woke up, he found me in the kitchen, prodding at a fluffy cheese-and-ham omelet. He suspected nothing.

I spent the rest of the day going through every little detail, searching for possibilities that might expose me. What if one of her neighbors had seen me arriving at her house or leaving it? No, I tell myself. I'd worn a wig and put on tinted glasses and applied my makeup a different way. Plus, it was so dark by then. But what if someone saw me in the desert? Unlikely, but still. So many what-ifs. I could only assure myself that I had done everything possible to clean up my tracks. After dropping the twins off at school, I came home, opened up my social media accounts, and almost had a heart attack. There was a new post from Mer. A video of her morning routine, posted at seven a.m. this morning. I choked so hard on my coffee that I had to thump myself on the chest. It took a while for me to realize what had happened: like every influencer worth her salt, Mer had scheduled posts in advance. Of course. So fucking obvious. I forced myself to calm down. And once I did, I realized this would work in my favor. I remembered, then, how Mer had taught me to schedule posts at least one month in advance. This meant that it would be at least a month before her viewers even realized she was gone.

Except now my month's grace is up. And Clara, who's been going crazy this whole time because Mer's left Luca with her without prior warning, is going to report Mer missing. My world is about to get blown up.

# Chapter 19

# ASPEN

I can barely look Liv in the eye when she arrives at the house the next morning. What with Clara's confrontation and knowing she's reporting Meredith missing, I haven't had much of a chance to think about anything, but now that Liv is here, right in the flesh, everything comes rushing back. Ben leaning into her at his open house. Her smiling up at him. My upper lip twitches, and I have to consciously stop myself from snarling.

"I brought croffles!" she chirps, waving a bag in one hand, carrying Rain in the other. "Cookie-butter croffles."

Well, goddamn it. I want cookie-butter croffles. But not from the woman I saw making out with my husband the day before. What is it about Ben that appeals to these women? There's Meredith, then Liv, amongst others. This morning, when I woke up, I turned to my side and just watched Ben as he slept. His mouth was drooping open, and he was breathing noisily, though I don't know if it counted as snoring. His jaw used to be nicely angled, but over the last couple of years or so, it's softened. He doesn't have a double chin yet, but there's definitely the threat of one. My point is, he is hardly the stud you would think he is, to have so many beautiful women throwing themselves at him.

Liv spots the frown on my face and her smile falls. "Uh oh," she says in a cutesy tone that makes me want to smack her. "Everything okay?"

Well, no time like the present. "Why don't you put Rain down in the playpen with Sabine, then we can heat up those croffles and talk about why you were going at it with my husband yesterday afternoon."

Liv's mouth drops open, but I don't even get to enjoy the sight of her shocked expression before it morphs into a different one. Acceptance, then smugness. It's like she's taking off a mask right before my eyes. Instinctively, my defenses clap into place.

"Ah," she says, walking past me to put Rain down in the playpen. Sabine coos when she sees Rain, and the two babies crawl towards each other, both of them drooling and grinning. "So you saw us."

"Yeah, I fucking saw you. What the hell were you—why?" I cry. God, I hadn't meant to lose my cool like this, but Liv's composure is really freaking me out.

Liv straightens up, and the anger on her face is so raw, I actually take a step back. "Because you don't deserve Ben. You don't deserve any of this." She gestures around her, at my Insta-approved home. "You know, some time ago, I saw your old friend Meredith and Ben together, and I was so shocked then. I totally judged Meredith. I thought she was a conniving bitch for doing that to you. I remember I couldn't tell you fast enough. But then over time, I slowly realized that, actually, Ben was right to cheat on you."

"Excuse me?" I don't even know what else to say. I stand there, sputtering stupidly.

"He's so good to you, so supportive. But you don't even see

that, do you? I do, because my own husband left me. But Ben stayed. And you don't even give a shit about him. Meredith had a thing for Ben because she was doing it to spite you. But for me, it's because you just plain old do not deserve him."

"How dare you stand there and—"

"Careful, Aspen," Liv says, and though her voice is still annoyingly cutesy, there is now a note of danger in it that makes me freeze. I feel like a skier who's just realized that they took the wrong turn and suddenly finds themselves on the precipice of a cliff, nothing underneath but a great, dark mouth. "You're really not in a position to be making demands or accusations."

"I don't understand what—"

"Because, Aspen, the past few months, since I started working for you, I got to know the real Aspen. The Aspen behind All Day Aspen. And boy, the real Aspen is a real disappointment." Liv glares at me. "You pretended to be this friendly, sweet person online. I've been following you, wanting to learn from you."

"Following me?" It hits me then: the figure I saw peeping into my car at the parking lot a while ago after leaving the meeting with Bodacious Babies. "You . . . were spying on me?"

Instead of answering me, Liv says, "You know how long I had to work for you before you even deigned to invite me into your home?"

"Wh—"

"Six months, Aspen. And you didn't even extend that courtesy to me, really; I had to make that chance happen for myself."

"What do you mean?"

"Your tires."

It takes a moment for it to sink in, and when it does, horror stabs at my gut. "That night, at the party, when I ran into you—"

Liv gives a bitter laugh. "Obviously you didn't 'run into' me. That was a party for mega-influencers. I was hardly going to be invited. I knew you'd be there, so I went, and I found your car and . . ." She makes a vicious slashing motion.

"You slashed my tires?" I squeak.

"Don't be so dramatic," Liv says. "I had to do something to get into your good books. And I even took you out for burgers afterwards. I felt bad about doing that, you know. And that was before I found out what a fake you are."

My head is swimming. All this time, I'd thought the slashed tires were just a prank.

"I was your biggest fan," Liv says. "I've been following you since your YouTube days. Remember those?"

Despite everything, the memory of my YouTube videos all those years ago, so amateurish, grainy and low quality, makes me wince.

"You shouldn't be ashamed of it, Aspen," Liv says. "Sure, they're not as polished as your videos now, but they were at least real. I was such a big fan; I was so happy for you when you got married and pregnant and became this viral sensation. You made motherhood look so easy!" Liv gestures around her again. "Look at your beautiful home. You make this entire lifestyle look achievable. You made me think that I could find the perfect man and have the perfect baby and live in the perfect home."

Dread uncurls in my belly, icy cold. I have no idea where Liv is going with all this, but this is my worst nightmare. Well, aside from someone finding out about Meredith, that is.

"I met a guy, got married." She shrugs. "You know how that went. When our troubles began, I blamed myself. I watched your videos over and over again. I thought to myself: *I just need to be more like Aspen. I need to get my ass in gear, stop whining about everything and clean the house! Bake bread! Exercise! Find cute outfits for Rain! And I'll be okay, my marriage will be okay, and everything will be great.*" Liv's face twists into a tortured grimace. "But it wasn't great. He left me. Do you know what it was like for me, thinking that all I had to do was try harder?"

How can I possibly answer that?

Liv takes a deep breath. "It wasn't great. Not great at all. I felt like a failure. No matter how hard I tried, I couldn't do anything the way you did. I couldn't make my morning routines anything like yours. I couldn't make bedtime routines as peaceful as yours. I felt like I was failing everyone. Adam. Rain. Myself. At some point, I thought: *I should just die. Then everyone would be better off.*"

"Oh, Liv," I gasp, horrified.

"Imagine how happy I was when you hired me as your PA. I thought: *ah, finally I'll learn from the guru herself. I'll learn how to be a good wife, a good mother.*" She levels her gaze at me. "Then I find out that it's all fake."

My breath comes out in a choked hiss. "No, wait a min—"

"All of it," Liv says. "Fake." She gestures at the kitchen. "Fake." She turns and waves at the living room, where Rain and Sabine are playing in the playpen. "Fake." She turns back and points at me. "Fake."

All of my senses turn to stone. I can only stand there, staring at her. A million answers whiz through my head, but none of them makes its way out of my mouth. I'm frozen, completely helpless. Because this whole time, my worst fear was for someone to discover that I am, in fact, not in the least bit #authentic.

That everything I post has been carefully produced and edited and curated to perfection. Because isn't that what social media demands?

This, then, is the answer I fall back on. "I'm not fake, Liv," I say, and I must be given some credit, because my voice somehow comes out steady. "I am a content creator. I'm running a business. I don't owe anyone the ugly truth. And no one wants that, anyway."

"Yes, but you're *lying*!" Liv shouts, and it is terrifying in its force. Spittle flies from her mouth and her entire face is red, and she's glaring at me like she's barely holding herself back from lunging at my throat. "You're not being upfront about anything. There are influencers out there who are obviously peddling highly curated content, and that's fine. We know what we're getting are just the highlights. But you pretend like this is your real life, and that's the problem, Aspen. That's why I think you're full of shit. You're actively harming people."

"But—no, I—"

"You are," Liv says, pointing a finger right at my chest. "You make it seem like this life is attainable, if you just try a little bit harder. Starve yourself a little bit more. Spend a little bit longer in the kitchen. Mulch your garden just that tiny bit more. Spoil your husband just a touch more. You make it seem so easy. Don't you? And when I found out that your life is really a pile of shit, you know how that made me feel?" She doesn't wait for me to answer. "Like the world's biggest fucking idiot, Aspen."

There is nothing I can say that will salvage the situation. I don't know if I even want to salvage the situation. It feels like it's as far beyond salvageable as any situation can get. Right. I need to recalibrate my goal. Move away from trying to convince Liv that she's wrong, and lean into finding out what she wants and how to get rid of her. Because, clearly, Liv is fucking insane.

"I'm sorry you feel that way, Liv," I say quietly.

Liv shakes her head. "Oh my god. Spare me the Gaslighting 101, okay? None of that 'I'm sorry you feel that way' crap. No, you need to be sorry that *you* made me feel that way. Understand?"

Hidden behind the island counter, my hands ball into fists. It's been a long time since anyone's talked to me this way. Well, anyone who isn't Ben. But this isn't the time for me to lose my temper. I need to play this smart. I force myself to nod. "You're right. I'm sorry I made you feel that way. What can I do to make it..." I hesitate. What I really want to say is: *What can I do to make you go away?* But I have a feeling that's not going to go over well. So instead I say, "... okay?"

Liv snorts. "How about giving me the last seven years of my life back? Give me the last seven years where I'm not desperately chasing after this unachievable life that you've made me think is a realistic goal? How about that?"

God, it's a struggle to keep a straight face. I want to smack this brat off my beautiful chair. "Well, as much as I would love to be able to turn back time, unfortunately, I can't do that. So maybe we can come up with something else?"

Liv narrows her eyes at me. How have I missed how truly ugly she is? Beneath the impeccable makeup and the vibrant clothes, she is repulsive. "How about I tell your followers the truth about you? How you pretend to dig up potatoes from your own garden?"

I make myself shrug. "And what will that give you, exactly?"

"Satisfaction, for one," Liv says.

"Okay, and that's going to last you about two seconds. Then it'll fade away, and you'll be left exactly where you were before."

*Think fast*, I hiss silently at myself. *There is a way out. There is always a way out. You are a survivor. You do not admit defeat here, not to this little upstart.* I look at Liv. Really look at her. Seeing her in her entirety. I put myself in her sad, Payless shoes. What does she want?

Then I find it. My way out.

"I have a better idea," I say.

Liv gives me a skeptical look, but I'm not so easily deterred.

"I know what you want. And I can give it to you." I smile at her, then I offer her dreams back to her on a silver platter. "Followers."

# Chapter 20

# ASPEN

Liv gapes at me. "I—I don't understand."

I resist the urge to laugh in her face and call her a moron. "It's simple. I have six million followers. You have . . ." I wiggle my hand at her.

"One hundred and fifty thousand," Liv mumbles.

"Right." I purse my lips. "Well. So I have a lot to offer you."

"You can't give me your followers."

Oh my god, how is it that this bumbling fool thinks she can be an influencer? "No," I say patiently. "But I can help to promote you. We can do cross-promo content, where you're in my videos and I tag you . . ."

Liv's face lights up as the idea takes root in her slow-moving mind. "We can cook together!"

"Yeah, exactly," I say with an encouraging smile. "We can do everything together. We can cook, like you said; we can do videos with the kids together; that would be really cute. We can—"

"We can do TikTok dances together!" Liv cries. "Oh my god, I've always wanted to be part of a dance duo. Those videos do real numbers on TikTok."

I wince. I'm good at pretending to garden and cook, less good at dancing. But it's not like I have much of a choice here. "I'm game; we can definitely try a few dance moves, yeah."

For the next few moments, Liv is quiet, though her fingers drum the countertop as she mulls over my proposal. "And you'll do cross-promo videos with me every day?" she says after a while.

I nod. "Sure. If you want."

"For as long as I want?"

"How about until you reach half a million followers? That should give you enough momentum to strike out on your own."

"No, I want six million followers like you."

This is a reminder of how young Liv is. How inexperienced. "Liv," I say gently, "I can't give you six million followers. It doesn't work that way."

"Why?" she says petulantly. "You've got six million followers."

"Yeah, but first of all, they don't all like the same thing. Some might like me because of my cooking. Others might like my morning routine. And others might like the kids. These are individuals we're talking about. Not all of them will like our cross-promo content. Once we get you to half a million followers, you'll find that your account will grow organically. The algorithm will feed your content out to people who will like it, and you'll get followers on your own. You won't need me anymore." Not strictly true, but it's true enough.

Liv nods grudgingly "Okay. Fine. But I want an open-door policy with the cross-promo stuff."

"I'm not sure I understand what that means."

Liv sighs theatrically. "I mean, if I ever ask you to do a cross-promo video, even if I have, say, two million followers, you need to agree to it."

I narrow my eyes at her. "Within reason. Sure. Once you hit half a million followers, I would like to cut back on the cross-promo stuff, but yes, if you need it, we can do it occasionally."

"Deal." Liv holds out her hand, and I shake it. "When can we start? Now?"

Despite everything, this almost makes me smile, because Liv's eagerness reminds me of myself. You have to have passion to make it as an influencer, and she obviously has it in droves. I need to use this to my advantage somehow. Can I? Maybe, but I can't think of it while she's here, studying my every move. I shrug at Liv. "Sure, why not?"

She grins and actually claps, like a little kid. It highlights just how young she is. Well, maybe not that young; she's only a few years my junior, but she is so inexperienced. Was I like that too? When I first met Mer? Did she see what I'm seeing in Liv now? Someone to take under her wing and mold in a way that pleases her? The thought stokes my anger towards Mer all over again. She could only handle me when I was pliable dough in her hands. But once I hardened into my own form, all Meredith could think of doing with me was to smash me onto the floor—to break me down so she could rebuild me all over again.

"Okay!" Liv says, her eyes shining. "What should we do? Oh, there's this dance I've been wanting to try; let me—" She picks up her phone.

Oh Lord. The thought of doing a TikTok dance with Liv is enough to make me want to stab myself through the head. "Actually, how about a gardening video? We could harvest a few veggies together?"

Liv makes a face. "No offense, Aspen, but that sounds boring as shit."

"None taken."

"And it's not really my brand, you know?"

I don't know, actually. Come to think of it, I don't really know what Liv's brand is. I haven't taken the time to study her social media accounts. "That's a good point," I say. "Let me see your profile." I settle down on a chair and scroll through her profile. It is a mess. There isn't a single cohesive thread throughout her posts. "What is your brand?"

Liv stiffens. "Well, it's—it's like your brand. Momfluencing."

"Yeah, but what's the angle? Are you the relatable mom whose hair is always messy and who forgets everything? Are you #momgoals? Are you career mom?"

Liv groans. "I just want to be myself. Nobody is ever just one of those things."

"True, but for the purposes of social media, it would be helpful for you to have a brand that people can recognize." I study Liv for a bit, considering the options.

"What's your brand?"

"Mom goals," I say simply.

One corner of Liv's mouth twitches into a smirk. "Oh yeah. Fake and unattainable."

I shrug, refusing to let her words sting me. "We could set that up as your brand, too, if you want. I could show you how." And for all her talk about fakeness and authenticity, I can tell that Liv is tempted. As she gnaws on her bottom lip, I add, "Think of how pissed off your enemies would be when they saw you living your best life."

"I don't want to be fake," Liv says.

"Stop looking at it as being fake. It's not fake; it's part of your life. Look, you can even do it your way. You could have a series of videos where you talk to your followers about how you pull everything off. How you can have it all. People would love that."

Liv's eyes widen. "You're right. Yeah, I would be helping people that way."

"Exactly. You could share mom tips on how to make their lives easier. There are so many ways you could help fellow moms."

A frown crosses her face. "Then why haven't you been doing that?"

I school my expression into one of regret and give a long sigh. "You're right, Liv. I . . . I guess I lost my way. I got too caught up in all the bullshit, and I forgot why I started doing this in the first place. But now you've reminded me what's important to me. I want to help other moms too. I don't want to make anyone feel like they're not good enough." My stomach clenches at the crap I'm spewing, but somehow, I manage to make my hand reach out for hers. "Thank you for reminding me of what's important. Let's do this together."

Liv grins. "You're welcome," she says, with such magnanimous pomp that it's all I can do not to hit her over the head with a wine bottle.

In the end, we do an outfit change video. "1 blazer, 6 looks!" We each pair the blazer with three different outfits, and Liv loves it because she thinks it'll somehow revolutionize how moms dress. I'm not about to argue with that. I show her how to edit it in a way that makes the video snappier and catchier, then I schedule to post it tonight, at prime social media time, and tag her as a collaborator. She leaves beaming, practically skipping out of my house with Rain in her arms.

After that, I slump onto the couch and stare blankly at the

ceiling until Sabine starts fussing, then I pick her up and rock her for a while until she falls asleep. I gaze down at my baby, taking in her features: the tiny nose, the curved lashes, the soft skin. I breathe in her scent and close my eyes, losing myself in the sweetness of her. I would do anything to protect my family. And I have done the worst thing, in fact, to protect them. Because in a way—a very big, very real way—I killed Meredith for them. It wasn't just about my social media accounts. My social media presence is what keeps a roof over my babies' heads, and when Meredith fucked with that, she fucked with my children. That is the real reason why she had to die. And now there's Liv to deal with, and Clara. What am I going to do about them?

I put Sabine down in her crib and pad softly back out to the kitchen, where my phone is. I send a text to Clara.

How did it go at the police station?

Three dots appear and I watch them for what seems like ages. Then, finally, the reply.

They took it rly seriously, because she's been gone for over 72 hrs. They're going to talk to all of her contacts. Expect a call from them.

All of the feeling seems to leave my legs. Standing becomes next to impossible. I stagger toward the nearest chair and sag into it, burying my face in my hands. *Expect a call from the police.* I need to get a hold of myself. Get my shit together.

Prepare myself for the coming interview. They must not see even a single crack.

I count to ten and breathe slowly. I'll be okay. They won't suspect me. Not All Day Aspen with her pumpkin sourdough focaccia recipes and her beautiful children. All I need to do is figure out how an innocent person would react to the news that her best friend has gone missing and commit to it.

I'm running through the dialogue in my head when Ben comes home with the twins. Elea drops her school bag in the front foyer before rushing into the living room and parking herself in front of the TV. Noemie hangs up her bag neatly and comes to the kitchen to give me a kiss. I hug her tight and breathe her in.

"Hi, baby," I say. "How was your day?"

"It was okay." Noemie looks around the kitchen. "Huh."

"What's up?"

"You're not cooking or shooting a video."

"Oh. Right, no, Mommy did that earlier today." *With Liv*, I think bitterly. I give Noemie another kiss and she toddles off into the living room to join her sister. I gaze at the two of them for a second, admiring, as always, how Instagram-ready they look. They're beautiful, my twin girls, with their long brown hair that turns gold in the sunlight, and their natural grace and peaches-and-cream complexions. I've been blessed; I know it.

Ben walks into the kitchen and the lovely moment crumbles into ash. I have to actively stop myself from scowling as I turn to face my husband.

"How's it going?" he says, opening the fridge and taking out an AriZona iced tea. He takes deep, loud glugs, and somehow the sound of him gulping down cold tea is repulsive, but I can't take my eyes off his Adam's apple bobbing up and down.

"Fine." I wrench my gaze away from him and busy myself with emptying the dishwasher.

"Liv left early?"

It's disturbing how good of an actor Ben is. The question comes out so casually, without any weight in it whatsoever. If I hadn't seen them at the open house, I wouldn't even have noticed anything off about it. *I am living with a seasoned liar,* I realize. The back of my neck prickles at the thought. I can't bear to look at him, so I focus on the dishes instead as I say, "Yeah. We got done early today." Then I look up and say, "Why?"

Ben shrugs. "Just wondering."

Something comes over me then. I know I'm playing with fire, but I can't help myself. "We had a really good talk today, Liv and I."

"Oh?" His hand tightens ever so slightly around the can. Again, it's such a minuscule tell that if I hadn't been looking out for one, I would've missed it. What else have I missed over the years? Who else has my husband slept with?

"Yeah, a real heart-to-heart." Careful, Aspen. I don't want to confront Ben. Not yet. And definitely not with the girls in the next room watching their cartoons, and Sabine napping in her room. "I should go wake Sabine from her nap." I give Ben a terse smile and bustle away, leaving him clutching his stupid can of tea. My stomach is clenched so tight, I have to remind myself to breathe. If only my world weren't threatening to fall apart at the seams, then maybe I would figure out how to deal with my philandering husband. But for now, I must remain patient. I must play the loving wife and beloved momfluencer. Only when the ashes from Meredith's case settle can I then scorch the earth of my own home.

# Chapter 21

# ASPEN

There are two things that America is obsessed with: guns and beautiful women who go missing. Meredith wasn't white, but she was beautiful, and she was a "huge TikTok sensation," or so the news calls her. I was very much hoping that the police would consider the last message she sent—"I need a fucking break"—as a hint that Meredith chose to leave on her own volition. But I quickly learn that was merely wishful thinking.

The very next morning after Clara reported Meredith missing to the police, two detectives show up at my house. One female, one male. Detective Garza and Detective Clarke. And far from popular belief, they haven't come as Good Cop, Bad Cop. They're both really nice, actually. I have them take a seat at the dining room table and make them each a matcha latte, then I sit down across from them with Sabine on my lap and say, in my most earnest voice, "How can I help you, officers?" My insides are twisting like trapped snakes, but I have prepared for this eventuality. I can do this. I must do this.

They smile at me. Detective Garza takes a sip of her matcha latte. I decide I like her more than Detective Clarke. "When was the last time you heard from Meredith Lee?" Detective Clarke says, flipping open a small notepad. I wonder why cops insist on writing things down on a notepad instead of typing into their phones like normal people do.

"Ah." I grimace apologetically. "It's been a while, actually."

"Really?" Detective Clarke's eyebrows rise. He still hasn't drunk his matcha latte, and I wonder if this means he thinks I'm a suspect. "How come? Meredith's sister said you're her best friend."

I press my lips into a thin, sad smile. "We were. But we drifted apart. You know how these things go." Last night, as I lay awake in bed, I considered not telling the cops that Meredith and I had a falling-out, but quickly dismissed it. It's more than likely that Clara would've told them about our fight, and if they caught me out in a lie, I would be in deep trouble. Still, I don't want them to know the extent of our fight. Best to minimize the damage unless they press hard.

"Did you two have a fight?" Detective Garza says.

"Sort of." I sigh and bounce Sabine a little, so their attention is pulled to my cute, chubby baby. No one can possibly suspect a mother holding a cherubic baby in her lap. "We're both momfluencers, and when I got big—"

"Sorry to interrupt," Detective Clarke says. "Momfluencer?"

"A mom influencer," Detective Garza says.

"Yeah, that's right. We're influencers who focus on mom-friendly content. You know, lots of life hacks about cooking and how to change a diaper efficiently—that kind of thing." I purposely focus on the least exciting parts of the job, counting on these details boring the detectives, and I think I see Detective Clarke's eyes glazing over ever so slightly. Good. He thinks I'm a dumb bitch whose life revolves around changing diapers. Dumb bitches whose lives revolve around changing diapers don't murder their best friends and dump their bodies in a pond. "And when I got big, I think Meredith felt a little bit insecure about it. She decided she didn't want to be friends with me anymore." I let out a small, apologetic laugh. "Oh god, that sounds so childish, doesn't it?" Ha ha, silly women and their silly little fights that definitely did not lead to murder.

Detective Clarke smirks. "A little."

Detective Garza takes another sip of matcha latte, but keeps her eyes on me. I think that maybe she's not quite convinced just yet. As though reading my mind, she says, "How bad was this fight?"

I purse my lips. "I mean, we weren't screaming at each other or anything like that." We definitely were screaming at each other. "No name-calling." *You social-climbing bitch*, Meredith had called me. *You pathetic jealous loser*, I'd called her. "It was more like, disappointment, I guess."

"And this happened when, exactly?"

I pretend to think. "I wanna say maybe five, six months ago?" It was four months ago, but who's counting?

Detective Clarke leans back in his chair, looking bored. Since our fight happened so long ago, it's looking less and less likely that I might have anything to do with her disappearance.

"I hope she's okay, detectives." I sigh, shaking my head. "After our last talk, she blocked me, and I haven't heard from her since. I sent her a few texts, apologizing, but she didn't respond. I could still see her posts, though, so I assumed she's fine."

"The posts were scheduled in advance," Detective Garza says.

My eyes go wide. "So . . . wait, so you're saying that for the last month, no one's heard from Mer, and she hasn't actually been posting to her social media accounts actively?"

Both detectives nod.

I sit back, stunned. "I—this whole time, I just thought she's been ignoring me."

"Didn't Clara tell you she hasn't heard from Meredith either?" Detective Garza says.

"Yeah, but I kind of assumed—well, Clara and Meredith's relationship is kind of choppy. You know, sisters."

"Sure, I understand," Detective Garza says, "but you're aware that Meredith also left her son with Clara, right?"

I nod.

"And you didn't find that strange? That she would up and leave her only child and not even bother calling to check in on him?"

Shit, shit. This interview is slipping away from me, and I need to grab it back under control, fast. I pinch Sabine's butt cheek and she squirms and starts fussing. "Sorry, I need to feed this one real quick. Could you?" I stand and hand Sabine to Detective Garza without waiting for her to agree. I note Detective Garza's discomfort, and Detective Clarke, surprisingly, holds his arms out, and Detective Garza hands Sabine over with obvious relief.

I bustle about, taking a prepared bottle of formula from the fridge and heating it up, my mind whirring away as I wait for the bottle to warm up. How best to answer this question?

"Sorry about that," I say, shaking the bottle as I return to the dining table.

"No worries; she's a cutie," Detective Clarke says, standing up and passing Sabine to me gently.

Sabine grabs the bottle with her chubby hands and starts sucking furiously. I smile down at her with unabashed affection.

I know exactly how I must look right now—loving and safe. Completely unlike their usual suspects. "Sorry, I totally forgot what we were talking about."

Detective Garza leans forward. "You're a mom, Mrs. Palmer," she says, nodding at Sabine. "As a mother, don't you find it strange that your friend left her child and never bothered to even text to ask about him?"

I let the sadness wash over me. "Well, yes. Obviously. It's unthinkable. My world revolves around my kids. But . . ." I sigh and look away for a moment, gearing myself up to say something difficult. Something ugly and harsh. "I'm not judging her; I swear I'm not. But Meredith . . . she wasn't ready to be a mom. Not really. She went through a bit of postpartum depression, and I got the feeling that she never quite bonded with Luca."

Detective Clarke sits up, suddenly alert. "Postpartum depression?"

Jesus, of all the things that he notices, it's this one?

"My wife went through that after our second was born," he says. "It was really rough. Did Meredith see anyone about it? Did she talk to you? Take any meds?"

Shit. I'd just thrown that out there without thinking. Why the hell did I do that? "No," I say quickly. "I'm sorry, I don't know if it was actually postpartum depression. I don't know much about the condition. I just meant like, she wasn't—she was emotionally unprepared to raise a baby on her own. So it was a struggle. Did Clara mention how often Meredith had to ask her to look after Luca?"

Both detectives nod.

"Yeah, so. Do I think it's weird for a mother to leave her baby behind with her sister and not even bother to check in on him?

Yes, I do. But do I empathize with that mother? Yes. It's tough, raising kids, and I can't imagine how hard it must be doing it alone."

"Hmm," Detective Clarke says, nodding.

My thoughts chase their own tails in a circle: *Did-I-fool-them-is-this-over-yet-when-will-it-be-over-I-need-this-to-be-over.*

"Do you know of anyone who might have a grudge against Meredith?" Detective Garza says.

I pretend to mull this over. "I mean, I want to say no, but it's a risk with our jobs."

"Mom influencer," Detective Clarke says.

"Yes. Well, any kind of influencer, really. It's different from being a celebrity. With influencers, people sometimes feel like they actually know you. Like complete strangers will think I'm their friend, because we have to post content throughout our days. And most of that content is sharing bits and pieces of our lives with everyone. Boundaries become blurred, fans feel entitled to getting closer and closer to you . . . I don't know of anyone specifically who might have something against Meredith, but we all have fans who cross the lines."

Again, the two detectives nod. Detective Clarke writes in his notepad.

I lean forward, frowning. "Are you saying that something might have happened to her?" My voice comes out with a touch of horrified realization.

"Well, we don't know yet, but we're taking this seriously," Detective Garza says.

I put a hand over my mouth. "All this time, I just assumed she'd gone to a retreat or—or a journey to find herself or something. Oh my god."

"Could still be a possibility. Don't get too worked up over it," Detective Clarke says, in what he probably thinks is a reassuring way. "But do keep an ear out for anything that might tell you where she is."

"Of course," I say quickly.

The detectives stand then, and I do, too, carrying Sabine carefully. As they walk out of the house, I stand there and wave to them with a worried smile. They wave at me from inside their car, and I wonder if I've played my part sufficiently. I look down at Sabine. She looks up at me but doesn't stop sucking on the bottle. They wouldn't suspect me. Not a mother feeding her baby. I will be okay.

Except the problem is, I saw the cops coming, but I didn't see America's obsession crashing down on me. Because Clara didn't just go to the police. She went online.

That very same day, as I log on to TikTok to do my rounds and leave nice comments on my friends' posts, the first thing I see is Kelly, one of my mom friends, talking about how worried she is about Meredith. I feel as though my scalp has shrunk and become too small for my skull.

"—I mean, it's one of us, guys," Kelly is saying to the camera, her Botoxed face showing something which I think is meant to be horror. "Meredith is such a huge part of our community, and what about Luca? This is crazy! She wouldn't have left him behind like that. You've all seen her videos. Luca was her whole world."

"Ugh," I say out loud. Luca was very definitely not Meredith's whole world.

"If she's missing, someone has taken her," Kelly says, her eyes filling with tears. Her nostrils flare. "Get this news out there. We all need to look for her."

"Jesus," I mutter. I scroll up. The next video is of a momfluencer friend doing yoga. I tap on the heart to Like it and type out "Slayyy!" I scroll up. A video of Meredith with the caption, "WHERE'S MEREDITH???" I shake my head and scroll up again. More Meredith. Where the hell is this coming from? Clara isn't even on TikTok. How did she get the news out so fast?

I type out Meredith's handle and tap on it. And my heart stops, because the latest post on Meredith's account is of Clara. She must've figured out how to log on to Meredith's TikTok somehow. Sisters. Who knows what other secrets of Meredith's Clara knows? I tap on the video.

Clara is looking straight into the camera, the angle unflattering. Luca is in her arms, sucking on a rubber duckie. "I'm Clara, Meredith's sister. I'm here to tell you that Meredith has been missing for over a month now." Her voice breaks and she pauses, looking up at the ceiling and blinking rapidly. The amateurish quality of the footage actually works for her, lending the video a kind of disarming sincerity. No one is going to scroll up, not before the video ends. "Thirty-six days ago, Meredith dropped her son Luca off at my house for the night. That was the last time I ever saw her. She was supposed to pick him up the next morning, but that night, she sent me a strange message, saying she needed a break. I need you all to know that this isn't like Mer at all. She's irritating as hell and irresponsible sometimes, but she loves Luca so much. She would never abandon him." Tears roll down her face, and she wipes them off angrily. She leans closer to the camera, her voice hardening. "Someone out there has taken my sister. Please, if anyone has any information, call this number." A number appears on the screen. "I've reported her missing to the police and they are taking it very seriously, but we need all the help we can get. I don't know much about social media, but I know Mer was doing it a lot. You guys are her world. She would want all of you to help. Please, help us find her. Luca doesn't deserve to grow up without his mommy." The final word hitches up into a shrill sob, and Clara shakes her head and whispers, "Please." The video ends.

Oh my god. Dread is an anvil crushing me, pulverizing my spine, squeezing every drop of air out of my lungs. How did this happen? Cops, I can handle. I handled them. I know I did. They walked out of my house convinced I have nothing to do with Meredith's disappearance. But the internet? Nobody has a handle on the internet. There is no way of knowing which direction TikTok will swing. In the age of conspiracy theories and fake news, no one is considered innocent. The wilder the story, the better. A momfluencer killing her best friend and rival? That's not even the wildest story out there, not by a long shot. TikTok will easily believe it. If they catch even a whiff of suspicion of me, I am done.

# Chapter 22

# ASPEN

What should I do? How do I handle this? Should I even be handling this? The front door opens, startling me so badly that I give a little shriek of surprise.

"Sorry!" Liv says, with a half grimace, half grin.

For a second, I just stand there, staring at her dumbly.

"You okay? Sorry I'm a little bit late. Someone was a grumpy-pants this morning," she says, turning to Rain and kissing the side of her head. "Weren't you, sweetiekins?" She looks up at me and frowns. "What's going on?"

"Mer's missing." It's only when the words are out of my mouth that the reality of them hits me. It's official. Out in the world. Meredith is missing.

"Oh my god, I know!" Liv cries. She hurries inside and plops Rain in the playpen. "Where's Sabbie?"

"Napping."

"Aww. Well, you'll just have to play on your own while Mommy works, okay?" she says to Rain. When Liv walks away from the playpen, Rain whines and crawls over to the fence, pulling herself up and reaching out for Liv. "Not now, sweetie, Mommy has to work." Liv sighs, then looks at me. "Any advice on how to handle this?"

"Oh." I shake myself a little. Focus. One thing at a time. "Uh, maybe give her a snack? I've got some veggie melts. Rain can use Sabbie's high chair."

"See, Aspen? You make it look so easy," Liv says.

I grit my teeth and go into the kitchen to fetch the snacks while Liv lifts Rain from the playpen and settles her in the high chair. I pour out a handful of veggie melts onto the tray, and Rain happily shoves one in her mouth. Liv turns to me and says, "So anyway, oh my god, Meredith! That is the craziest thing. You guys were so close! Did she say anything to you before she was—oh my god, I can't even say it." She lowers her voice into a scandalized whisper. "Before she was taken?"

God help me. I swear if I don't control my temper, I'm going to end up shaking Liv so hard that it snaps her skinny little neck. "No. We weren't really talking by then."

"Oh yeah. You guys had that fight."

"Well. I wouldn't call it a 'fight.' It was more like a disagreement."

"Po-tay-to, po-tah-to."

Again, I grit my teeth. I almost flinch when Liv reaches out and squeezes my shoulder. "You must be distraught," she says.

Must I? I don't know what I must be. If I were distraught, would it come off disingenuous, especially since Meredith and I hadn't even talked to each other for the last few months? No. Liv is right. I must be distraught. No matter what, Meredith was my best friend. Any normal person would be devastated if their best friend disappeared, even if they weren't talking at the time. I nod, pressing my lips into a tight line to make it look like I'm trying to hold back tears. "Yeah, I'm a mess." I turn away and sniffle.

"Oh my god, of course you are. You poor thing!" Liv says. "What are you going to say about it?"

"Say about it?"

Liv waves her phone in my face. "Online? You're going to post about it, right?"

Fuck. Of course I need to post about it. It's obvious, now that Liv's said it. I can't just keep quiet and continue posting recipes for diabetic-friendly quiches. "Right," I say quickly. "I don't even know. I mean, like I said, I've just been a mess about it, and the police came over this morning, and—"

"The police came by?" Liv squeaks, not even bothering to cover up her excitement. "What did they say?"

"Not much. They asked if I know of anyone who might have a grudge against Mer, and then they told me if I think of anything, I should call them. And it's so . . . it's just so surreal, you know? I don't—it hasn't really sunk in yet."

Liv nods slowly. Then something dawns on her face, and she turns, stands next to me, and holds up her phone.

"Wha—"

"Come on, we're going to do a post now. Together."

"What? No."

Liv glares at me. "Your best friend is literally missing. Probably kidnapped. You need to say something about it. And you promised that you'd help me gain more followers, so I don't see why we shouldn't kill two birds with one stone."

"Because—" I gesture vaguely, scrambling to try and come up with a legit reason, other than that she's being a complete psycho. "I don't even know what to say yet."

"Aspen, this is exactly what you need to do. No more being fake, remember?" Liv raises her eyebrows and gives me a pointed look. "Say something straight from your heart. No rehearsed lines."

"I—but—"

"You're supposed to be hashtag authentic."

She's really going to force me to do this. And maybe she's right. Maybe it's better if it doesn't seem rehearsed. But what if I say something wrong? Something that can be used against me? And I don't want to do it next to Liv. But I can't think of anything to say to deter Liv, and I also don't want to make Liv angry, and god, how the hell did I land myself in this mess? Even as I stand here, gaping, Liv holds up her phone again.

"Ready?" she says.

I open my mouth to say no, but then I see us on her phone. I see how shocked I look. Genuinely shocked. Stricken, flustered. Shattered. Like someone who's just learned that her best friend has gone missing. No matter how hard I try later, how many takes I do, I know that I'm never going to achieve this level of authenticity. So despite everything inside me screaming *Nooo!* I nod and say, "Okay."

Liv rumples up her hair and shifts her hold on the phone to find a more flattering angle. Then she taps the red Record button. "Hey, guys, I'm here with Aspen from All Day Aspen, and we've just heard that Meredith, @MerryMeredith, is missing."

I take in a shuddery breath. "Hi, everyone. Meredith w—is my best friend. Although we haven't spoken to each other in months, she will forever be my soul twin. And I—I can't believe—" My whole face feels like it's just burst into flames. When the tears come, they're genuine. Genuine tears of fear, that is. Because holy shit, I have never been this close to being found out—to losing everything. My self-preservation instincts are going insane. It is overwhelming.

"Oh, Aspen," Liv gasps, "You poor thing." She squeezes my shoulders and I lean into her.

"I just want my best friend back," I sob, and this I truly mean, with all of my being. I want the old Mer back. The one I spent every day with. The first person I texted when I woke up, and the last person I texted when I went to bed. The person with whom I shared a million inside jokes. With whom I could just sit and do nothing in particular with. Someone I could be quiet with. "I miss her so much. Please, if you have Mer with you, please let her go. Let her come home to us. There are so many people who need her."

Liv starts sniffling, and to my surprise, she's actually crying. What the hell? She's never even met Meredith, and here she is, honest to god crying. "Yes, please let her go. She's such a beautiful soul." A beautiful soul? How the fuck would Liv even know what sort of soul Meredith was?

But I make myself nod.

"And Mer," Liv says, looking straight into the camera, "if you're watching this, don't lose hope. We're looking for you. We're not going to stop until we find you." She taps at the screen and ends the recording. "Phew!" Liv says. "That was intense, huh?" She wipes at her face.

"Yeah." I turn away and find a napkin to dab at my cheeks so I won't wipe off my makeup. I still feel shaky, like the rug has been pulled out from under me. I've just carved out my insides and offered them up to the camera, and I think I should feel empty, but I don't. I feel exhilarated. Did I really just pull that off?

"I think that was good," Liv says. "I'll post it now, yeah? I don't think we should wait for optimal posting time; what do you think?"

"Yeah." I want the video to get out there as soon as possible. To join the chorus of voices pleading for Meredith's return. The sooner we post it, the better. I watch as Liv opens up TikTok and uploads the video.

"What should I say in the caption?"

"How about 'Please help us find Meredith! Hashtag WhereIsMer'?"

"Perfect." Liv types it quickly, tags me, and hits Post.

My chest flutters as it is sent into the ether. It's done. My reaction video is out there now. I have officially plunged into the Find Meredith crowd. Even as Liv uploads the video to Instagram, both of our phones are already exploding. Mine *boops* endlessly with Likes and comments. I open TikTok on my phone and scroll through the comments, my belly tight with dread.

FreyaSSS: OMG this is so crazy!!! I hope you guys find her!!!

TaokeY: Aspen! My heart is breaking for you. #whereismer The sick fuck who took her will meet JUSTICE!

CrispyPie: 😭 I am literally crying right now. Poor Aspen!!

I can't read the comments fast enough. They stream in like a river, endless and fast. As I read them, my heart swells to fill my entire chest. They bought it. Everyone is in love with me. Enraptured by my grief. I realize that part of me has been bracing for the troll comments, but maybe, without Meredith to incite the trolls into attacking me, they've lost interest and found another target. I have to fight hard to keep myself from grinning. I repost the video from my own accounts, and even more Likes and comments cascade in.

"Oh my god," Liv says. "I've just gained like, a hundred followers in the last ten minutes—holy shit."

Am I supposed to congratulate her? I settle on giving her a grim smile instead. I click on the #WhereIsMer hashtag, and with a sickening feeling, I see that it's already got more than two million views on TikTok. Mer has gone viral. I look at her profile. Three million followers. She's gaining followers like crazy. I shake my head, unable to suppress my snort. I'm torn between laughter and tears. If only this growth had happened sooner. Months and months ago, before Meredith's jealousy grew so large that our friendship couldn't support its weight. So many if-onlys. What I wouldn't give to have my friendship with Meredith back.

The irony is, Meredith would've killed to see these kinds of numbers on her page.

# Chapter 23

# ASPEN

It's my turn to pick the twins up today. The moment I turn into the driveway, I know that the news has hit the school. Parents stand in clumps, talking animatedly. Many of them are shaking their heads. As I slide into a parking spot, one of the moms, Pamela, spots my car and strides over.

"Oh crap," I mutter. I get out, keeping the windows open, as Sabine is still inside her car seat. "Hi, Pamela."

"Aspen, oh my god, you must be crushed," Pamela says. "I actually started crying when I watched your video."

"I . . . yeah. Thank you for the kind words."

The rest of the group has joined her now, crowding around me like a pack of hyenas.

"Do the police have any idea where she is?" someone says.

I shake my head. "I know about as much as you all do, I'm afraid."

"I can't believe it," someone else says. A mom named Marla. She's always hated me, but now she's pouting at me in sympathy. "Your best friend. Oh, is there anything I can do?"

*Leaving me the hell alone would be nice*, I think. "Try to get the message out. The more people we have looking for Meredith, the better."

They all nod. "Of course, yes," Marla says.

"Did you hear what her sister said, though?" Pamela says. "Apparently, she sent a text message? Saying she was sick of everything, right? I mean, is there a possibility that she decided to leave? You know her best, Aspen; what do you think?"

I think you are all a bunch of vultures who don't deserve a shred of my time. I take a deep breath. "Ah—I don't know. Maybe? It's possible."

Pamela leans closer, like a predator sensing blood. "But surely you know something. You two were so close. Best friends. Like sisters, even. She must've told you something?" Her eyes glitter with barely concealed glee.

The familiar fear rises up within me, its jagged edges slicing into me. Do they know? Are they just toying with me the way a cat plays with a wounded mouse?

"I really don't know much." God, someone get me out of here. But there's no one. No help. If I want to get out of this unscathed, I need to rely on my own wits. And haven't I been doing that for years? My resolve hardens, and I look Pamela in the eye. "But here's what I know: motherhood is so tough. So much tougher than I thought it would be."

There is a round of nods and *mhmms*.

"And she's a single mom, so it's even harder on her. I don't blame her for wanting to get away. Don't we all, at some point? I mean, I don't know about you ladies, but sometimes I feel so overwhelmed I just want to go on a retreat, you know? I hope that Mer is at some beautiful resort, sipping a margarita. The alternative is . . ." I gulp and shake my head, and everyone murmurs their agreement.

The bell rings then, and I scan the kids streaming out of the school and—thank god—spot the twins. "Girls, over here!" I call out, barely able to keep the relief out of my voice. "Excuse me, ladies." With a few meaningful glances at each other, the group of moms disperses, and I hold out my arms to hug Elea and Noemie. Thank god I got through that.

I half expect Elea to duck underneath my arms the way she usually does, but to my surprise, both girls fling themselves at me and hug me tight. Then it hits me. Of course. They must've heard too. A couple of the kids in their class already have their own phones. By now, Meredith's disappearance would've gone so viral that it would be impossible to be in the dark. The realization slams into me with ruthless force. Of all the people I'd hoped to keep out of this whole mess, it's the kids. It's always been about protecting the kids. But now, here they are, singed by the fire I've created.

"Is it true? Was Aunt Mer kidnapped?" Elea whimpers, looking up at me with wide eyes. I'm not used to my little firebrand looking so vulnerable, and the sight of it cracks my heart wide open.

Noemie doesn't say anything, just hides her face in my leg. I go down on my knees and hug them tight. "I'm so sorry, pumpkins. Aunt Mer is missing, but you know what, it probably wasn't a kidnapping or anything like that. I think that maybe she needed some time to herself."

"But why did you beg her kidnapper to let her go in your video?" Noemie says.

Well, shit. "I . . ." Nope, I can't think of a single answer that would allay their suspicions. "You're right. I don't know. Maybe she was kidnapped. Maybe she left to discover herself."

"So she could be tied up in a dungeon right now?" Elea says, her eyes wide.

"I—I really hope not. I don't think so. I don't know." I stroke their little faces and straighten up. "Hey, shall we go grab a smoothie?" There is a place nearby that does veggie smoothies, and they are less atrocious for diabetics than fruit smoothies, so it's okay for Noemie to have some once in a while.

"No," Noemie says, while Elea shakes her head. "We just want to go home."

They both look so terrified that I almost burst into tears then and there. I crouch down again and look them in the eyes. "Listen to me. You girls are safe, okay? Mommy isn't going to let anything bad happen to you."

They nod and a little bit of the fear leaves their faces, but as I buckle Elea into her car seat, she suddenly grips my hand tight and says, "But how will you stop the bad guy from taking us too? Aunt Mer is a grown-up and she couldn't stop the bad guy from taking her."

My mouth sets into a thin line. "I'm a lot stronger than Aunt Mer. And don't forget, we've got Daddy. So there are two of us looking after all of you."

The irony of the situation doesn't escape me. I know how awful it is—the fact that the person my kids are afraid of is me. But what other choice do I have? I can't say, "Don't worry, kids, I was the one who kidnapped Aunt Mer, and I'm hardly going to do the same to you, am I?" Instead, I turn on some music and we drive home without saying another word, letting the music drown out our thoughts.

Once we get home, the twins, as usual, park themselves in front of the TV while I change Sabine's diaper. But when Elea turns the TV on, the first thing I hear is some announcer's voice saying, "—has been reported missing. Meredith Lee is a thirty-two-year-old mother and TikTok star. As of this morning, she has over three million followers on TikTok, and one million on Instagram. She was last seen by her sister, Clara Lee, on the night of the fourteenth of last month."

I hurry over and turn it to a different channel.

"Aww, Mommy!" Elea says. "We were watching that."

I shake my head at her. "I don't think it's appropriate for you to watch it."

Surprisingly, the next plea comes from Noemie. "Please, Mommy. Aunt Mer is our godmother. We want to know if she's okay."

*Forget her!* I want to scream. She's not okay, not at all, and it's best for everyone if you just pretend like none of this is happening. I never once considered that I would be in this situation, trying to comfort my girls about a murder I committed. "I don't want you kids to scare yourselves."

"We won't," Noemie says. My sweet, shy girl is being so brave, and I have never hated myself as much as I do right now. "We want to know so that we can help too."

I know when I'm defeated. I hand the remote control to Noemie. "I—I'll fix you girls a snack." As I walk out of the living room, I hear the TV coming back on, but instead of the announcer's voice, it's my own voice coming out of it. "Please, let her go . . ." It sounds like a ghost coming out of my TV. I turn around and dart back as Noemie and Elea shout, "Mommy, you're on TV!"

It's the video that Liv took of us this morning. My face is crumpled in sorrow and I'm ugly-crying. The caption underneath the image says: "Missing woman's friends make a plea to whoever has her to release her." Thankfully, it switches to a different video of some other influencer, also crying and begging the fictional kidnapper to let Mer go.

"Wow, Mommy," Elea says, looking at me in wonderment. "You were on TV."

"Yeah," I mumble, and walk out of there in a daze. This has blown way out of proportion. What is going to happen now? *Nothing*, I tell myself. Nothing will happen, because nothing will be found, and in a week's time, some other awful piece of news will break, and everyone will forget about Meredith. They'll assume she's either on an *Eat, Pray, Love*-type journey and has found herself on some exotic paradise island, or that her kidnapper's killed and buried her, in which case they'll probably be looking at people who are most likely to kill attractive women. First, they will look at convicted felons in the area. Then they'll . . . I don't know. Look at the men in Mer's life? Who knows? The key part is that they won't look at me. They have no reason to look at me as a suspect.

Still, no matter how many times I repeat it mentally, I can't quite get my mind to believe that the FBI isn't about to kick down my door and arrest me. They'll dig, and dig, and they'll find something. Our fight. The stolen meetings. A witness who saw me leaving Meredith's apartment, carrying her dead body. Anxiety crawls through me.

I'm pouring out some baby carrots into a bowl when I hear a key sliding into the front door. Panic flares up my chest, but then the door opens and it's Ben. Of course it's Ben.

He strides in without bothering to take off his coat, dropping his briefcase to one side. His expression is stricken, and I know that he's heard the news too. "Aspen," he says, "oh my god." He wraps his arms around me and pulls me into a tight hug. It's the first real hug we've had in a long time, and I close my eyes and let myself fall into the embrace, savoring the solidity of him. "Are you okay?" he murmurs.

I lean back and give him a brave smile. "Yeah. No. Well, I'm about as okay as I can be, I guess."

Ben sighs and pulls me back into the hug, and now I want to cry because this is what it takes to get my husband to show me some love and concern? A possible kidnapping? Then it strikes me that, no, it's not quite that. It's the fact that he can once again take care of me. It's the fact that I'm in distress, that I'm helpless, and he, big manly Ben, can stride in and finally be the man of the house.

Am I being ungenerous? Maybe. Probably. But I can't shake the feeling that Ben's only being affectionate because he thinks I'm flailing. I pull away from him and say, "I'm fine. I'm okay."

And immediately, his expression cools, just a little. The walls slide back into place. I'm not a broken woman that he can try to fix after all.

I hug myself and shudder. "Honestly, I think I'm kind of in shock." Ben's face softens, and now it's my turn to harden, though I don't show it. But he's just proved me right. He's a man who doesn't understand how to love a woman who isn't in need. I let a note of fear bleed into my voice. "What do you think happened to Mer?" I stare at him, wide-eyed, a silly woman waiting for a man to explain his theory to her.

"She must've been kidnapped by some guy she knew," Ben

says, with so much conviction that, if I didn't know better, I would probably believe him. "I read a statistic once that says that most kidnappers are people who are already in the victim's lives. My money's on it being some asshole who probably has a crush on her. Maybe her personal trainer . . ."

Mer's PT is gay, but I'm not about to ruin Ben's fun.

"Or maybe even the barista at her local café. Someone who sees her every day and is secretly in love with her."

I want so badly to believe that this is what everyone will assume. I wrap my arms around myself even tighter and grimace up at him. "My god, that's horrifying. The thought of it being some guy who's like, serving her coffee or whatever, secretly plotting to take her . . ."

Ben nods solemnly before rubbing my arms. "Hey, it's going to be okay. With all the technology we have today, they'll catch the sick fuck who did this. They'll find Mer, and years down the road, this is going to be a story that she will tell at every party." He actually smiles at this, like he has utter confidence that Mer will be found safe and sound, and this will be behind us within a week—two at the most. Oh, to have the confidence of a mediocre white man. "Listen, I want you to take the rest of the day off, okay?" Ben says. "Don't worry about fixing dinner; I'll take care of it."

"Really?" Now I really am surprised. Ben hasn't bothered cooking anything in the last three years. Whenever I asked, he'd say something along the lines of, "Are you sure? It's not going to be 'Insta friendly.'"

"Yeah. You go take a hot bath or something. Go relax." He steers me out of the kitchen with a bright smile.

"Okay, okay. Thanks, babe." I kiss him on the cheek and head down to the bathroom. I could use a hot bath. I'm halfway down the hallway when I remember that I was supposed to get the twins a snack. I walk back toward the kitchen and catch a glimpse of Ben with his hands braced against the countertop, his head drooped like a wilted flower. The expression on his face is one of anguish.

*That's right,* I recall belatedly. Ben had kissed Meredith. In fact, he'd kissed her the day she was last seen. Surprisingly, jealousy flares up. A weak flare, more like an ember than a flame, but just enough to make me think, fleetingly: *Serves him right. I hope he stays worried.* I must have made a noise then, because Ben's head snaps up and he quickly rearranges his features into less tortured ones. I grab the bowl of baby carrots and say, "Just getting these for the twins." As I head out of the kitchen, I turn around and say, "You okay, babe?"

He nods and smiles.

What must be going through his mind right now? I try putting myself in Ben's shoes. A woman I kissed is now missing. Confusion. Terror. Disbelief. Fear that someone might have seen us and point to me as the kidnapper. Poor Ben. Despite myself, I feel slightly sorry for him. I know exactly what it feels like to have the weight of a deadly secret bearing down on you.

# Chapter 24

# ASPEN

How's this for a turn-up for the books? Meredith's disappearance going viral is good for everyone involved. Well, except for Meredith, of course. But that can't be helped. For everyone else who is still alive, the news cycle brings wave after wave of amazing surprises.

Mere days after Meredith's disappearance was announced, my account is very nearly at seven million followers on TikTok, and is already at over six million on Instagram. It's a growth rate unlike anything I've ever seen before. Like I said, America is obsessed with beautiful missing women. Liv's account has boomed too. She's now at over three hundred thousand followers. She and I are posting content at a furious pace: three to five videos a day, most of them related to Meredith. I share past videos and photos of myself with Meredith—easy to do since there are literally millions of them in my folder.

Liv is surprisingly helpful. She often serves as the "interviewer" in my videos, asking me specific questions about Mer (*What's her favorite food? What's her favorite outfit?*) and coming up with theories of how these little tidbits of information might help us find Mer (*Do you think maybe the police could keep a lookout for people ordering vegan pizzas, since that's Mer's favorite food?*). They're absolutely useless, of course. The food thing, for example. What kidnapper in his right mind is going to be spoiling his victim with her favorite food? Still, the videos do ridiculous numbers, spreading like a Californian wildfire. The comments are full of people trying to be helpful, reporting that they saw a shady-looking guy buying vegan pizza in Brentwood, or that they caught a glimpse of someone wearing something similar to Mer's favorite jumpsuit. All of it useless in terms of actually finding Mer, but extremely useful in bumping my follower count up.

The kids, too, are behaving beautifully. Well, Noemie has always been well behaved. But Elea has done a complete one-eighty. She doesn't talk back to me anymore. Her anger has been replaced with fear, which honestly sounds more horrible than it really is. Because when she was angry, I didn't know how to deal with it. But her fear is easy to handle. I even cherish it, in a twisted way, because it's what brings her back to my arms. At night, she cuddles up sweetly to me, baby-like, and asks me to read her bedtime stories once again. And when we walk to the park, Elea holds my hand tight. I hold my baby girl close to me and pray that when the fear does fade, I won't lose her like I did before.

Even Clara is doing well. I went to her place and shot a video of her with Luca, and the outpouring of sympathy was so overwhelming that I set up a GoFundMe to help support them. It surpassed its goal of fifteen thousand dollars many times over, and is still ticking up every time I check on it.

And, in a way, even Meredith is doing well. Her TikTok now has over five million followers. Ironically, even her old videos are getting millions of new views every day. People are watching them on repeat, trying to look for clues in them—a glimpse of some guy watching Meredith intently in the background—or trying to find a pattern in her daily routine so they might guess whose attention she might have caught. As a result, her accounts are growing faster than mine. Her wish has come true, and I'm honestly crushed that she's not able to see it happen.

Because the thing that really breaks me is that I was perfectly content trailing along behind Mer. My whole life, I've been more comfortable as the sidekick. I never wanted to best anybody. I didn't have big dreams of becoming a huge star or anything. I just wanted to have enough followers to get by. I was happy when I blew up, of course I was, but all the success came with so much baggage. The more I earned, the more I spent on my family, and the more I needed to earn. I always thought that one day I could save up enough to cut back on posting, but somehow, I was unable to ever get there. There are so many bills, each one staggeringly huge. Meanwhile, Mer was secretly becoming embittered, the bond of our friendship growing more and more strained, until one day it snapped, and the tension sent us both reeling back.

I always wanted Mer to succeed. I wanted her to do better than me; I really did. If I had to be a star, then I wanted my soul twin to be an even bigger star, to take some of the limelight off me. I cried when I saw how fast Mer's accounts were growing, and I hoped that if there is an afterlife, then she would be gazing down and smiling at the number of followers she has now.

This morning, after making the usual school run, I go straight to a meeting that's been set up ages ago. It's one that I'm particularly excited about: a meeting with Damien Kim, the producer who's doing a Netflix show about influencers. I've prepared myself well for this meeting. I need this to work out. I need this to save me from the never-ending demand of content creation—to give me some sort of stability so I can finally take a step back and go, "Okay, that's enough." *Let's not get too far ahead of ourselves,* I remind myself. *One step at a time.*

We'd agreed to meet at a trendy café—your typical LA fare, sun-kissed and filled with plants everywhere, and serving things like organic matcha lattes with burnt rice milk. I get there five minutes early, settle Sabine in her high chair, and order myself a matcha latte. I hate to admit it, but the burnt rice milk is delicious. Sabine cheerfully stuffs Cheerios into her mouth. The server tells me Sabine is the cutest baby he's ever seen, and I make a mental note to tip him generously. I take another sip of my matcha. By now, it's half gone. I look at my phone. Damien is fifteen minutes late.

My ribcage closes up like a fist. Not again. I open up my calendar and check the event. According to this, I'm at the right place, and at the right time. Since I killed Meredith, I went through all of my appointments and corrected them. Or so I thought. Because there were still mistakes made. Appointments I missed, like the one with Sunflower Cheeks. And I don't understand it. I know I corrected them. It was one of the first things I did the days after coming back from the desert.

I close my calendar, find Damien's number in my contacts, and call him. He picks up after three rings.

"Hi, Aspen. This is a surprise," he says.

My mouth goes dry. A surprise? Why would it be a surprise if we were supposed to meet up today? Unless, of course, we weren't. "Hi, Damien. Ah, were we supposed to meet today? Because I'm sitting here at For Goodness' Sake . . ."

There's a moment of surprised silence. Then he says, "Aspen, you canceled our meeting, remember?"

"What?" Did Mer do that?

"Yeah, you sent a text and said you're no longer interested in the show."

I swear every drop of blood drains from my head. I almost faint then. "N-no," I manage to choke out. "I didn't—that was definitely not from me. I'm still very much interested in your show."

Damien groans. "Oh man, that really sucks. I would've loved to have you, but when you turned me down, I reached out to other influencers. The roster's full now. I'm sorry, Aspen."

I feel so heavy, like my bones have been replaced with lead. I want to collapse in a defeated heap and never get up again. "Is there a way to uh, slot me in?" I ask weakly.

"I'm afraid not at this point, but tell you what, if anyone drops out, you'll be the first person I call. Okay?"

"Okay. Thank you, Damien." After I hang up, I stare at the phone for a long time, my thoughts a confused blur. I know I didn't send a text to Damien to cancel our meeting. But then who did? Who could've done it? I open up my text messages and do a search for my DMs with Damien. But all of my messages to him have been erased, the thread wiped clean. I lose sensation in my hands. My phone thunks onto the table. Heads turn, eyes looking at me, but I don't care.

Someone went into my phone and erased my messages. Could it have been Meredith? Was this something she did before I killed her? Unlikely. I can remember that the last message I sent to Damien was a week after Meredith died. Someone else did this.

My mind sifts through every possible suspect. Ben. Liv. Clara.

My online trolls. Maybe they managed to hack into my phone. Is that possible? Of course it is. Anything can be done nowadays. What else has been tampered with? The back of my neck prickles, bursting into goosebumps. I peer over my shoulder, half expecting someone to be watching me. My phone feels sullied, like a hidden camera designed to spy on me. With a shudder, I turn it off. I can't get out of the café fast enough. I take out a twenty-dollar bill and leave it at the table, then lift Sabine out of the high chair and practically run out of there.

Inside my car, I force myself to pause and catch my breath. I can't drive in a panicked state. I won't allow myself to do that. Deep breaths. In and out. Count backwards from ten. I can deal with this. I dealt with Meredith, didn't I? And look how well that's going for everyone now. Whoever is sabotaging me, I'll find out. I'll work everything out.

Finally, I feel calm enough to drive home. I do so slowly, my mind still prying away at the locked box that is the mystery of my sabotaged calendar. I imagine Ben doing it, tapping away at my phone while I'm in the shower. The image swims to my mind easily, painfully vivid and clear. I swallow and force the image away. I move on to Liv. The times I had to change Sabine's diaper while Liv was at my house. The times I had to leave the room for whatever reason. I think of Liv picking up my phone. Again, the image is incredibly easy to conjure up. I can see her doing it as easily as I see Ben. Then I think of Clara. I think of the time I went to her place to shoot videos with her. At one point, Luca woke up from his nap, and Clara asked if I could get him and maybe change his diaper while I was at it. I'd agreed without a second thought; after all, I was still carrying the guilt of killing Meredith and saddling Clara with Luca. Luca turned out to be a squirmy kid;

it took me an interminably long time to get his diaper changed. Could Clara have gone into my phone then? Then I think of some anonymous troll sitting in some dank basement, typing away on their keyboard. Smiling when they finally break into my phone.

The problem is, I can see each one of these possibilities so clearly. Every single one of them is plausible. And where does that leave me? My breath is coming in and out rapidly again, and I have to remind myself to calm the hell down. Panicking isn't going to solve anything. Okay, one step at a time. I'll start by questioning Ben and Liv as casually as I can, since I see them every day. But carefully. Oh, so carefully. And before I even do that, I need to make sure that all of my appointments are in order. I'll call up every single person I'm supposed to meet and confirm our meetings, then I'll—ah, I'll get a notebook and jot them down manually. Yes. That'll work. And when I find out who's behind this . . .

My hands tighten around the steering wheel, strangling it. I've killed once, and you know what? It wasn't too bad, actually. I could do it again if I had to. I really could. How's that for #authenticity?

Except when I get home, Ben rushes to meet me at the door, his eyes wild. "Where've you been?" he cries. "I've been calling you like crazy, and you didn't—what happened to your phone?"

"I turned it off. Why?" I haven't seen Ben this panicked in—well, ever. And it's contagious. My neck grows warm. "What is it, Ben, what's wrong? Is it the girls? Are they okay?"

"Yes, they're fine." Ben swallows. I watch his Adam's apple bob and try to squash the hysteria that's threatening to bubble up my throat. Ben licks his lips and holds out his hands, gesturing at me to hand Sabine to him. For a split second, I almost refuse, clutching her protectively. But then I tell myself I'm being silly, and I hand Sabine to him. "Come. I think you should sit down."

"Ben, you're scaring me. Just tell me, damn it. What is it?"

Ben drags his eyes to meet mine, and his expression is so haunted that it pushes me back physically. "I'm so sorry, Aspen. Meredith is dead. They found her body."

# Chapter 25

# ASPEN

If it's possible to black out while still standing, then that's exactly what happens when Ben tells me that they found Mer. One moment I'm there, listening to Ben; the next moment, it's like I've plunged underwater. Every sound is muted and hollow, every movement thick and slow. I stay there for a while, in that peaceful, quiet space between one second to the next, not wanting to resurface. From afar, Ben's voice calls out my name. I ignore him until he reaches out and shakes my arm, jerking me back to the present.

"Aspen!" he shouts. "Are you okay?"

I look at him, dazed, and let him lead me to the couch.

"Sit down." He pushes down on my shoulder gently, as though I've forgotten how to sit down on the sofa. And maybe I have, because one moment I'm standing, and the next moment I'm sitting, and I have no idea when that happened.

"How?" I manage to choke out.

If Ben thinks it is a suspicious question to ask, he doesn't show it. "Some divers came across it."

Divers. I should've seen this coming. As Ben takes Sabine into the nursery, I stare blankly at the wall. My mind is still struggling to catch up with everything that's happening. The past few days, I somehow managed to convince myself that everything would be all right, and now, all of a sudden, everything is crumbling. I place my hand on my inner thigh and pinch, hard, digging my nails into the skin until I suck in my breath in a hiss. The pain is a sharp lance spearing through the fog in my mind.

*Get a grip,* I snarl mentally at myself. *This is not the time to fall apart. You cannot afford to be weak, submissive Aspen. There is no room for that Aspen. Not unless you want to land in prison.*

I keep pinching until the pain is all I'm aware of. By the time I let go, I'm panting slightly, and my thigh is throbbing. It worked, though. I'm no longer underwater. Okay. Let's think.

So they found her body. How the hell did they find her body? This would never have happened if I could've buried her in that hole I'd prepared. It's so unfair how I had to derail my meticulous plans because some asshole found the hole I'd dug out in the desert.

*Stop that,* I scold myself. *No use harping on that. The most important thing is to figure out what they know.*

Another wave of despair threatens to overwhelm me, but I shove it away. They know that Meredith is dead, obviously. Okay . . . so what will they think? Who would they suspect? Well, there's no reason why they wouldn't still think it was a Joe Goldberg situation. Right? That's the most obvious suspect. Meredith was an attractive single woman. She was on most dating apps. She partied a lot. Chances are, they'll still think it was some guy who was obsessed with her. Definitely not me, the best friend who created a GoFundMe page for Meredith's sister and child. I'll still be okay. Nothing has changed.

God, I'm coming up with some really desperate bullshit. Everything has changed. Before, there was still a chance that Meredith left of her own accord. There were even rumors about it flying around; people who insisted they saw her in Bali or the Maldives #livingherbestlife. Now, all those theories have been smashed to hell. And the focus will shift from finding Mer to finding her killer. The noose around my neck is tightening.

But there's nothing I can do, aside from sit tight and maybe post a couple of videos about how distraught I am over the news. With shaking hands, I take out my phone and turn it back on. The notifications come in a never-ending cascade of beeps; so many all at once that it almost turns into one long beep—an alarm shrieking straight to the center of my skull. And for the first time in my life, I feel a desperate need to get away from my phone. I grip it tight, wanting to fling it away as hard as I can and watch it shatter against the wall, but somehow, a part of me remains that hasn't been whittled down into an animalistic state. A part of me hangs on to its senses. A part of me swipes up on my phone and turn it to Silent mode.

Sweet, blessed silence. Still, the top part of the phone screen is constantly moving as more and more notifications come in. I lick my lips. Bone-dry. What to open first? Definitely not social media. I can't deal with that just yet. I open my messages.

Clara: Aspen, call me ASAP
Clara: They found Mer's body
Clara: My sister is dead
Clara: Where the fuck are you???

My breath comes out in a tiny whimper. I close her text messages. There is a string of messages from my other friends, and the school moms' text group is blowing up. I skip over all of them. I tap on my message chain with Liv.

Liv: OMG ASPEN??!!! DID YOU HEAR??? HOLY SHIT!!!
Liv: Rain has a cough so I'm at the pediatrician's but BE RIGHT OVER ASAP
Liv: OMG YOU MUST BE DEVASTATED. ILY HANG IN THERE!!

Shit. The last thing I want is Liv to be—

Well. Is that really the case? No, not anymore. Over the past couple of weeks, she's gone from someone threatening to reveal the real me online to someone who's an actual asset. Her content ideas are refreshing, and she coaxes out the best in me when we make our videos. With a start, I realize that I actually would like to have Liv by my side, especially when I make my reaction video to the news of Meredith's death.

Ben comes back into the room, sighing. "I can't even imagine what Clara and Luca are going through right now."

Bile rushes up my esophagus. The last thing I need is to think about poor, sweet Luca growing up without his mother. I feel a sudden inexplicable rage surging toward Ben. Why would he bring up Luca right now? To rub my guilt in my face? I want to shriek: *But I made a GoFundMe account for him! What more do you want from me?* My fingers grip the mug so tight that they start trembling.

*Get a grip*, I think to myself. What Ben said has nothing to do with you. It's a normal train of thought. Whenever a mother dies, the world focuses on her children. And in Luca's case, he didn't even have a father figure in his life to begin with. Then there's Clara. How is she going to manage everything now? It's normal to be thinking about these things. It's not meant to be a hidden commentary about me. He doesn't know I had something to do with Meredith's death.

"Yeah," I mutter. "I don't know. But hopefully the donations from the GoFundMe will help them get through this."

"Oh my god, yeah, the GoFundMe. I checked it just now and . . ." Ben shakes his head. "It's at over a million dollars."

"What?" I'm shocked speechless. There are no words. Only yesterday it had been at under one hundred thousand.

"Yeah. When news about Meredith being dead broke, people just started donating like crazy," Ben says. "You should be proud of yourself, Aspen. You did this. You made sure to take care of them. Mer would be smiling down at you right now."

A shrill, choked laugh burbles out of me, and I bite my tongue to stop myself. Mer would definitely not be smiling down at me right now.

The front door opens then, and Liv rushes in with Rain in her arms.

"Oh my god, Aspen!" she screams. "Aspen, are you okay?"

"Uh, can you keep it down?" Ben says. "Sab's napping."

"Oh. Yes, sorry."

Despite everything, I catch the way they look at each other—guilt and shame and attraction entangled in their gazes—and my insides boil once again. I had forgotten, in the whirlwind of everything, that Ben and Liv had a thing as well. I'm not sure how far they went; I only saw them kissing at the open house.

Have they gone all the way? After how attentive Ben has been the past week or so, I wanted to believe that our marriage was healing. But now, here is a reminder that, underneath it all, there are still festering sores, open and suppurating.

"Are you okay?" Liv says, sitting down next to me. Rain paws at my mug and I pull it out of reach just in time.

"I—no. I mean, how can I be okay right now?" I say, and I hate how accusatory I sound. I can't afford to lash out at anyone right now.

"Oh god, of course. I'm so sorry. I'm such a mess, too, oh my god. I've been crying the whole day." Liv is frantic, her face tear-stained. Why does she care so much? She barely even knew Meredith. But this is LA, isn't it? The land of over-the-top emotions. When it comes to emoting here, you've got to go big and fake, or go home. I want to scream at her to shut up, but then I realize: this is it. This is exactly what I need. Liv is showing me the blueprint of how Meredith's friends would be reacting. All I need to do is mirror Liv and dial it up a few notches, and I'm golden.

"Let's do a video," I say.

"What?" Ben says, and when I turn to look at him, his face is twisted into shocked revulsion.

"I need to release a video," I say, as calmly as I can. "I can't just stay silent, Ben. She was my best friend."

"She was your best friend," Ben hisses, "which is why you shouldn't be using this to get views."

"I'm not doing this to get views!" I cry. "How can you even think that?"

"Then why are you doing it?"

"Because—" I gesture wildly. "She was my best friend." We're going round in circles, and I know it. But how can he not understand why I need to post a video about this? Shouldn't it be obvious?

"Forget it," Ben mutters. His upper lip curls into a sneer. "I thought maybe this time you'd put something else first. Your family, your friendship, or, hell, your mental health, even. But of course, nothing can come before our lord and savior, TikTok." With that, he marches out of the living room, leaving behind a heavy, suffocating silence that's only broken up by Rain's little coos and gurgles.

Liv clears her throat. "Um. I'm just going to put Rain down in the playpen." She rushes off, and I try my best to calm myself down.

Fucking Ben. He's been so nice the past few days that I forgot how vile he could be. How contemptuous and belittling. When Liv comes back, I look at her with desperation. "He's not—he doesn't—he's wrong. Right? I need to post a reaction video."

Liv nods, frowning at me with sympathy. "Yeah, I don't think Ben gets it. I mean, how weird would it look if you just all of a sudden went silent? You can't not post about this."

"Exactly!" I cry. I take a deep breath. "Okay. Let's do this."

"Yeah? Okay."

Before Liv, I would've written down a whole speech and rehearsed it several times before I even started recording. And I would've recorded multiple takes, until my voice was hoarse—until I got everything down perfectly, down to every little detail. Thanks to Liv, I've since learned that, sometimes, it's best to shoot in the moment, when the emotions are raw and the words come as a surprise, even to my own ears.

Liv holds up her phone and adjusts the angle so we both look even skinnier, then she hits Record.

"Hey, everyone," she says quietly. "You've all heard the news. Meredith is dead."

I utter a choked sob, and Liv points the screen toward me. "Sorry," I moan, and I take the memory of all that pain and anger I have, most of it aimed at Ben, and I let myself break on camera. "I can't believe it. My best friend—my soulmate—she's gone. Some sick asshole killed her, and I—I can't. I can't, I'm sorry." I bury my face in my hands and let the bone-shaking sobs wrench through my whole body.

"Oh, Aspen." Liv puts a hand on my back. "Sorry, guys. Be right back." I hear her put the phone down and I rein the sobs back. "Here," Liv says, handing me a tissue.

I struggle to get control over myself, taking the tissue from her and dabbing at my eyes. "Thanks."

"Wow," Liv says, wonderment shining in her eyes. "That was powerful."

"Really? It was short."

"Yeah, but you conveyed so much emotion in like, three seconds. That's amazing. People are going to love it. I'll post it now." She picks up her phone and uploads the video, hesitating when she comes to the caption. "What should I put as a caption?"

I blow my nose and think for a bit. "Um . . . maybe, 'We just heard about Meredith, and we are devastated. Hashtag RIPMeredith hashtag WeLoveYouMeredith.'"

"Perfect," Liv says, typing rapidly. She tags me and posts the video. "Okay, let's do another one? Maybe a longer one this time. I'm thinking over three minutes, since the algorithm likes that length now?"

I nod. Three minutes sounds like an awfully long time, but I have so much to share—so many overwhelming emotions that

I need to let out. This is exactly what I need to do right now. This is exactly what Meredith would've wanted me to do. It's the least I can do for her.

Liv and I spend the next hour making more content. We do everything: Stitches with news reels, where we share a snippet of news and then react to it ("The body of thirty-two-year-old Meredith Lee has been uncovered in a pond a hundred miles outside of Los Angeles." Cut to me and Liv, in tears. Me: "A pond. I can't believe it. Someone took my best friend out into the middle of nowhere and left her there." Liv: "It's sick. It's disgusting. Who would do such a thing?"). We share more photos and videos of Meredith where I wax on about what an amazing mom and friend Meredith was, and how I vow to help look after little Luca for the rest of my life. (Me: "I swear to Meredith—I know she's up there listening, I love you so much, Mer—I swear to you, I will take care of Luca. Don't you worry. He will be loved." Liv: "Meredith would be smiling down at you right now.") We post about women's rights, and how important it is to raise little boys into good men. (Me: "She was killed by some sick fuck who thought he was entitled to her life, just because she was a woman. You are going to be caught, you asshole. You're going to be behind bars for the rest of your fucking life. Justice for Meredith!" Liv: "Justice for Meredith! That's right.")

At one point, Ben comes out of the home office and strides toward the front door. He pauses long enough to say, "I'm going out for lunch. I'll pick up the twins from school." He only glances at us for a split second, just enough for me to catch the sneer still snug on his face. My cheeks grow warm. I have no doubt that he's been listening to Liv and me this whole time, probably judging every word we say. Well, he can fuck right off. Easy to take the high road when you know you've got someone on the ground to count on.

But I don't dwell on Ben's contempt. There is no room in my attention span for Ben right now, because everything is blowing up. We are reaching numbers previously unheard of. The little ten-second video of me breaking down, posted a mere hour ago, has already reached nine million views. My follower counts are shooting up in real time. Seven and a half million followers on TikTok. #JusticeForMeredith is already trending everywhere. My phone is still on Silent mode, and I get missed call after missed call. A few of them are from Clara. She'll need to wait; I'm busy getting her even more donations for her GoFundMe account.

"Oh my god, we are growing so fast," Liv says, echoing my thoughts. "This is amazing. I'm so glad that we're able to help Meredith."

The absurdity of her statement does not escape me. Surely, Meredith is beyond help now. But I know what Liv meant, and I can't be mad at her because I'm so grateful that she's here. Every detail that is revealed about Meredith sickens me, and without Liv here, I would've lost it for sure. But because of her presence, I'm forced to keep myself together, and I'm thankful for it. Sabine stirs then and starts to cry.

"Break time, I guess," I say. Good timing, as I feel so empty after all that crying and talking in front of the camera.

"I'll order us lunch," Liv says. "Kale salad okay?"

"Yeah."

"With or without avocado?"

"With." I need the extra calories to keep shooting videos. I'm just picking Sabine up from her crib, inhaling the sweet warm scent of her, when I hear Liv curse.

"Uh, Aspen?"

Something in Liv's voice makes my ears prick up. "Yeah?"

"I think you need to come out and see this."

Sabine smiles at me, cherubic and delightful and so utterly distracting. "What is it?"

"It's Tanya. And she's saying some really bad stuff. About you."

Tanya. It takes a second for me to place the name. When I do, my insides turn to ice. Tanya Dylan. The influencer who had posted videos with Meredith months ago, declaring herself as Meredith's BFF. The mega-influencer who, for whatever reason, seems to hate my guts.

# Chapter 26

# ASPEN

I can't get to the living room fast enough. Sabine whines, but I barely hear it as I run down the hallway with her bouncing in my arms. I pause just long enough to deposit her in the playpen, ignoring her complaints, and leap to Liv's side. Liv looks up from her phone, and the expression on her face is unreadable, but one thing's for sure: she's not looking at me the way I'm used to.

"Um, let me just—start it from the beginning," she mumbles.

She taps at the video, and Tanya appears: her face perfectly done up as usual, her bee-stung lips glossy, her skin smooth as silk. "I can't keep silent anymore, you guys," Tanya says. "I haven't said anything out of respect to Meredith, and also because . . ." She pauses, sighs. "Okay, I guess part of me was scared. Aspen has a huge following, and I didn't want to turn myself into a target."

What? My lips part. What in the world am I listening to right now? With just one sentence, Tanya has turned me into a villain.

"But I heard the news about Meredith's death, and then I saw all these videos that Aspen's been posting about how they were best friends, and they were soulmates who did everything together, and I can't stand it anymore. I've just—I've had it with all the lies. You guys deserve the truth. So here it is." She pauses for dramatic effect, and in the short silence, my blood pressure shoots up. "Aspen and Meredith were *not* best friends. In fact, Aspen had hurt Meredith. Hurt her deeply. See, when Meredith found Aspen, she was nothing more than a wannabe YouTuber, floundering, going nowhere. Meredith was the one who showed her the ropes. She reached down the ladder and basically heaved Aspen up. That was the kind of person Meredith was. She was—" Here, Tanya's voice cracks, and she pauses to take a breath. "Meredith was one of the most generous and kind people I knew. But when Aspen became big, she ditched Meredith completely. Like, we're talking complete ghost mode, you guys. She'd overtaken Meredith by then, and she started being condescending towards Meredith. She only had time for her new influencer friends. This bitch dropped Meredith like a pile of hot bricks. And you know she is perfectly capable of it. Nobody buys that helpless nice person act she puts on. You've all seen that video of her screaming at some poor woman and calling her a ghoul by now, right?"

Again, that feeling of the floor giving way under me, so familiar now, washes over me. I have to focus to keep myself on my feet.

"Anyway, Meredith didn't even hold it against her. I was like, 'You should do something about it,' and she said, 'No, I'm happy for her. I'm just sad about our friendship.' That's how sweet Meredith was."

I want to scream. Rage bubbles and froths, and I want to grab Tanya's stupid face and shriek the truth at her—that Meredith did do something about it. She did a lot. She did everything. And that's precisely why we're all in this mess right now.

"And when Meredith went missing, Aspen couldn't pounce

on that news story fast enough," Tanya snorts. "I stayed silent because I thought like, well, you know what? The more eyes we get on this story, the more likely someone will find Meredith, so I let Aspen capitalize on it all she wanted. But now we know that Meredith's dead. And I can't keep watching this bitch fake-cry all over TikTok. Y'all deserve the truth. So here it is. Aspen is a fake-ass bitch. And I bet that she knows more about Meredith's death than she's letting on." With that, the video ends.

The silence in the room is so thick it has its own presence. My eyes are glued to Liv's phone, but I can sense her stare on me. When I finally meet her eyes, she actually takes a small step back.

"This is crazy," I hear myself saying.

Liv nods. "Yeah, totally."

"It's pathetic. She thinks she needs to get in on the story, and this is the only angle she can find." My voice rings in the silence, too loud. Too shrill. In the playpen, Sabine and Rain stop playing and look up at us, surprised.

Liv is quiet, chewing on her bottom lip.

"What?" I say, and even I hear the raw anger in my voice.

"Well . . ." Liv winces. "I mean, obviously I don't believe Tanya. She's totally full of shit, especially about you dropping Meredith because you got big."

"Yeah, I didn't 'drop' Meredith," I say. "She dropped me. She was the one who completely freaked out at me and then blocked my number. And all because I got more followers than she had. I only ever wanted what was best for Mer. I can't believe this is how Tanya's spinning it."

"Well, yeah, except, um . . . you know, it's true that you and Mer weren't exactly talking anymore when she disappeared," Liv mumbles.

"Yeah, so?"

Liv sighs. "I think it might look weird to people. Because we've been posting all this stuff about how you guys were best friends."

I rub the palms of my hands against my forehead with a groan. "Obviously, I wasn't going to air out my fight with Meredith. Because it didn't matter! We were best friends. Best friends fight; that's normal. I didn't want to distract from the fact that she was missing. I was only ever trying to help."

"No, I totally get it," Liv says. "I'm just saying, that's how some people might take it."

I know she's right. I want to fight Liv on this, because she's the only person around, but I know there's no use. Liv doesn't control how others are going to perceive me. But maybe Liv can help staunch the damage. If there is any damage to be fixed, that is. With luck, people will see Tanya for the attention-hungry fraud that she is and stick up for me. But when I open up TikTok, I see that I'm being way too optimistic. The first video that shows up on my FYP is from another influencer ranting about how fake I am, and how they should look into the GoFundMe page that I'd set up for Clara and Luca because she's willing to bet money that I really set it up for myself.

"Unbelievable," I mutter. "We need to post something now. A response to show that we're on the right side here."

Liv nods hesitantly. "What will you say?"

"I don't know, just shoot the video. It's better if it comes from the heart."

Instead of lifting up her phone as I expected, Liv continues standing there, chewing her lip. "I don't know, Aspen. I think this time you need to pause and really think about what to say."

"You were the one harping about being #authentic this

whole—" The doorbell rings then, the sound slicing through the air like a scythe. We both jump. Who the hell could it be? I walk to the front door and open it, and light explodes in my face. Cameras flashing, blinding me. I stand there, blinking owlishly, my mind short-circuiting.

"Aspen!" a reporter calls out. "Can you say a few words about Meredith's death?"

"I—what?" I heard his question perfectly clear, of course I did, but my mind is refusing to comprehend what the hell is happening. The thing with social media fame is that there is a clear divide between social media and mainstream news media. The paps rarely ever follow people like us, not unless we've got fifty million followers. Or, as it turns out, unless someone in our circle is found brutally murdered.

"Do you have any responses to Tanya Dylan's claims about you and Meredith being sworn enemies?" another reporter shouts.

"We weren't sworn enemies," I snap back without thinking. Immediately, the knot of reporters shouts out another barrage of questions. *Shit, I shouldn't have said anything.* I'm about to retreat into the sanctuary of the house when I see a familiar car pulling up on the curb. The doors open and my heart sinks. It's Detective Garza and Detective Clarke. The reporters swing their cameras round and click away as the two cops walk up the driveway. Oh my god, how must this all look right now? Cops coming to my house? I must appear innocent. I mustn't look scared, even though everything inside me is shrieking in pure terror. I summon up a smile, and the cameras flash away at me. Belatedly, I realize how wrong it looks, smiling at a time like this, and quickly drop it, but it's too late. I'm now the psycho who stands at the door and smiles as cops come to question her about her best friend's murder.

"Hi, Mrs. Palmer," Detective Garza says. "Sorry to disturb you. Can we come in?"

I can only nod and step aside. The last thing I see as I close the door is the crowd of unforgiving lenses trained at my face, the shutters clicking away. I lock the door and take in the blessed silence of the house, trying my best to grasp at any semblance of calm. The detectives stand before me, and Liv is right behind them, carrying Rain.

"Uh, I just remembered I have a lot of errands to run," Liv says. I think she's trying to smile, but it comes off more as a grimace. "I'm just gonna—sorry, 'scuse me, detectives." She slides past them. "See you!" She scoots past me and is out through the door in less than five seconds.

The two detectives' eyes never leave me. "She looks familiar," Detective Garza says after a beat.

"She's my PA. Liv Boyer."

"That's right. @LivBoo," Detective Clarke says. "She's been in most of your recent videos."

"Mm, yeah, that is her. Wow, I didn't recognize her in person," Detective Garza says. "Would've liked to have a chat with her. But I suppose we can just drop by her place after this."

Sabine, finding herself alone in the living room, begins to fuss. "Sorry, I need to—"

"Yes, of course," Detective Clarke says.

I rush to the living room and pick Sabine up. Her onesie is soaked through with pee, and with a rush of guilt, I realize that I didn't change her diaper after her nap. I was going to, but Tanya's video had sidelined me. "I'm so sorry, baby," I whisper. When I turn around, I jump. The two detectives have followed me into the living room. "Uh." I catch myself and force a polite smile. I gesture at the sofa. "Please, take a seat. I need to change her diaper."

"Take your time," Detective Garza says.

As I hurry off, I analyze our short interaction. Are they behaving any differently toward me? Is there suspicion in their eyes? A note of accusation in their voices? I can't tell. I force myself to focus fully on changing Sabine's diaper, hoping this mundane task will calm me down. More than anything, I need to be in full control of my emotions right now. I can't afford to lose my shit. I take a deep breath and let it out slowly. Then I pick Sabine up and walk back into the living room.

"Can I make you a drink? Maybe another matcha latte?" As soon as I hear the words leave my mouth, I want to kick myself. Who the hell would be offering a matcha latte when she's just found out that her best friend has been murdered? I make my chin wobble. "Sorry, I know that sounds ridiculous. I'm just trying to hold on to any semblance of normalcy."

Detective Clarke nods sympathetically. "I understand. Please, Mrs. Palmer, take a seat. Don't worry about us. We won't be here long."

*Really?* I want to squeak.

"We're sorry for your loss," Detective Garza says.

I nod, not trusting myself to speak.

"We saw your videos. You were obviously heartbroken," Detective Clarke says. "We had hoped to find Ms. Lee alive." He shakes his head and sighs. "We know how tough this must be for you, but could you walk us through the last time you saw Ms. Lee alive again?"

"I—I don't understand. I told you, the last time I saw her was months and months ago. Isn't Clara the one you need to be talking to?"

"We've talked to Clara Lee," Detective Garza says. "Don't worry about that; we are talking to everyone and anyone that Meredith might have come in contact with in the last six months."

Maybe that's true? Maybe this is just routine questioning? Or maybe I'm just a fool who's being overly optimistic.

"What can you remember about the last time you saw Meredith?"

"It's been so long . . ."

"Any details you can think of will be helpful," Detective Clarke says gently.

I nod, trying to sift through the jumbled mess in my head. "Um, well, I told you she was unhappy about how fast my social media accounts were growing. She told me she felt we weren't good for each other anymore and she wanted to take some time away from our friendship." God, that sounds so bad. Does it? I make sure to keep my tone as neutral as possible. "It's just a silly little argument."

"Doesn't sound little to me," Detective Garza says. "If one of my friends told me she didn't want to see me anymore, I would be devastated. Did it not upset you?"

"I mean . . ." I grope around for the right words. "I wasn't happy, obviously. But I understood. I wasn't going to try and stop her or anything. I have a lot on my plate." I nod at Sabine, who's babbling away happily on my lap. "I've got three kids. Two of them are twins, so I haven't slept in years. I have a booming career to manage. Honestly? I was kind of relieved when Meredith said she needed some space." I grimace. "Sorry, I know that makes me sound like an awful friend."

"Not at all," Detective Garza says. "You have your own life; I get it."

I nod and smile sadly.

"But . . ." she continues. "In your latest videos, you didn't mention any of this. You made it seem like you've been in constant contact with Meredith."

My cheeks and forehead and neck grow hot and sticky. It's exactly what Liv pointed out earlier. But you know what? Being fake online isn't a crime. I need to remember that. "Yeah," I say. "I hate that I had to do it that way, but I hope you understand; my main concern these past few days was getting word out there about Meredith's disappearance. I didn't want to distract people from the real purpose, which is to find her."

Detective Clarke nods. "Makes sense."

"Um, can I ask?" I say, "What was—um, did she—um, did she suffer?" My voice breaks then, and I cover my mouth with one hand.

The two detectives look at each other. "The coroner's report isn't out yet, so we can't say anything definitively," Detective Garza says.

"Oh my god," I moan. "Meredith."

"I'm sorry this is so hard for you," Detective Garza says. "But we do have a few more questions. Do you think we can keep going?"

I nod, my face still a picture of sorrow. "Yeah. I want to help any way I can. I—do you have any suspects yet?"

"We're looking at a few leads. With cases that are as high profile as this, there tend to be a lot of voices thrown into the mix." Detective Garza studies me, and I can't tell if she's buying my act. "Can you recall, at any time after your falling-out with Meredith, did your paths ever cross?"

I mull her question over. The answer, of course, is yes. They crossed multiple times. We were often invited to the same events, the same parties. I decide there's no point in lying; they'd find this out soon enough. "Yes, here and there. We sometimes were invited to the same parties. But I respected her space. I knew she didn't want to talk to me."

"Other than parties?" Detective Garza says. "Anything else?"

I shake my head. "I can't think of anything."

Her eyebrows raise. "We've been studying Meredith's movement in the weeks leading up to her disappearance. And there were a few things we found somewhat interesting."

There's that sense of danger again, the lizard brain stirring, tensing up at the presence of a predator's attention. "Oh?" I say.

"We've been talking to a lot of her contacts," Detective Garza says, "and a few of them mentioned that they got to know Meredith because they happened to run into her while they were waiting for a meeting with you. Apparently, you didn't show up to these meetings, and Meredith happened to be there, too, so they ended up working with her instead. Does that strike you as strange?"

Oh god, oh god. Run. Run now. Run fast. Somehow, I manage to sit still, though my fear is an all-encompassing entity, swallowing me whole into its red mouth. I shake my head slowly. "I'm sorry, I don't understand."

"If it happened once, that would be nothing—just a coincidence that she happened to be at a place where you were supposed to meet with a sponsor. But we've now talked to three separate people who said this happened to them. That's more than a coincidence."

"It's a pattern," Detective Clarke agrees. They both look at me, and I swear they're not blinking.

"I—yes, I suppose that is strange. But I'm not sure what to make of it," I say, adding a stupid, girlish laugh. Look at me, I'm just an airhead.

"Do you tend to miss important appointments, Aspen?" Detective Garza says. "Because these people seem to be bigwigs in your industry."

No, you condescending cunt, I don't tend to miss important appointments. Nobody gets to where I am by missing important appointments. I give that stupid, self-deprecating laugh again—the one that makes me sound like I have an IQ of seventy—and say, "Oh, you know how it is. Like I said, I have three kids, and the inside of my head is like, argh!" I mime a head explosion.

"I get that," Detective Garza says, not letting up. She's like a dog with a bone. "But don't you think it's strange that Meredith was at all of these meetings? What are the chances of that?"

"Yeah, that is strange." I nod, my mind whizzing ahead. How do I play this? Act ignorant. "I don't really—I'm not quite following. I don't understand how she could've possibly been at these places."

"It's curious, that's for sure," Detective Clarke says. Of the two of them, he's still the more sympathetic one, so I focus my poor, confused gaze on him.

"I really don't know what to tell you, I'm sorry." I look down at Sabine and stroke her back.

"Fair enough," Detective Garza says. "That's for us to figure out. But one more question before we move on from this." She leans forward, going in for the kill. "What did you do when you found out that Meredith got these sponsorship deals and partnerships over you?"

When is a question not a question? When it's an attack. It slices right into my gut, carving me open, exposing all of my insides to the world. For a second, I just sit there, frozen, with no idea how to respond. Then I give myself a mental shake and force a confused smile to my face. "I don't know what you mean, Detective. I didn't really do anything."

"Walk me through what happened on your end. You had these meetings set up, yes?"

I nod.

"And you didn't turn up because, what, you forgot?"

No, it's because Meredith sabotaged me. God, I need a way out. I can't sit here and be attacked like this anymore. But then it hits me. The perfect answer. "Well, actually, it's more like I realized they weren't the right partner for my brand. Branding is very important in my line of work. I'm all about being authentic to my fans. I can't be selling products I don't believe in."

Detective Garza narrows her eyes. "And you didn't bother calling to cancel the appointments?"

I give an apologetic grimace. "I probably meant to, but then forgot. Like I said, it's a mess up there," I say, pointing at my head.

"So when you found out that Meredith got the sponsorship deals instead of you, were you upset?"

I widen my eyes. "Gosh, no! To be honest with you, I wasn't even aware that she'd gotten these deals. I told you before, I have so much on my plate. And even after we fell out, I always hoped she'd do well. I loved her. She was the one who taught me how to succeed as an influencer. I only ever wished the best for her." The thing with the best lies is, they all have a kernel of truth in them. And this one is no exception. No one can deny the sincerity in my voice because yes, I did want what was best for Mer.

Detective Garza leans back, still studying me. I've thrown

her off balance for a bit; I can tell. But she's not convinced. She thinks there's something fishy here, and she's right. What are the chances that Meredith would happen to be at the places where I was supposed to meet with sponsors, over and over again? Zero, that's what. Then she takes out her phone, scrolls for a bit, and plays me a video.

A crushing grip catches hold of my midsection. Because it's a video of me at the pediatrician's office, from that time I missed Sabine's vaccine appointment. I watch, wide-eyed, as I stride over to the camera and hiss at the woman recording me.

"You seemed pretty upset here," Detective Garza says when the video ends.

I shake my head, trying to clear it, trying to come up with a good explanation. "I—well, yeah. That was me missing my baby's vaccine appointment. Of course I was upset. That's different from missing a meeting with a sponsor."

"Is it?" Detective Garza exchanges a glance with Detective Clarke. "I wouldn't know; I'm not a mom. But seems to me they would both be very frustrating."

"I'm a mom, first and foremost," I say, and it's a wonder how I manage to make my voice come out even. "My priority is taking care of my girls." There is nothing more I want than to look away, but somehow I keep my eyes trained on Detective Garza.

Her mouth opens, like she's about to say something, but the front door opens and there's the sound of running feet.

"Mommy? Mommy!" The next moment, Elea and Noemie appear in the living room, both of them crying. Ben follows behind them, looking haggard, an empty shell of a man. When he sees the detectives, he stops short, his mouth parting.

I stand, thanking my lucky stars. With the twins home, there is no way that this cursed interview can go on. And next time, I'll be much better prepared. I'll be lawyered up by then, for one thing. "These are Detectives Garza and Clarke," I say to Ben, right before wrapping the twins in a hug. "Oh, babies. It'll be okay."

"It won't be!" Elea cries. "Aunt Mer is dead! Everyone's talking about it at school!"

The two detectives stand there, looking uncomfortable. Noemie—shy, sweet Noemie—is the one who looks up at them and says, "Are you going to catch the bad guy who did it?"

Detective Clarke nods, his face softening. "We will."

Ben still hasn't said a word. He's just staring at them like a stupefied little kid.

"We'll leave you to it," Detective Clarke says, nodding at me. "We'll let you know if we have any follow-up questions. And don't hesitate to call us if you think of anything."

I nod, and we all stand there, clutching at each other, as the detectives leave the house.

# Chapter 27

# ASPEN

Everything has shifted. In the space of a single day, I go from Meredith's champion to her villain. More people are coming out and corroborating Tanya's claims that Meredith and I were fighting. Worse than fighting, actually. "Sworn enemies," one of them called us. "Jealous bully," another called me. "Meredith's nemesis," said another. And on and on.

I lose followers and gain others, but I know that the new ones I've gained aren't my supporters; most of them are here to enjoy the carnage. The trolls start up again, and all my posts are inundated with rape and death threats. I report them to TikTok and Instagram, but there are so many of them that I'm soon overwhelmed. I try calling Liv to ask her to delete them for me, but she doesn't pick up the phone. How's that for irony? Mere days ago, she'd been begging me to do cross-promo content with her, and now she's ghosting me.

I spend the rest of the day trying to ignore the incessant clamoring online and outside my house. And at the back of my mind, there's still the question of who the hell had messaged Damien to cancel our meeting. I know it feels frivolous to be worrying about that now, but I can't stop picking at it, like a wound that's refusing to heal. Someone did this, and that someone is still around. A loose thread, hanging there for anyone to pull. And if someone did pull at this thread, what is going to be unraveled?

We close all of the blinds in the house, shrouding it completely, and whenever I peek through the slits in the blinds, the knot of reporters remains, like a tumor that refuses to be excised. Ben calls an old college friend of his who is a lawyer, and he promises to come up with a referral for me. I swing back and forth between wanting to post a response and wanting to lie low. What the hell should I do? I need crisis control. For the first time in my career, I wish I'd signed with a talent manager. Many influencers do, but so many agencies have predatory contract clauses that I've shied away from signing with one. Boy, do I regret that decision now.

I'm about to put down the phone when it rings. I snap it back up and hit answer before belatedly realizing that the name on the screen is Clara. Oh shit. This is the one call I do not want to take.

"Aspen?" Clara's voice calls out.

Argh. I raise the phone to my ear. "Hey, Clara."

"Where have you been?" she demands. "I've been calling and calling."

"I'm sorry, it's been kind of crazy around here. The cops came by—"

"Yeah, they came here too."

"I'm sorry," I say again. There doesn't seem to be anything else to say.

"Aspen—" Clara sniffles. Her voice shakes. "The things I'm hearing . . . they're not true, are they? I mean, I know you and Mer weren't exactly close the last few months, but you didn't—you need to tell me the truth: do you know anything?"

"How can you ask me that?" The hurt in my voice isn't made up. I am truly offended. Does she understand just how much I've done for them? That GoFundMe page is going to set her up for the rest of her miserable life. "You know how much I loved her."

She sobs. "I know, I'm sorry, I'm just a huge mess right now. I can't believe she's gone. Can you—um—I need to go to the coroner's office to identify the body. I can't go alone, Aspen. I just—I can't. Please come with me?"

I swear I'm about to throw up right now. *No*, I want to scream. *I do not want to go with you to a coroner's office where I will see the half-decomposed body of your sister who I killed.* But how can I say no to Clara? *And*, a little voice adds, *this is good for your image. You need to go. Think of how good it'll look to have Clara's faith. To have the victim's sister trust in you so much that you are the person she turns to for support. The reporters will eat it right up. Confidence in you will rise.*

Yes. Of course. Once I think of that, it seems obvious that I must go. "Of course," I say to Clara. "Um, when are you going?"

"First thing tomorrow morning."

"What are you going to do with Luca while you go to the police station?"

There is silence, then Clara gives a broken sigh. "God, I didn't even think of that. It really is relentless, isn't it? Having a kid. They're just there, all the time!" She's getting shrill, panicking again.

"Don't worry about it," I say in a soothing voice. "Just come by my house and you can drop him off here. Ben will look after him and Sabine. It'll be good for Luca to have some playtime with Sabine. You and I can even drive to the station together."

"Really? Oh, thank you, Aspen. You are a lifesaver."

My mouth crooks into a small smile. *I am the opposite of that,* I think bitterly as I hang up.

In the morning, Ben does the school drop-off with the twins. He doesn't even complain about it; he just nods somberly and herds the girls into the car, his face pale, his mouth set in a grim line. He still can barely look at me, and every time he does, I catch that disgusted twitch in his lips, but at least he doesn't say anything. I guess he's probably worrying about his own little secret—he kissed Meredith. I wonder if the detectives will find out about that at some point. They seem to be doing a whole lot of digging. If they do, it's going to look bad on both of us. It'll give me a motive to kill Meredith, for one. How cliché it would be; me stuck in the role of an insecure wife who, in a jealous rage, kills her best friend. If it comes to that, I'll tell them the truth: that it wasn't about Ben at all. It was about friendship.

Clara arrives ten minutes after Ben leaves, and I see her shocked expression when she spots the clump of reporters outside my house. I open the front door and wave at her to come right in. She bundles Luca in her arms and hurries up the driveway, ignoring the reporters shouting her name, asking her what she's doing here, and whether she believes I had anything to do with Meredith's murder.

"Holy shit," she says, once she's inside the house.

"I know." I shift my attention to Luca and force a smile. He looks so much like his mother, it's eerie to look at him. But I need to keep up appearances, so I hold out my arms and take

Luca from Clara, fussing over him. "Oh, look at this little angel. You poor, poor thing. My poor, sweet baby boy." I kiss the top of his head and try not to gag at the thought that I killed this poor kid's mother. "Sabbie will be so happy to see you, yes she will." I carry Luca into the living room where Sabine is already in her playpen. "Sabbie, look who's here." Sabine looks up and her whole face brightens. She raises her arms and gives an elated cry. Luca sticks his arms out and writhes in my arms, and I put him in the playpen. The two babies immediately fall into each other's arms amid giggles and coos.

Clara bursts into tears. "I'm sorry," she wails. "It's been so hard. I don't know how to be a mom. It's not at all like babysitting. He's been absolutely miserable. The only way I've kept myself going the past month was to tell myself that she'll be back, and now—" Her sobs are so hard that they rack her entire body, bending it like a banana.

"Oh, sweetheart," I say, wrapping my arms around her. "There, there. You're okay. You're going to be okay. We'll get through this." I stroke her back the way I do with the kids, firm and soothing.

Ben arrives home then and stops short when he sees Clara crying away in my arms. For a second, he looks unsure, like he's thinking of running away. But then he clears his throat. "Um, hey, Clara."

Clara lifts her head and sniffs. Ben comes over, his arms stretched out. "I'm sorry for your loss," he says.

Clara accepts the hug stiffly while I grab a tissue for her. "Thanks," she mumbles, wiping at her face. "Um, and thanks for looking after Luca while I—you know."

"Yeah, of course, anytime," Ben says, stuffing his hands into his pockets. The atmosphere in here is so awkward it's almost painful.

"Shall we go?" I say. I want to get this over and done with as quickly as possible.

Clara looks over at Luca. "Are you sure you'll be okay with him?"

"He'll be fine," I cut in. "He and Sabbie are so happy with each other. They won't even realize we're gone. And Ben is great with kids."

Ben gives a nervous smile. "Call me if you need anything," he says as Clara and I head for the side door to the garage.

Once we're inside my car, I struggle to think of something to say. What does one even say at a time like this? I back out of the garage slowly, being careful to avoid the reporters. They crowd around like a pile of red ants, taking a million pictures of me and Clara in the car. Even though all the windows are closed, I can still hear their questions.

"Are you going to see the body?"

"Clara, did you know that Aspen hated your sister?"

"Aspen, were you bullying Meredith?"

It's a relief when I finally drive out of earshot. I release my breath and glance over at Clara. "You okay?" Well, that was a stupid question to ask. She's obviously not okay.

"Not really. You?"

"Same. It's just so surreal."

Clara's mouth turns into a thin line. "I'm sorry that the vultures have turned on you."

"Yeah, it's not great, but when they find the guy who did this, they'll go away. I have faith the police will catch the sick fucker."

Clara nods, looking out the window.

"Do you have any ideas who could've done this?" I say, sneaking glances at her from my peripheral vision.

"I don't know," Clara sighs. "You know what Mer was like. Always rushing someplace. She didn't really tell me the details of her life. She was always too busy for long chats."

"Right."

"Although she did mention she was maybe interested in some guy . . ."

"Oh?" I grip the steering wheel, trying to contain my curiosity.

"She didn't tell me anything about him, though. Not even his name."

"How did they meet?"

"Who knows? She met so many people from 'the industry,'" Clara says, using air quotes. She smiles wryly at me. "God, I used to hate that word. The 'industry.'"

I snort. "We can be pretty pretentious at times, huh?"

"Yep." She lets her head fall back against the headrest. "I keep obsessing about it. Trying to remember any details she might've mentioned about the guy, but I got nothing." There's a tremor in her voice again. "My little sister was murdered, and I know nothing."

"Don't do that," I say softly. "Don't blame yourself. It's not your fault."

She nods, sniffling. We drive the rest of the way in silence.

Somehow, there are reporters in front of the police station. I stare dumbly at them, wondering how they beat us here. Then I realize, of course, that they didn't. They're probably colleagues of the ones camped outside my house. Not that it matters. A reporter is a reporter is a reporter. Clara and I brisk-walk from the parking lot through the throng of cameras clicking in our faces and shouts of "How do you feel right now, Clara?" and "Are you ready to see the body?" I put an arm around Clara's shoulders, and the cameras click away with ferocity. *Good,* I think. *Let them see what a supportive friend I'm being. And how innocent I am, obviously, because what killer would march into a freaking police station to identify the body of her own victim?*

Of course, it's easier said than done. Inside the police station, the tiny kernel of unease in my belly grows into a lump as Clara speaks to the reception officer, telling her why we're here. We're told to have a seat, and so we do. I look around me at the depressing state of the place, and at all the officers at their desks talking, typing away. They're probably working Meredith's case, I realize, and the lump grows into a rock.

"Ms. Lee?" someone calls out, and I jump. It's a clean-shaven man in his mid-forties. "Hi, I'm Matt, the coroner. Can you follow me please?"

We hurry after him down a long corridor until we reach a door that says "AUTOPSY ROOM 2." Matt stops in front of the door and regards us solemnly. "Before we start, I'd like to warn you of the nature of this procedure. It'll be disturbing. There's no other way of saying it. And I'm sorry for your loss. Now, are you ready to identify the body of Meredith Lee?"

The rock metastasizes into a boulder. *No,* I want to scream. *Leave me out here in the hallway. I'm not even a family member.* Next to me, Clara slips her hand into mine.

"Yes," she says, so quietly I almost don't hear it.

Matt nods and leads us into the room. It is lit by harsh fluorescent lights and smells so strongly of formaldehyde that my eyes start to sting. And there, in the middle of it, is an examination table with a figure lying on top of it. There is a thin blanket covering the figure. Matt steps toward the corpse and places both hands on the top edge of the blanket.

"Are you ready?" he says gently.

*No!*

Clara nods. Matt lowers the blanket. I avert my eyes. Clara squeezes my hand so tight I wince. I hear her strangled moan. "Oh god," she says. "Mer. Oh my god. Mer!"

I realize Matt is looking at me for confirmation too. I'm trapped. No other way out. I have to make myself see her body. Slowly, painfully, I drag my gaze toward the table.

The first thing I notice is how shockingly gray Meredith looks. I never gave much thought to the amount of pink and yellow there is in our skin, but the absence of pigment is striking. She is not the color of a human being. Bile rushes up, and for a second I think I might vomit. My hand is on fire. I pry it loose from Clara's death grip. Now I see more details, ones I will carry with me forever. The signs of Meredith's flesh breaking down. Her eyelids and her lips look like little creatures have been nibbling away at them gently, revealing enough of her teeth to make it look like she's grinning at us. It's too much. I wrench myself away and stumble out of the room.

Outside, I take deep gulps of air, trying to convince my lungs to keep working. Clara joins me, still sobbing. Matt comes out a second later, carrying a stack of papers. "Come with me, please," he says, and leads us to a different room. There is a single desk with four chairs around it. "Please, have a seat. There are a few forms I need you to sign."

Clara accepts the papers and a pen with shaking hands. As she signs the forms to confirm that the body is, indeed, Meredith, I struggle to keep the screaming in my head down.

Matt clears his throat. "It looks worse than it really is, due to the state of decomposition. But um, I think she died a relatively painless death."

"Painless—" Clara seems to have lost the ability to speak. She leans back in her chair, breathing hard.

"It's a good thing," I say. I need Clara to understand this one kindness I have afforded her.

"The killer probably drugged her before putting something over her face—probably a pillow—and asphyxiating her," Matt says. "I'm sorry, I know this must be hard to hear."

"Why would anyone do that?" Clara screams.

Matt grimaces. "I'm very sorry for your loss, Miss Lee. But I can't answer that. I hope the team finds the killer. Thank you for your time. You can have the room for as long as you need." With that, he slides the forms back and leaves the room.

I sit there wordlessly while Clara howls. I try to will the tears to come, but in the face of her unimaginable sorrow, my own tears seem to have dried up, so I sit and wrap my arms around Clara's shoulders and whisper meaningless, soothing words to her. My own emotions are a hurricane inside me. I don't know what I should be feeling, but every emotion feels wrong. Do I have the right to mourn my best friend's death when I was the one who caused it?

It's an eternity before Clara calms down enough for us to finally leave. I walk her out of the station and into the car, where I make sure she's buckled in before I start the engine. I take a moment to ground myself. *Focus,* I remind myself. *Getting into an accident right now isn't going to be cute.*

As I'm pulling out of the parking lot, my phone rings. I glance at it, see Ben's name, and immediately leap to the worst-case scenario: something has happened to Luca or Sabine. I hit Answer, putting him on speakerphone.

"Aspen," Ben says, and there is so much urgency in his voice that both Clara and I stiffen.

"What is it?"

"Where are you right now?"

"Just leaving the police station. Why?"

"You need to come straight home," he says in an acidic tone.

Fear claws at me, ripping into my skin. "What's happened? Is everyone okay?"

"Is it Luca?" Clara cries.

There is a pause. Then Ben says, "Am I on speakerphone?"

"Yes, oh my god, Ben, just tell me what it is; I'm driving."

"Pull over and put me off speakerphone," he says, and it comes out practically as a snarl.

Clara's mouth drops open. "What is it?" she's practically screaming. "Is Luca okay? Just tell me that right now!"

"Luca is okay. The kids are fine," Ben says, obviously fighting to put his anger in check. "I need to speak with Aspen privately."

I shoot Clara an apologetic look and pull over, my stomach churning like I'm about to be sick. I pluck the phone out of the holder, turn it off speaker mode, and press it to my ear. "What is it?" I hiss. "I hope you know you're being really rude right now."

"Fuck being rude," Ben hisses back. "What the fuck did you do, Aspen? Someone posted a video of you."

My insides turn to ice. "Wh-what video?" In the second it takes Ben to answer, my mind whizzes ahead, coming up with a thousand answers, each one more dire than the last. Does someone have footage of me killing Mer? No. It can't be that. They would've released it way before.

"It's a video of your morning routine." Accusation drips from every word.

"Oh." That doesn't sound too bad.

"Except . . . it's not a morning routine."

"Oh." I squeeze my eyes shut. Now I know what he's talking about, and it's so much worse than I thought. I want to dig a hole for myself and cover it up and never come back up.

"Yeah," Ben says. "It shows you getting the twins off the couch and into their bedrooms to pretend to wake up. It has you snapping at Elea. I mean, for fuck's sake, Aspen, this is what I've been warning you about. I've been telling you that people will find out how fucking fake you are, and now—" He pauses, his breath coming in a sharp hiss, "And the person who posted it—Tanya—she's saying that Meredith sent it to her months ago. You know how bad this looks, you stupid—you—fuck! I can't—"

My stomach is twisted so tight that I think I might actually faint. I manage to mumble, "Okay, be right there." I hang up and stare out the windshield.

"What was it?" Clara says. "Aspen?"

I can't bear to look at her. "It's fine. The kids are having a great time." My voice sounds like it's coming from afar.

"Bullshit it's fine," Clara shoots back. "You look like shit. What is it?"

I don't bother replying. Instead, I put my phone away and resume driving.

"Are you serious right now?" Clara says.

"It's nothing," I say.

"Unbelievable." She shakes her head and gazes out the window, taking in a shuddery breath. Then, shaking her head again, she mutters something and takes her phone out of her bag. For a few blessed moments, there is silence. I pray that it lasts the rest of the trip home. But then Clara goes, "What the fuck?" And she turns the volume up on her phone.

A video is playing. A video with my voice.

"—you get in bed please? Just for a second," my voice says.

"I'm busy," says Elea.

"It'll take a second. I just need you to pretend that you're waking up, okay? You'll get a star for this."

"What the hell is this?" Clara says, glaring at me.

I clamp down on the steering wheel and keep my gaze forward. My guts twist into tight knots, making me want to throw up, but somehow I manage to keep driving. The video continues playing. I hear myself scolding Elea for rolling her eyes. I hear myself chirping at them to rise and shine. Then it ends, and out comes Tanya's hateful voice.

"This is the video that Meredith sent to me. She wanted to show me what a fake bitch Aspen is, and I've held on to this video for months because y'alls know I'm not one for airing dirty laundry. But Aspen's lies have gone too far. She knows something, you guys. I mean, come on, Meredith sent me this video, and months later she's brutally killed? You're going to sit there and tell me that Aspen had nothing to do with it? I call bullshit. Justice for Meredith. Lock Aspen up!" The video ends there.

There is a shocked silence. Then Clara says, in a soft, dangerous tone I've never heard her use before, "Is this true?"

I shake my head, not trusting myself to speak. I can barely breathe. Please, let this be nothing more than a bad dream. Please.

"But it is you in the video."

I nod and clear my throat. Get a freaking grip. "Yes. We make things up; you know that. It means nothing."

"How did Meredith get a hold of it?" Clara says.

"I don't know," I cry. "I—look, I promise you, Clara, I had nothing to do with it. Nothing!"

For a second, it looks as though Clara is about to say something. Then she thinks better of it and sits still, though I notice that her right hand is now clutching the armrest of the door, as though she's preparing to open the car door and jump out at any moment. It's the longest drive of my life, the air thick and toxic with tension.

When we finally arrive at my house, Clara leaps out before the car rolls to a full stop and dashes inside, calling out, "Luca? Luca, where are you? Luca!"

Ben hurries out of the living room. "Hey, you—" Clara rushes past him. I hurry behind her. Ben looks at me questioningly, and I give a small shake of the head. We watch as Clara scoops Luca out of the playpen and shoulders past us, refusing to meet our eyes. At the door, she pauses long enough to say, "Don't come near us ever again."

"Clara—" I say, but already she's opened the door.

She practically sprints away from our house, her shoulders hunched, her expression probably thunderous. The reporters are clamoring at her, shouting, "Clara, did Aspen kill your sister?"

I slam the door shut and let my head fall back against it. Oh god. How could I possibly have thought that things couldn't get any worse? *Anytime now, I'm going to be arrested,* I think. I open my eyes and the first thing I see is Ben, still staring at me with that awful expression on his face, like he's seeing a particularly disgusting centipede crawling across his meal.

"Did your friend get back to you with the lawyer's number?" I manage to say.

Instead of answering, Ben's mouth twists, his face turning ugly. "I'm only going to ask you this once, Aspen." He steps closer to me, and now I feel afraid. I am a tiny animal trapped by a hungry wolf. Ben might feel small, but physically he is anything but. The muscles in his arms ripple as he raises them, and I shrink back.

"Don't—"

"Did you kill her?" he snarls, his face so close to mine that I feel the heat of his breath on my skin.

I can only shake my head. Ben stays there for a few seconds, taking me in, his face completely devoid of any affection. Nothing but the detached look of a hunter wondering how best to cut open the carcass of his latest catch. Then he says, "If I find out that you've been endangering our family, Aspen? You'll be on your own." He turns and stalks off.

I'm shaking. My legs give out from under me, and I slide to the floor. For a few moments back there, I was convinced that I'm not the only one in this house who's capable of murder.

# Chapter 28

# ASPEN

As I walk through the impressive lobby of the office building, I scroll through my inbox. There are a lot of emails. Many of them begin: "We regret to inform you that, due to recent events, we will be terminating our partnership agreement . . ." Even more of them begin: "You are a lying fake murdering bitch; you better watch your back . . ." Followers on TikTok: eight million, though anyone would be hard-pressed to call them fans. What do you call people who hate-follow you? Trolls? Stalkers?

The receptionist tells me that Prasad, Carey, and Associates is located on the twenty-second floor. I pretend not to notice the judgmental look on her face as I head for the elevators. I can't stop picking at my fingernails as the elevator goes up. At least the receptionist here is more professional. She doesn't even bat an eyelid when I tell her my name. I'm taken to a meeting room and given a glass of water. I'm just about to take a sip when Helena Carey walks in.

"Aspen?" she says, and her voice is somehow soothing and yet firm. The kind of voice that makes you immediately trust her. She is a blonde woman in her mid-forties, stunningly beautiful, in a silver skirt suit that looks like it was designed specifically for her. "Hi, I'm Helena. Nice to meet you."

"Thank you for agreeing to meet with me," I say nervously. I'm a successful businesswoman myself, but the kind of success that Helena has is something else entirely, and I don't know how to present myself to someone as intellectual as her.

"Of course. I've been following your case. It's quite something." She settles into the chair adjacent to mine and folds her hands over her lap, giving me her full attention. "Now, tell me everything."

I came prepared, of course. I rehearsed what I could tell her—went through every detail until I was sure what I could and could not say. "Well, my friend Meredith died, and everyone thinks I did it," I begin. I tell Helena a lot more things than I told the detectives. I tell her how bad the fight with Meredith really was; that it wasn't just a minor disagreement; that it was a screaming fight—the kind that left both of us destroyed. I tell her how hard it was for me afterwards to have that Meredith-shaped hole in my life, an open wound that is still seeping blood. I tell her everything except the one crucial fact about me killing Meredith. It goes without saying, of course, that I also leave out the part about Meredith stealing Elea's iPad.

Helena listens without saying anything, nodding here and there, but otherwise showing no reaction. When I'm finally done speaking, she says, "Well, that is certainly a lot." She considers me for a bit, then says, "My retainer is two thousand dollars. My hourly rate is eight hundred dollars. And here is what you will get from me in return: I will be your champion. It will be a bloodbath, and you're going to want a fighter, and that's who I am. I don't like to fight dirty, but if I have to, I will."

"I want to work with you," I say quickly.

She smiles. "Good. I want to work with you too. All right, now that we've got that out of the way, let's talk strategy. Do you have any idea how Meredith could have gotten access to your personal videos?"

My mouth goes dry, and I shake my head.

Helena taps her chin with a manicured finger. "Are your photos and videos uploaded to a cloud?"

"Yes."

"Change the password."

"I did that already."

"Set up a two-step authentication for everything. I'll have the team look into how Meredith got a hold of it. On your end, what you need to do is damage control. You need to get your followers on your side. You stopped posting two days ago. That's not good."

"That was when Tanya's video came out. The one where I—" I grimace.

"Where you faked a morning routine video," Helena says. Ouch. "Right. We are going to use this to our advantage."

"How?"

"Lean into it. Release more videos that show the reality of your life. Behind-the-scenes videos. People love those."

"But they're going to hate me!" I cry, wondering if I've made a mistake hiring Helena after all.

"They won't, because you're going to be talking to them, and you're going to be real and vulnerable and above all, authentic. You'll tell them about how difficult it is to be a momfluencer. Talk about how everyone sets such unrealistic standards that you feel like a failure. You're always messing up, you're depressed, anxious—everybody is depressed and anxious; they'll relate to you. One of your daughters has diabetes, right?"

I nod. "Noemie, yes."

"Talk about that. The burden of having to earn enough to pay for her healthcare. I assume you're paying out of pocket?"

I nod again.

"Have Noemie be in the shot with you. Appeal to the sympathy of your fellow mothers. You know how to do that."

I stare at her, open-mouthed. The woman is a magician. Holy shit. "What do I say about Meredith?"

"Say nothing about Meredith. This is about you shedding light on the industry. It's about you fighting for authenticity. Let me handle the subject of Meredith. Got it?"

I have to bite down hard on my lip to stop myself from bawling. The past couple of days have been nothing short of a nightmare, and here, finally, is someone who's reaching down into the depths of the hole I've been thrown into. Handing me a lifeline.

"You've got this, Aspen. I've seen your videos; you're good. You can do this. You can make the world love you again," Helena says, and when she says it, I believe her.

When I get home, Ben is slouched on the sofa with the twins and Sabine, *Peppa Pig* playing on the TV. I fleetingly think of how, before our world imploded, I would've gotten irritated if he'd allowed Sabine to watch TV. Our rule is simple: no screen time before the age of one. How laughable it is, now, to be concerned with such meaningless rules. Ben barely bothers to lift his head from the couch, even when I greet them.

"How did the meeting go?" he says, still staring at the TV. I want to scream at him. He could at least pretend to give a shit about my life. But since that god-awful moment when I'd been convinced he was about to hurt me, he's retreated into a thick shell, barely existing on this plane of reality.

"Really good. She says I need to keep posting videos."

He scoffs, a hateful sound that reaches deep into my core and ignites me. "Of course she did. The answer to everything."

I'm this close to lunging at him and grabbing him by the collar and screaming, *Well I don't see you coming up with a better idea*, so I turn and walk out of the living room. I go to the bathroom and splash some cold water on my face, then I take a long look in the mirror. God, I look so tired. This isn't the face of All Day Aspen. But maybe that's a good thing. Maybe this is exactly what people want to see.

I go to the living room and say, "Hey, Noemie, can you come here and help Mommy with something, please?"

She looks hesitant, but slides down the couch and follows me. I lead her to her bedroom, an aesthetically pleasing space painted in pastel shades of brown and pink, with a white cotton tent hanging down from the ceiling between the girls' twin beds. I sit down on Noemie's bed and pat the spot next to me, and she settles there, leaning against me.

"Are you going to prison?" she says in a small voice.

Tears prick my eyes. "No, baby. I'm never going to leave you."

Noemie wrings her hands. "It's just that . . . all the other kids at school are saying you're going to prison."

"Well, they don't know what they're talking about. Mommy had a little adventure today. She went to meet with someone called a lawyer."

Noemie gives me a tired smile. "You don't have to talk to me like I'm a baby. I know what lawyers are. They taught us during Career Week."

God, this kid. How can one heart possibly love anyone this much? "Sorry, my bad. I hired a really good lawyer, and she gave me some homework."

"But lawyers aren't teachers. Only teachers can give you homework."

"Not true, actually. But never mind that. The homework she gave me is to make a video with you."

Noemie's little face scrunches up into a frown. "Why?"

"Mommy needs to tell the world the truth about our situation. Why Mommy has been working so hard. And you're part of the family, which is why I need you to be in the video too."

"What about Elea and Sabbie and Daddy?"

The thought of having to herd everyone into complying to a long, heartfelt video makes my head throb. "Just you, sweetheart."

Noemie looks down at her lap. "It's because of my diabetes, isn't it?"

My heart tears itself apart. "Yes and no. But listen, sweetheart, I would not have you any other way. You are my perfect little angel, do you hear me?"

"I don't want everyone to know about my diabetes," she says, wringing her hands.

"Oh, sweetie, there's nothing to be ashamed of. It's going to help so many people to know that you're going through it. You're raising awareness about the disease, and that's a really good thing."

Noemie raises her face and looks at me, her eyes round and worried. "I don't know," she mumbles.

It's a struggle to keep calm. *Please,* I want to beg her, *do this for Mommy. You don't know how much I stand to lose.* But I know

I need to remain confident. In control. "Okay, how about this? You don't need to say or do anything. Just be next to me while I make the video. Is that all right?"

She leans her head against me, and I give her a fierce hug. "Okay, you ready?" She nods, and relief floods my senses. I've got to move fast before she changes her mind. I turn my phone camera on and aim it at us, adjusting it slightly for a more flattering angle.

"Hi, everyone," I say. "I think it's time I tell you all the truth." I pause, sighing, but still stoic. No overt emotions. "By now, you have all seen the video that Tanya posted. The one where I was, ah . . ." I have to pause to control my emotions, "where I was faking a morning routine video." I look down reassuringly at Noemie. "That video isn't a deepfake of me or anything. It really was me in there, running around like a madwoman, bribing my own kids into making a fake morning routine video. There are no excuses for why I did what I did. I'm here to say sorry to all of you, especially to my loyal fans, for lying to you.

"When I first started posting online, all I wanted to do was to share bits and pieces of my life with all of you. I didn't want to be anyone's role model. I just wanted to be me. More and more people found me, and I'm so grateful to all of you for your support. Then I had the kids, and . . ." I squeeze Noemie closer to me and plant a kiss on the top of her head. "I've never known love like this before. And fear. I've never known fear like this before. Suddenly, I had everything to lose. And when we found out that Noemie here has diabetes, I think . . ." I pause and look up at the ceiling, blinking furiously. "Something in me broke. I would do anything for my kids. It's no secret that when you get a certain number of followers, you can start monetizing your accounts. I had to earn enough not just to get by, but to pay off our healthcare, to make sure Noemie gets her insulin every day. And I needed to save up money, because we all know how fickle social media is. I just want to provide for my family.

"I tried being authentic, for a while. But—" I give a rueful laugh. "The real me? Is a mess, you guys. I don't get up at five in the morning to do sun salutations before making sourdough focaccia from scratch. Who does that? Well, you know who does? Everybody on Instagram and TikTok, it seems. I felt like everyone else, every momfluencer on here, has their shit together. And I'm the only one missing the puzzle pieces to make it all make sense. I watched all this mom content and tried so hard to be like them, but I couldn't do it." And here, I let the tears come. "I don't have my shit together like the other momfluencers do. I'm a mess. The only way I can keep up with everyone else on here is to fake it. So that was what I did. What you saw in that video of me pushing my kids into getting in bed at four in the afternoon? That was sheer desperation. And I hate myself so much for doing that. I am sorry. From now on, I promise, no more filters. In fact, I'm going to start showing you the real stuff. I'll show you a curated, edited video, followed by the real, full-length video to show you just how much it takes to come up with good TikTok- or Insta-friendly content. Until then, thank you for watching."

I end the recording and look down at Noemie. She looks up at me. "That was good."

"Really?" I wipe the tears from my face and smile at her.

"Yeah. Did you really mean it? About showing them the real stuff?" Noemie says.

"Yeah."

She gives me a small smile. "Cool. Can I go watch *Peppa Pig* now?"

"Yes. Thank you for being here for Mommy." I hug her tight and then let her go, smiling as she skips out of the room. Then I send the video off to Helena with the message: "How's this?" Two minutes later, she replies: "Perfect. I knew you could do it."

I swallow, hesitating, then I open up TikTok and upload the video. For the caption, I type out: "Real talk. No more filters. #authenticity." I take a deep breath. Here goes. I hit Post.

I don't sit there waiting around for the responses to come in. As soon as it's up on TikTok, I close down the app and post the video to Instagram. Then I close that, too, and go out of the twins' room and into the kitchen, where I open the fridge and start taking out ingredients to make dinner. As I take out a few bell peppers, it hits me that, for once, I don't need to pretend that they're freshly picked from my backyard, nor do I need to worry about the position of my arms as I chop the veg, because there isn't a phone camera hovering over the cutting board. For once, all I need to do is simply cook.

I'm chopping the bell peppers when Ben saunters into the kitchen. Right away, from his body language, I know to expect a fight. My guard goes up, though I'm careful not to show it. I keep my eyes on the chopping board, refusing to give him an opening for an argument. He strolls past me to the fridge. By the clicking of the glass bottle, I know he's taken out a beer. I bite my tongue. *Just focus on the bell peppers.*

"What's for dinner?" he says. There is a clink as he opens the bottle.

"Just a simple roasted butternut squash and bell pepper soup. We've got half a loaf of ciabatta that'll go really well with it."

"Hm," Ben says, taking a big gulp of beer. He leans against the countertop, uncomfortably close to me. As I chop, my left elbow grazes his arm, and goosebumps break out across my arms. It's not a pleasant touch, not a romantic one. It feels as though I've touched an eel. But I won't be the first one to move away.

Since when did I start fearing my husband? I don't understand when this shift happened. Has he always had this meanness in him? Have I just been so preoccupied with everything else that I failed to notice his sharp edges? Or did this whole thing break him, and in doing so, created jagged pieces that are now attempting to slice me open?

"I saw your video," Ben says. Another swig. The bottle must be half-empty already, and he only opened it half a minute ago.

"Oh?" I won't ask him what he thinks about it. I won't. "What do you think about it?" Damn it.

"'Sgood. Is that what your lawyer told you to do?" The words "your lawyer" are said in a very pointed tone.

"Yeah. She said it's important for me to win back the public opinion."

"Well, you should be used to that by now," Ben says.

*What's that supposed to mean?* I want to snap, but I know perfectly well what he meant by it. I refuse to show him how needled I am by that statement. Smiling, I say, "Yeah, I guess I am."

"What else did you and your lawyer talk about?"

This feels more like an interrogation than a conversation. I finish chopping up the last of the bell pepper and move on to the squash. "Well, it was mostly me filling her in on everything. I guess that's what most first-time consultations are. But I liked her. I think I'm in good hands."

Ben scoffs, and I pretend not to hear it. "Did you really tell her everything?"

"Yeah, of course I did."

Ben takes another swallow of beer. "Because you shouldn't hide things from your attorney."

This time, I turn to face him, the knife I'm using to chop vegetables gripped tight in my hand. "What are you trying to say, Ben?"

He shakes his head. There is so much mistrust and judgment in the way he looks at me that I instinctively want to hide behind the counter to put as much between us as possible. After a beat, he says, "See, the thing that keeps niggling at the back of my mind, Aspen, is . . . where were you that night?"

Ice trails down my spine. "What night?"

"About a month ago, we had a fight. One of many," he snorts. "You said you were going to sleep in Sabine's room. I went to get a beer, but we were out, so I went out and got some. Went to bed. In the morning, I woke up, and there you were: my beautiful, perfect wife, cooking breakfast for the family as usual."

"I'm not sure what you're getting at." I turn away from him and start chopping up the butternut squash so he won't see the guilt that must be written all over my face. My very hot face. My gaze is kept with laser focus on the squash I'm slicing into, but my brain isn't registering anything aside from his words.

"Well . . ." He drinks the rest of the beer and sets the empty bottle next to the chopping board. "Sabine woke up at around four, maybe five in the morning. Her diaper was full. I had to go in and change it. And you weren't there."

Chop, chop, chop. As long as I keep chopping, everything will be okay.

"I thought about confronting you. I assumed you were

sleeping with some other guy. Might as well; it's not like we ever do anything in bed with each other." He takes out another beer. "But now I'm starting to wonder. Maybe it wasn't another guy. Because the timing with Meredith's death . . . it's all a bit too much of a coincidence, isn't it?"

I straighten up and face him, fixing him with a cutting glare. "If you're accusing me of murder, Ben, I think our marriage is well and truly done."

He wavers a little, but stands his ground. "So where were you that night?"

It's time for my trump card. "How come you never told me that you saw Meredith at your open house?"

His mouth drops open, and I wonder at how utterly stupid he looks right now. How ugly and stupid and hateful. "Who told you that?"

"Doesn't matter. Maybe you were the last one who saw Meredith alive."

Ben takes a step back as though I've just hit him. "Do not go down this path, Aspen. I'm not fucking around."

I stare at him just a moment longer before turning back to the cutting board. For a few excruciating moments, neither of us speaks. Then I say, neutrally, "Dinner will be ready in about half an hour."

Ben turns and strides out of the kitchen without another word.

I'm scared that dinner will be a silent, awkward affair, the tension between me and Ben painfully visible. Elea and Noemie are old enough now to sense when we're fighting, and the last thing the girls need is an unstable home. But then I hear the front door open and close, and a minute later, Ben's car starts up and drives away, and I breathe a sigh of relief even as anger stirs in my chest. He's just left without even telling me. But then again, good riddance. I find myself half-hoping that he'll get into a car crash. Then, of course, I feel awful for even thinking that. What kind of monster wishes for her husband to die? The kind that is being cornered by said husband.

I push the hideous thoughts away. After putting the squash and bell peppers in the oven, I finally pick up my phone and open TikTok. The video I posted less than an hour ago already has nine hundred thousand views and two hundred thousand Likes. With no small amount of trepidation, I tap on the comments.

LightYurr: This is the realest thing I've seen today. Love U, Aspen!!!

Elleies: GUYS IM CRYING THIS GOT ME IN THE FEELS

Seeweed10: Srsly it's impossible to keep up with all these momfluencers, I wish more ppl would be this real

Tears sting my eyes. Oh my god. Could Helena be right? That this was all I had to do to get people on my side? That in the end, what might save me is showing them the real me? I check Instagram, and the responses are just as good as the ones on TikTok. There are a few haters here and there, but they are drowned by all of the heartfelt comments from moms gushing about how I'm keeping it real.

While waiting for the vegetables to roast, I scroll through my old videos, trying to find one that's authentic without being too damning. I reject many of them before finally finding one. It's of me cleaning the house. If someone had said to me ten years ago that videos of people cleaning their own houses would be a huge thing, I wouldn't have believed them. But they are, and so here I am, recording myself cleaning up. But the thing is, while I do it, I'm also bitching about how much mess there is in the house. How nobody ever helps me tidy up. The twins are forever leaving their toys everywhere, and Ben's shit is all over every available surface. Multiple times throughout the real video, I slump in a chair, exhausted, and bury my face in my hands.

In the edited video, I fast-forwarded the original footage by a multiple of eight, cut out all the depressing parts, and replaced the audio with relaxing classical music. The result is a one-minute-long video that is both therapeutic and satisfying to watch. The house starts out untidy, the house ends up beautifully clean, and the viewer doesn't even have to lift a finger.

I stitch the edited video with the original video and add a voiceover of me narrating. "Here is a video I posted a while ago of me cleaning my house. It looks quick and fun and relaxing. Here is the real footage of me cleaning my house. It wasn't quick, or fun, and it definitely wasn't relaxing. As you can see, I lost hope various times. I sat down and thought about giving up. I cursed a lot. I cried. I resented my family for not helping me. And you might be wondering why they don't help me. The answer is: they think it's my job. Because my career is a lifestyle brand, and so they think keeping a beautiful home is part of my career. I don't know, I mean, obviously that's bullshit, and I could probably force them into helping me if I really wanted to, but I just wanted the house to be cleaned, you know? So yeah. And, to be honest with y'all, I thought that this way I would be able to clean the way I want to clean. And get a video out of it. But it's so tiring to keep this up for social media. I want you all to know that your houses don't have to be pristine. Mine is rarely pristine. This is the real me. Later, you guys."

I send the video to Helena, and as I'm taking the vegetables out of the oven, she replies: "Genius!" Smiling, I post the video, then blend the vegetables up into a creamy soup.

Dinner without Ben is actually a relief. Elea and Noemie are beautifully behaved, and Sabine loves dipping her ciabatta into the soup and smearing it all over her face. My phone is face down as per our no-gadgets-at-the-table rule, but my watch is silently buzzing nonstop as Likes and positive comments pour in. I take a peek at my watch once in a while, and my god, how adoring the comments are. The watch only shows snippets of them, but they are glowing.

`My husband never helps me with . . .`

`No but why is this so relatable . . .`

`OK this one got me crying, you . . .`

After we finish eating, I give Sabine a bath. The twins shower, and I help dry them and change into their pajamas. Sabine gets a warm bottle and falls asleep before I even put her in her crib Then I go into Elea and Noemie's room to tell them a bedtime story. I snuggle into Elea's bed, and Noemie joins us, one twin on each side of me.

"My favorite sandwich," I say.

"Oh, Mommy." Elea rolls her eyes, but she's smiling, and I never want this moment to end.

"Is Daddy going to be okay?" Noemie says. "He seems so . . . mean all the time."

That makes me want to cry. And hit Ben and scream at him. "He'll be fine. It's just been a tough time for everyone."

"Will the cops catch the bad guy who killed Aunt Mer?" Elea says.

"Yes." Then, to my surprise, Elea nuzzles her head into my chest, and I think my heart might actually burst with love for this girl. "It'll be okay." I think of how my fans are coming to the bat for me now, their loyal chorus overwhelming all of the trolls, and I think of how Helena is busy putting together a battle plan, and I really do believe that everything will be okay.

I tell the twins that I love them and leave their room. I go out to the kitchen, pour myself a glass of wine, and open up TikTok. A video pops up on my FYP. The wineglass slips from my hand and shatters on the floor.

# Chapter 29

# ASPEN

I don't know the couple in the video before me. I've never seen them a day in my life. And yet here they are, destroying it.

"We didn't know any of these so-called influencers—" the man says. "We're not really social media people."

"We mostly use Facebook," the woman says. "Then we started seeing Meredith Lee's face everywhere. And I thought she looked so familiar. But I couldn't place her for the longest time. I thought maybe she just had one of those faces."

"Then over dinner one night, she came up on the news—we watch the news while eating dinner," the man says. "And there's her photo, and Shelley says to me, 'Don't you think she looks familiar?' And I said, 'Oh, I know her. She's that lady we bumped into at the open house. The one in Alhambra.' And Shelley went, 'Oh my god, that's it!' That was probably one or two days before she was murdered. I mean, how creepy is that?"

"Very creepy," the man says, nodding.

"I downloaded TikTok," Shelley says proudly.

"She did."

"I did a deep dive, and I watched all the videos about Meredith and Aspen, and I said to Andrew, I said, 'I don't trust this Aspen. There's just something about her that's rubbing me the wrong way.'"

Andrew nods. "Yep."

"So I watched Aspen's videos, and that's when I saw him!"

"The realtor," Andrew says, just a beat before Shelley says the same thing. She glances at him, annoyed at giving it away.

Shelley leans forward, her eyes wide, "The realtor who was holding the open house where we saw Meredith shortly before she went missing is Ben, Aspen's husband."

That's it. The silver bullet. All the stuff I just did, Helena's brilliant strategy—all of it is shattered just like that. I stand there, ignoring the broken wineglass and spreading puddle of wine at my feet, and I start doomscrolling.

The responses are swift and unforgiving. Theories sprout like wild grass.

Ben was sleeping with Meredith!!!

Aspen killed Meredith because Ben was sleeping with Meredith!!!

Aspen was following Ben and spied on them!!

No, Aspen was stalking Meredith!!

The last one makes me laugh a thin, mirthless sound. *No,* I want to say to them, *she* was stalking *me*. And how has all of this ended up centered around Ben? Can we please have a single story that doesn't center around a man? God, it's going to boil down into me killing Meredith because I got jealous about her and Ben, isn't it? Come the fuck on. As if I would do such a thing. I've always said, if a husband cheats on his wife, revenge should be taken out on the husband, not the mistress. Not that anyone would believe me. It's too familiar a storyline. Someone cheats, so the spouse offs the other man—or the other woman, in this case. People like familiar storylines. And I suppose at the end of the day it doesn't really matter why I killed Meredith.

I video-call Helena. I don't expect her to pick up the phone—it's eight-thirty p.m.—but she picks up on the first ring. She's wearing a silk robe, but still has full makeup on.

"I was just about to call you," she says.

"You've seen it?"

"Would be hard not to; it's everywhere. They're likable too. Relatable. People believe them."

"Everyone thinks I killed Meredith because she was sleeping with Ben."

"I'm going to ask you this once, Aspen. And I will trust you."

I brace myself.

"Did you kill Meredith?"

I shake my head. "No." The lie comes out surprisingly easy. Because, in a way, I didn't kill Meredith. She did it to herself. She left me with no recourse.

"All right." She tilts her head to one side and thinks for a bit. "We'll need Ben to work with us here. We need him on camera, telling the world why Meredith was at the open house. What's wrong?"

I realize I'm frowning. "Um . . . Ben and I are not really on good terms right now."

Now it's Helena's turn to frown. "That's not good, Aspen. That's a really bad idea. You don't want a pissed-off husband right now. You need to show a united front. He needs to be right there by your side, convincing everyone that his loving wife couldn't have murdered an ant, never mind her best friend."

"Yeah, the thing is, he . . . kind of thinks I killed her?" I close my eyes. God, that sounded so bad.

"Oh dear," Helena says. "And why does he think that?"

It's a fight to keep myself from squirming in my seat. "I—we've been having problems for a long time now. The resentment's been building up, and some nights, I like to go out for a drive on my own because the atmosphere at home just gets so thick and unbearable. Anyway, I did that about a month ago, and—"

"You went for a midnight drive around the time Meredith was killed?"

"Yes."

Helena sighs. "And I'm assuming you don't have an alibi."

"No. I was driving around aimlessly, singing sad songs."

"Right. And that's why Ben thinks you might have something to do with Meredith's death."

"Yes."

Helena sucks in her breath through her teeth. "All right. You need to get on his good side. There's no way around it. He has to show support for you. He has to get on camera and explain why Meredith was at the open house. Preferably the answer is because she was there looking for a house to buy."

I give a weak smile. If only that were the reason why she was at the open house. "What if people don't believe Ben when he says that?"

"Of course they won't. It's too good a story to have him sleep with her. Sorry for my bluntness."

"It's fine. Ben hasn't been faithful for a long time."

Helena's eyebrows rise. "Has he—? With Meredith?"

"No, that was new. I know he's been with other women since we got married."

"Hm." Helena taps her chin for a bit. I can practically see the gears in her mind clacking away. "And you don't seem to mind this very much. Are you in an open marriage?"

The way she asks this makes me pause before answering. "Would it . . . be a good thing if we were in an open marriage?"

"Well, it'll show that you were less likely to get angry when you found out he was sleeping with Meredith."

"Ah. Then yes, we are in an open marriage."

"Okay. But you haven't—"

"No."

Helena nods. "Good. As much as I hate to say this, society is a lot less understanding when the wife partakes in an open marriage."

"Hah. Yeah, I know that much. No, I haven't had time to have flings."

"All right, Aspen. Try to get a good night's sleep. Record a video first thing tomorrow morning, preferably with Ben. And run it by me before posting."

"Always." Against all odds, I actually feel slightly better after hanging up. Helena is clearly a sorceress, and I'm thanking my lucky stars that I have her on my side. I put down the phone and start cleaning up the spilled wine and broken glass. As I do so, I think about my task. Convincing Ben to admit to everyone that he's been cheating on me? It's going to be a tough one, but I'm sure that when I explain to him what's at stake—my freedom—he'll do it for me.

It's nearly midnight when Ben comes home, reeking of cheap beer and sweat. I get up from the couch and hurry to the kitchen, where I pour him a glass of cold water.

"Here."

He takes it from me and glugs it down sloppily, rivulets of water pouring down the sides of his mouth. When he's done, he gives me a wary look and mumbles, "Thanks," before plopping down onto one of the counter stools.

"Um, I'm not sure if you saw, but there's been a not-so-great development—"

"I saw. I was at the bar when some punks started shouting at me, asking me if I killed her."

"Oh my god." This whole case is quickly spiraling out of control. "I'm sorry, Ben."

He grunts and peers up at me. "I didn't do it, you know."

I nod. I want to tell him I know, but then I wonder if, at the bitter, drunk state he's in, he'll use that against me and demand to know how I know that he didn't kill her. Instead, I say, "I trust you."

He breaks eye contact, looking away guiltily.

"So Helena says that it would be good if you could make a video with me. Tomorrow, after a good night's sleep."

"What? Why? Nobody wants to hear from me."

"She said it's really important to show that we're a united front."

"What am I supposed to say?" he demands, like I'm asking for the world when all I need is a one-minute video. It's a struggle to keep my temper in check.

"Um, she thinks it would be a good idea if we told everyone that we're in an open relationship."

Ben gapes at me like I've just asked him to stab his own mother.

"It'll show that I'm less likely to have gotten jealous about your affair with Meredith, because I'm okay with you being with other women."

"Wh-what the fuck, Aspen?" he says. "First of all, we are not in an open relationship. And second of all, even if we were, I'm not going to tell the whole world about it. What's everyone going to think? I'll be fired from the agency. My whole family would disown me. *My* reputation would be ruined."

Anger overwhelms me. My asshole of a husband, who's always strived to keep me small, who's always ready with cutting remarks. My husband who never once showed me appreciation for everything I've done for this family. Who doesn't seem to be able to understand what's at stake, even when it's staring him right in the face. I have three little kids to look after, and a man-child is the last thing I want to be spending time on. "Oh, okay, never mind then," I hiss. "We'll just tell everyone that you have a long history of cheating on me, and each time, I've just looked the other way. Would that be more accepta—" The rest of the word ends in a gasp as Ben grabs my arms in a merciless grip and shoves me against the kitchen island. My lower back slams into the overhang and pain shoots up and down my spine. It feels like my spine's just been snapped in two. The pain is so bad that I don't even scream out loud—I can't; the breath's been knocked out of me and only an agonized gurgle comes out.

Ben's face is right up against mine, our noses grazing. His teeth are bared, and everything inside me is telling me that this is it. This is how I die. "Don't be a fucking bitch, Aspen," he growls. "All these years, there's never been any room for me in your life. First, it was the Mer and Aspen show. Then, when you decided you got too big for her, it became the All Aspen show. It's always been about you. You love the attention so much, you can deal with all of this shit yourself. This mess is yours. Do not drag me and the kids into it. Just–" He shakes me, once, and this time, I do cry out. "Don't," he says with finality. Then he pushes me away, and I slide down to the floor in a crumpled heap.

I'm not sure if what I'm doing counts as crying. Tears are rolling down my face, but I'm not sobbing, because it's too painful to sob. I just lie there, gasping for breath until the fire in my back recedes, then I curl up into a ball, and that's when I do cry. For some ridiculous reason, what I'm feeling right now is shame and guilt. A very significant part of me is ashamed for pushing Ben into doing this. I was the one who goaded him, who kept pressing even after he'd said he didn't want to shoot a video with me. I did this. It's all my fault. But even as I think that, I know how messed up the thought is. Hot on the heels of the guilt is fury. How dare he lay his hands on me? How dare he–

He's right. It sinks in with awful clarity. Ben is right. All these years it's always been my show. There has never been any room for him. Not for clinger-on Ben. He's like the appendix in our lives, and now he's infected, and it's clear what I need to do.

I stay on the kitchen floor until weak morning light streams in through the windows and the birds begin to chirp. Slowly, gingerly, wincing at every move, I uncurl. My back spasms with electricity, and my breath comes in and out in little whimpers. I push myself up and stagger to the sink where I drink straight from the tap. The water revives me a little, just enough to lurch to the bathroom where I open the medicine cabinet and take two Tylenols. I lean over the sink and stare into the mirror.

The woman who stands before me looks utterly broken. Pale, with dark circles under her eyes, and a tremor in her arms, like they can't bear the weight of her upper body. I blink slowly. Ben did this to me. My husband, who fell in love with me because he saw me as a helpless, young, naive thing. A thing to spoil and protect. My husband, who, when I stopped being a thing and started coming into my own person, became embittered and small. My husband, who's spent the last few years of our marriage belittling me, reminding me at every turn of how empty-headed I am. How frivolous my job is. Scoffing every time I call my job a "career." Refusing to celebrate any of my milestones. My husband who has always underestimated me.

It's easy, I suppose, to underestimate influencers. We're often minimized as these shallow, featherbrained creatures. What people fail to see is how cutthroat we have to be in order to make it in the industry. We have to think outside the box to come up with creative content. And not just one or two times but every fucking day, multiple times a day, we have to scour our brains and extract creativity from them. We need to be disciplined. We need to be organized. And above all, we need to be charismatic.

I spread my mouth into a smile. The Tylenol is beginning to kick in, numbing the pain in my back slightly. I straighten up slowly, wincing, running my hands up and down my spine. Nothing's broken. No slipped discs. I square my shoulders and lift my chin. My smile, previously looking more like a grimace, turns into a real one.

My husband has just made the worst mistake of his life.

# Chapter 30

# ASPEN

Liv's face is a picture when she opens her door to find me and the girls standing on her front porch. "Oh my—" she squeaks. Then she lowers her voice. "What are you doing here?"

"We didn't have anywhere else to go," I whisper back with just the right amount of fear and vulnerability in my voice to incite pity.

Liv stands back, chewing her lip. I bend down and say to the twins, "Go on inside, sweethearts."

Elea and Noemie grin and say, "Hi, Liv!" as they slip past her into the house.

"Wait—" Liv sighs and gives me a look before stepping aside. "Come on in. Hi, Sabbie. Rain will be so happy to see you."

Liv's house is a lot smaller than mine, but it's well on its way to being Pinterest-worthy. The decor is simple but pretty with plenty of house plants, which gives the space some color and life. One corner of the living room is enclosed into a playpen, like mine. Rain is toddling around inside, playing with various toys. I head straight for the playpen and plop Sabine in it. The two babies look at each other and laugh.

Liv is standing with her arms crossed in front of her when I straighten up, wincing. "You really shouldn't be here," she says.

"Can we talk in private? Please?" I look at the twins pointedly. They've made themselves at home on Liv's sofa, and Elea has located the TV remote control.

Liv breathes in deeply. "Come on into the kitchen."

Unlike my house, Liv's house is an old build, and therefore doesn't have an open-plan kitchen. Which, as it turns out, has its good points. Privacy, for one. Once we're in the kitchen, I turn to Liv and say, "Liv, I need to tell you something really big. I don't know what to do about it, and I don't know who else to tell. You're my closest friend, the only person I can trust."

"Wh—wait—what?"

"Please, Liv. I have no one else." I grasp her hand tightly, my chin trembling.

"Okay. Yes, of course. What is it?" She leans closer to me, and she's so eager to hear what my awful secret is that she seems to have forgotten how to blink.

"I—" I glance around to make sure no one is listening, then whisper, "I think Ben killed Meredith."

"What?" Liv leaps back like I've just hit her.

"Shh!" I hiss, putting a finger to my lips. "I don't want the twins to hear."

"Sorry!" Liv whispers back. "I just—no, that's not possible. Everyone says you—" She licks her lips and falters.

I utter a soft sob. "Yes, I know. Everyone thinks I did it. But you know I didn't, Liv. You know I couldn't possibly have done anything like that. Otherwise, you wouldn't have let me into your house. Trust your instincts. What are they telling you? The last few weeks, we were so close. We were best friends. You know me better than anyone. Do you really think I could've killed someone?"

Liv hesitates, uncertainty wrinkling her forehead. "But—"

I turn around and lift my shirt.

"What are you do—oh my god." Liv's protest ends in a horrified hiss. "Aspen, what happened?"

I know what she's seeing. The bruise in the middle of my lower back, an obscene-looking blob, the color of an eggplant, spread across my skin like an ugly continent. It looks all the more grotesque because, ever since killing Meredith, I haven't had much of an appetite. I've lost weight, and my spine sticks out of my back, each knob visible under the skin, and the outline of my ribcage can be seen clearly too. To put it plainly, my back looks terrible. When I'm confident that Liv has fully absorbed the true horror of my situation, I lower my shirt back down and turn to face her. Then, I roll up my sleeves and show her the bruises around my arms where Ben had grabbed me. Liv covers her mouth with both hands, blinking rapidly.

"Ben happened," I say softly.

"No," Liv moans.

I lower my sleeves, taking my time. "He did. I know you like him. I know . . . you and Ben had a thing. I don't blame you," I say quickly. "Trust me, I really don't. Our marriage has been over for a long time. I only stayed with him because—well, I thought the girls needed their father, and stability. But now I have to be honest with myself. I feel safer when Ben isn't around. I'm actually relieved whenever I sense that he's found someone else to sleep around with, because it means at least he's not at home with me."

Liv is gaping at me, and I can't tell what she's thinking. "But—why?" she squeaks after a while.

"Why did he beat me?" I swallow and step closer to her. "That's the thing. The past few weeks, he's been acting so strange. You know how you have these instincts as a woman? Like, a survival instinct or something. Mine was going off, telling me something was wrong, but I kept ignoring it because Ben's—well, it's Ben! My husband. The father of my kids." I shake my head, grimacing. "But I can't deny it anymore. And when Meredith's body was found—oh god, Liv—the look on Ben's face . . ." I utter a sob. "I knew then that he had something to do with it. I couldn't—I didn't know what to do. I've been so scared this whole time. When that couple came out and said they saw Meredith at Ben's open house, I couldn't hide my suspicions anymore. I asked Ben if he killed Mer." I cover my mouth right after I say this, horrified at the awful words I'm saying.

Liv gasps, her expression aghast.

"I never expected him to do this to me. I thought he'd laugh and tell me I was being ridiculous. But he . . ." I shake my head, lost in the memory of that horrific night. "I thought he was going to kill me. If the kids hadn't been in the house, I think he would've."

"You should go to the police!" Liv says. "Why did you come here?"

"I'm scared," I cry. "I didn't know where else to go, and would the police even believe me? All the things that people are saying about me online—I'm scared, Liv. What if they think I'm making it up? There are so many lies about me on social media. I didn't have anyone else to turn to other than you. You're the only person I trust."

Despite everything, I can see that Liv wants to believe me. She wants to see herself as the heroine of my story.

She nods slowly and murmurs, "You're right to trust me."

I smile at her. "I know. You of all people understand—truly understand—what it's like to be me."

"I'll help you," Liv says. "Do you want me to come with you to the police station?"

"Yes. But before that, there's something else you can do for me."

"What is it?"

I lick my lips. "Well, um, my lawyer says it's really important that everyone online knows the truth."

"What are you saying?"

I close my eyes and take a deep breath before opening them. "I think we need to make another video."

Liv's hand is so shaky that, in the end, we have to prop her phone up on a stand. "I don't know—" she says in a wobbly voice.

I pat her arm. "You're doing the right thing. Think of all the women you'll be saving from Ben. I doubt Mer was his only victim. She's the only one who was found."

Liv's chin trembles, then her jaw moves and tightens. "Okay." She flips her hair behind her back and squares her shoulders. This time, we're doing a live video. Something I haven't run past Helena, but I know in my gut that I need to do it this way. The kids are all playing quietly outside the bedroom. It's now or never. I open up my TikTok account.

"Ready?" I say.

Liv nods.

I hit the Live button. The screen counts down, and I swallow the lump in my throat. Three, two, one. And we're streaming. At first, only twenty-four people are viewing. But within seconds, the view count goes up. And up.

Liv looks at the camera and swallows. "Ah . . . hi, everyone. I have to make a confession. I think I owe you all an explanation and an apology." Her tongue darts out and licks her lips. For a second, she seems frozen.

"It's okay," I whisper. "It'll be okay." Six hundred viewers.

"I had a thing with Ben!" Liv blurts out. "Um. I'm so sorry, everyone, but especially Aspen. I'm so, so sorry."

I shake my head. "No, don't be sorry. I'm sorry. Because I sort of knew—I could tell there was something between the two of you. Some vibes. But I never said anything because . . . I didn't care about that. Ben has slept around the whole time we've been married. I never blamed it on any of the women he slept with. Not Meredith, and not you. Of course not. I care about you. I cared about Meredith. I would never have held it against her. But Ben . . ." I brace myself. "I'm scared of Ben." I turn from Liv to face the camera. We're at over three thousand live viewers already.

"I also have something really hard to tell all of you. It's something I've been suspecting ever since Meredith was found. I . . ." I take a deep inhale, bracing myself. "I think my husband killed her."

I have to bite my lip then to keep from crying. The comments section is a furious blur now, too many of them coming in at once for me to read. Twelve thousand viewers. "Um—sorry. I just need a second." Next to me, Liv puts her arm around my shoulders, and I wince, clearly in pain.

"Oh, sorry!" Liv says. Sixteen thousand viewers.

I shake my head. "It's not your fault." I train my gaze at the camera once again. "Ben did this to me." I roll up my sleeves and show the camera the bruises around my upper arms. Twenty-one thousand viewers. Slowly, I stand and turn around so my back is now facing the camera. I lift up my shirt and resist from looking over my shoulder to check if they can see the awful bruise on my back. I just have to trust that there is no way anyone would miss it. I count to three under my breath, then lower my shirt and sink back gingerly onto the side of the bed. We are at over forty thousand viewers now. "This is what Ben is capable of. I've known for a long time that my husband has a dark streak in him. That he's able to hurt people. But for the longest time, I tried to convince myself that everything's okay. I'm just so scared of him."

Liv rubs my arms gently. "You're so brave."

I nod at her, pressing my lips into a tight line to keep from crying. "I thought that if I were better—if I cooked better food, cleaned better, was the perfect mom, and made sure the kids never misbehaved around him—that it would all be okay. And after a long time of this, I no longer trusted my own instincts. I believed everything Ben said about me." A choked sob escapes me. Seventy thousand viewers. "I'm so scared," I whisper.

"Oh, Aspen," Liv gasps. "I can't believe how hard this must be for you. But you're okay. You're safe now."

"I owe everyone the truth. I'm not staying silent anymore. So here it is. The thing is, sometimes, everything gets too much, and I just have to leave the house. Some nights, when everyone's asleep, I go in my car and I drive around aimlessly, wishing I could disappear. About five weeks ago, I did that. I went for a drive and sang sad songs and cried. The usual. But this time, when I came home, Ben wasn't there." A tear slips down my cheek. "It was around the time that Meredith went missing." One hundred thousand viewers.

Liv moans. "I can't believe it. He was always so nice to me. I can't believe I fell under his spell."

"It's what he does. He's so charming. He has a way about him that makes everyone fall in love with him. That's why I never said anything this whole time. I didn't think anyone would believe me. But I can't keep it to myself anymore. I have to protect my children. I have to tell the truth, get Meredith some justice. Even though it means my kids will grow up without a father."

Liv hugs me. "You are so brave. Meredith would be so proud of you if she were here."

I nod through my tears. We say a few other things and end the live stream. I squeeze Liv's hand. "Thank you for doing that. That was amazing."

Before Liv can answer, there's a small voice at the door. "Mommy?" My heart stops.

Noemie is standing at the door. The door that I had left cracked open so I could hear if any of the kids needed me. I jump up and plaster on a smile. "Hi, honey, is everything o—"

"Was that pretending?" she says, her eyes wide and scared.

I kneel down in front of her. This is the part I dreaded the most. But it's inevitable, and it's better if it comes from me than their friends at school. While I think of the right words to say, words that could soften the blow, Noemie says, "Is it because you're mad at me?"

"What? No, Mommy isn't mad at you. Why would I be mad at you?" Noemie's little face scrunches up, and she begins bawling. I gather her in my arms. "Oh my gosh, sweetie, I promise, I'm not mad at you. I can never be mad at you. You are my perfect little angel."

"I'm not!" she cries. "I did something bad."

"Oh, honey. I'm sure it wasn't that bad."

"I messed up your calendar."

I freeze. "What?"

"You were going to meet with that Netflix person and have a reality show about us, and I didn't want to be on a reality show, Mommy. I don't want people to see me getting my shots every day," Noemie says through her sobs.

"Oh god." I swear my soul is tearing itself apart like tissue paper.

"I heard you tell Daddy that your calendar got all messed up somehow, so that gave me the idea to do it. I went onto the family calendar, but I didn't know which one was the Netflix person, so I . . ."

"Changed the dates on all my meetings," I say.

"And when I told Elea, she said we should do more."

The sinking sensation in the pit of my stomach goes even deeper. "You sent an email to them telling them I wasn't interested in working together?"

Noemie nods.

"How did you even—how?"

"When we tapped on each appointment it showed us their phone numbers and email addresses and we just . . ." Her voice trails off.

*You're not even seven years old*, I want to shout. *You're not supposed to be doing shit like this already!* But at the end of the day, the fault is all mine. I was the one who pushed them in front of the camera. Sure, it may have been necessary, but I should've seen this coming.

Noemie's face crumples up again. "I'm sorry, Mommy!" she wails.

"It's okay, it's fine," I manage to say.

"But it's not! You're punishing me now. You're taking Daddy away."

"No!" I say quickly, stroking her little back. Oh god, they can't think that. They can't. "Listen to me, Noemie, I am not doing this to punish you. Your daddy has done something really, really bad, and I had to tell the truth about it."

"But what's going to happen to him?"

I brace myself. "It's out of my hands now. He did something terrible, and he has to pay for it."

Noemie wails, "Is he going to prison?"

I nod. "Yes. But we'll be okay. Because I'm not going anywhere. I will always be here for you girls. Mommy will take care of everything." I hug her tight and feel her breaking in my arms, and I make a promise to myself that despite this moment, despite the hurricane that is about to sweep us all up, my kids are going to come out the other end okay. They will be scarred, there's no avoiding that, but they will end up stronger for it.

# Chapter 31

# ASPEN

I thought I was ready for this, but when the officer brings Ben out, he looks so awful that I actually gasp out loud. Ben has always been a vain man—always took care to do his hair just right and keep his jaw clean-shaven. Back home, the cabinet in the bathroom has a whole shelf of products dedicated to keeping him looking great. He said it was important, in his line of work, to look good. But now, his skin is sallow and greasy, his facial hair is left sprouting unevenly, and his hair is a tangled mop. When he sees me, his jaw clenches. He lowers himself to the chair behind the screen and picks up the phone.

His first words to me are: "You fucking bitch."

Not a nice way to greet your wife, but I've had seven unhappy years of marriage to get used to it. I give him a tight smile, biting back my retort. Even here, even now, I am always careful. You never know when someone might recognize me. I have eleven million followers on TikTok now, and ten on Instagram. That's more than a lot of celebrities. I get recognized everywhere I go—Whole Foods, the post office, the gym. People are always coming up to me and telling me how brave I am, and telling the twins what an amazing mother they have.

"You won't get away with this," Ben is saying.

I want to laugh. I'm not the one sitting on the wrong side of a prison screen. But that's the thing about Ben, isn't it? He can't help but underestimate me, even now. Even after all the evidence that's conveniently popped up. The burner phone that was found in his car, tucked snugly under the lining of his trunk. In it, a message sent to Meredith's phone: "Mer, it's me. I miss you so much. Please talk to me. I need my best friend."

The internet had exploded when that little piece of evidence was revealed.

> He pretended to be Aspen to lure Meredith to him, the sick fuck!

> Poor Meredith. Poor Aspen! I can't believe she had to deal with him for so long.

The phone on its own would've been enough to put Ben away for life, but like I said, influencers have to be very organized. I also made sure his prints were all over the phone. It's simple, really, planting prints on an object. There's a whole wikiHow page with step-by-step pictures; I'm not exaggerating.

The day that I killed Mer, I made sure to throw out all the beers in the house. Then I picked a fight with Ben. A bad enough fight so I could tell him I was going to sleep in Sabine's room. I waited until I heard Ben rummaging around the kitchen for a beer. Predictably, he went out soon after in search of more beer, and of course he left from the front door, in full view of our cameras. I left from the back door, where I'd disabled the camera hours before. It was bad luck that Sabine woke up in the middle of the night and alerted Ben that I wasn't there, but it's okay. I have a lot of practice rolling along when things don't go my way. Every momfluencer has had a ton of practice with that.

Then there are the messages from Ben's phone to me over the past few months, sent over Google Hangouts, not our usual chat app. When did I start doing this? When I first found out about his affair, years and years ago. As much as I tried to turn the other cheek, I knew then that he was no longer my rock. At the time, I wasn't sure what I was doing this for; I only knew I had to document as much of his abuse as possible.

> You stupid, useless cunt. I'm going to end you. I should never have married you, you ugly fat bitch.
> One of these days, Aspen, you're gonna piss me off one too many times and I will fucking kill you, I swear it.

I deleted them all as soon as I sent them, before closing the app. Ben never even noticed; he doesn't really use Google Hangouts. It fits the narrative—Ben, the charming, manipulative mastermind. Of course he would be careful enough to send abusive texts using a different app. He's always so careful to cover up his tracks.

I can't even take credit for the rest. I got the ball rolling, and now it's snowballed before my very eyes. I hadn't counted on the other women, but they came out, one by one. Some went to the press. Others, who have more online presence, did their own explosive live streams. The messages were all pretty much the same.

> I slept with Ben Palmer. I didn't know he was married. He led me on. After a while, I could sense that there was something off about him, so I ended things. Thank god I did, because otherwise, I might've ended up like poor Meredith.

> I came this close to sleeping with a murderer.

> He hit on me at a club, but I could tell with just one look that he was dangerous. You can tell, with some men. Women have had to hone their senses for centuries to avoid men like Ben.

I enjoy watching all of their interviews and their videos. I listen to every word and play a game: Spot the Lies. Sometimes, they're obvious. Did Ben really hit on that particular woman at a club? Unlikely. She's not his type. But, god knows, I can't begrudge someone trying to hop on a trend for views.

"Why the fuck are you here, Aspen?" Ben says. "I've got nothing to say to you."

Funny, that. He's said a lot to me already. I lean forward. It's time for me to have the final say. "I came here to tell you not to worry," I say slowly. I need him to hear every word. "About the kids. The house payments, the healthcare bills, the school fees. Look after yourself. We don't need you, Ben. I'll take care of everything else. Like I always do."

Ben's mouth stretches into a growl, but I replace the phone in its holder gently and stand. He screams something. I don't hear it.

The thing about being a momfluencer is, I've had to get very good at doing everything with a smile. And I'm not about to stop now. Right before I turn and leave the room, I give Ben my final parting gift. My prettiest smile, not just my mouth moving but my eyes twinkling, joy and victory dancing in my expression. A smile worthy of Instagram.

# Acknowledgements

All of my usual suspects are to be thanked in the making of this book. My wonderful, joyous, insightful, kind, accommodating, pure magic of an editor, Cindy Hwang. Katelyn Detweiler, who is so much more than an agent at this point (she is therapist, friend, fellow empathetic mom of littles, fellow author, everything as well as superagent). My team at Berkley—Jin Yu, Angela Kim, Dache' Rogers, Danielle Keir, Anika Bates, and Tina Joell for being the dream team to work with. The rest of the team at Jill Grinberg Literary Management—Sam Farkas, Denise Page, Jill Grinberg for making the publishing journey so seamless.

My author soul twin, Laurie Elizabeth Flynn, and I went on a virtual writing retreat while I wrote this book and she wrote her novel *Till Death Do Us Part*. It was a magical experience to be able to do a retreat with her, and the best part: Somehow, our two books are coming out in the same month. It feels kismet, and I am so fortunate to have Laurie's support every step of the way. If you liked this book, you are going to *love* Laurie's book. It is haunting, dark, twisty, and heartbreakingly beautiful.

Thank you also to the rest of my writing community—my

Menagerie folks (Tilly Latimer, SL Huang, Elaine Aliment, Toria Hegedus, Rob Livermore, Emma Maree, Maddox Hahn, and Mel Melcer), May Cobb, Lauren Ho, Nicole Lesperance, Grace Shim, and Kate Dylan. Since this book is about female friendship, I would be remiss to not thank my amazing female friends. These are the people I wouldn't be able to survive life without—thank you to Lauren Davies, Leah Madeleine, Tina Simatupang, Jocelyne Tjandra, Roshi Mahtani, and Melissa Chairul.

This book is dedicated to my best friend, Anji. We meet so many people in life, and yet it is so rare to find the best friendship that Anji and I have found in each other. We met in college, at Berkeley. We were babies, our faces bright with laughter and our minds fizzing with sharp ideas and possibilities. We giggled over everything.

After college, life took us in vastly different directions, with us living on opposite sides of the world, and for a while, I feared that this was it. That our friendship would fizzle out and be nothing more than a sweet memory that grew fuzzier with each passing year. But that didn't happen. Somehow, we endured.

Through weddings and babies and time zone differences, we remained, always, each other's rock. One year, we decided to take a trip, just the two of us, to Japan. It was the start of our annual girls' trip; a tradition we now look forward to every year. For one week each year, we travel to a beautiful location, just the two of us, and confide in each other our deepest secrets. People say the words "no judgment" so easily, without much thought, but with Anji these two words are meant to their fullest extent. These are trips where, through hour-long talks, we feel like full persons, not just mothers or wives, but flawed humans with dreams, fears, disappointments, and joy.

Anji made it easy for me to write about Aspen and Meredith; I knew exactly the kind of friendship that Aspen and Meredith longed for, the kind of friendship they pretended to have with increasing desperation as everything around them crumbled.

It is such a privilege to experience a friendship like this. Love you always, Anji!

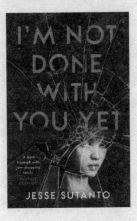